Feinstein's Theory of Relatives
and other
HESSEL STREET
Stories

Withdrawn

Eric Levene

D1440200

For my grandsons Leo, Ollie and Ike.
Carry on being silly.

Acknowledgements

My special thanks and gratitude go to Barbara 'Bibi' Brown for editing the stories without losing their flavour and absurdity. And, of course, for her understanding and patience with me.

I should also like to thank my son-in-law, Gareth 'Gaz' Thackeray for his proof-reading and enthusiastic feedback.

In addition, may I thank Tristan Wickham for creating what I think is a great front cover, and Jill Furmanovsky for finding time out from photographing the good and great of the world of Rock 'n' Roll to take a photograph that makes me look like a mench.

I am also grateful to Rory Isserow for collating and producing the book.

A very special thanks to my family and friends for putting up with me during this mishigus. Without their support this book would never have come to fruition.

Finally, my warm thanks to Arnie Kransdorff for continually bullying me into putting the stories together in book form. So, if you want to have a go at anybody, have a go at him.

Front cover - Hessel Street 1938 – Geoffrey Spender
TristanWickham. Tristanwickham@gmail.com

Contents

Introduction

For over 50 years, Hessel Street in the heart of the East End was *the* Jewish street market in London, if not the country, despite what shop-owners and stallholders in other markets might say to the contrary. Even those who weren't Jewish were Jewish by association, so everybody was Jewish.

All the stories in this collection are completely fictitious and are based in and around Hessel Street during the late 1940s and 50s. With a bit of luck, none of them are anywhere near the truth, but you can never tell. My memory often plays tricks on me and it is possible that what happened in one of the fictional stories actually took place, albeit in a slightly different way.

Furthermore, with so many Morry Cohens and Issy Levys, and Sadie Golds and Silvers, plus a shulful of Goldbergs and Greenbergs about, it's not easy to come up with the name of a new character. And when I do come up with what I think is a new one, I find dozens of them, so if by some odd chance I have used the name of one of your relatives in a negative or derogatory way, I apologise half whole-heartedly. It certainly was not my intention.

In addition, if I have insulted anybody by omission or saying something positive about them when it should have been negative, the same apology stands. So please do not issue a writ for defamation or praise of a fictitious character even though the character may have the same name as one of your relatives or friends.

And another thing...before you start emailing or texting or writing to me complaining that this one or that one didn't live in Hessel Street in the 1950s or before or after, don't bother. Don't even bother to tell me that somebody called what-ever-his-name-is didn't have a butcher shop or a fish shop or a fruit stall in Hessel Street, I know. Remember, these stories are completely fictitious, apart from the one about…

My grandfather, okay, zayda, have it your way, was a kosher butcher and poulterer in the street - don't ask his name as refusals often offend. But for those of you who do know who he was, I beg you not to say a word to anybody else. You never know, there might be a family debt outstanding. He was, however, the inspiration for one of my characters, as was a great aunt, a couple of so-called aunts and a so-called uncle. And no, I'm still not mentioning any names.

I lived in Hessel Street from 1944 until 1956, when I moved to Langdale Mansions - may it also rest in peace - with my mother and step-father. Sadly or fortunately, my memory of those days in both places is not as good as it should be - which is why this book is a work of fiction and not fact. If you're looking for facts go check on Google.

Now, I was going to put in a glossary of Yiddish words but decided against it. Somebody would only complain that the transliteration and translation were wrong and within days there would be a broigus - 'a bitter dispute or feud' if you believe the Oxford English Dictionary definition. That's up to you, I'm not getting involved. I don't want to get involved in the whole 'you say bagel and I say beigal' pronunciation business either. But having said that, those of you that say 'bagel' should be named and shamed in public.

Finally, I have used times and genuine places to add a certain amount of authenticity and credence to the stories. However, if some of these facts are wrong they are of my own doing, but please feel free to blame somebody else from Hessel Street.

Eric Levene

When Solly met Harry

In the beginning, there were no Jews.

But by the 1920s, Hessel Street market, in the heart of London's East End, was full of them. There were butchers, bakers and chicken soup makers; fishmongers, costermongers and a host of wheeler-dealers and luckless shpielers. A 200-yard long and maybe 10-yard wide sardine tin, crammed full of vibrant Jewish life and, as nature would have it on occasion, death. They had come from all over. There were Poles and Russians, Latvians and Lithuanians, Moldovans, Ukrainians, Rumanians and Georgians, plus a multitude of others who had escaped the pogroms that had been raging across Eastern Europe.

And, remarkably, they all got along with each other without the need to argue; unless they needed to. And, of course, it goes without saying, they needed to. They needed to argue in Yiddish and they needed to argue in what they thought was English and they needed to argue in their mother tongue and they needed to argue in a mixture of all three or maybe four if they could find another language they thought they might be able to understand. They just needed to argue.

The main reason being was that if they agreed with each other, there would be nothing to argue about, and if there were nothing to argue about, there would be nothing to tell their wives or husbands.

"You know who I had a row with?"

"Who this time?"

"That shmendrick from Lvov, Yunkel, Shmunkel or whatever his name is. He wanted to charge me 3d for a lousy tea strainer."

"But we've got a tea strainer."

"What's that got to do with it? He still wanted to charge me 3d. So I gave him a little suggestion what he could do with his fakakta tea strainer, and that's what started the whole shlemozzl."

The Russians were cheating the Poles, or so the Poles thought, whilst the Poles were doing the poor Rumanians out of their hard-earned money. The Latvians were doing the Russians out of every penny they had because the Latvians were so poor, which stopped them from becoming poorer, and the Moldovans were being done by everyone. The Lithuanians would have cheated the Georgians if they weren't so busy cheating other Lithuanians, and the Ukrainians were being swindled by the Poles when the Poles could find time out from arguing about the price of everything with the Georgians. And as for the English...what English? This was Hessel Street.

And there were, of course, plenty more arguments to be had.

"How can a man of mine statue in the community make a surviving living if I can't be making a profit for a person of mine proper importance?" asked a Moldovan.

"If you didn't try to make such a gantze profit, maybe, please God, you'd have made a bisl profit, but still a profit," said a Pole, or was it a Russian?

"The trouble mit you is that your prices are higher than a giraffe. I have to make a big enough profit to buy even the smallest nothing from you," replied a Lithuanian, or it could have been a Latvian.

"Who's asking for you to buy from me anything?" questioned an irate Georgian.

"Did you ask for me not to buy from you something?" asked another Pole.

"Stop driving mine kop meshuga. I didn't ask you to buy from me and I didn't ask you not to buy from me, even for one lousy stinking penny. Can't you be understanding a void of the English from what I'm speaking to you?" cried the Georgian.

"Dat's it. Dat's the final strawberry. I'm never going to buy anything from you ever again ever, as I stand here on my own two foots in shoes," said a furious Ukrainian.

"But you've never bought anything from me, ever, not even in Yiddish," came the response from a Bessarabian.

"I never came all the way from Plotsk just to make a loss," interrupted a near penniless eighty-two year old man from Minsk.

"Omain," said everybody else from everywhere else.

Another argument stopped by an 'omain' before a fight could break out. And so life went on, even during the war, when times were difficult for everybody, except the black-marketeers and wheeler-dealers. Oh! And the butchers and maybe the bakers and the fishmongers and … Somehow they all got by. Even when bombs were dropping all around, people survived. And by some glorious miracle or divine intervention, Hessel Street was untouched by Hitler's aerial bombardment.

Somebody suggested it was God's will. Morry Gold said it was bad bombing by the Luftwaffe. Some crazy person with a lokshen pudding for a brain said it was Hessel Street's own defence system, the 'Luft Wafter' that saved them - the smell of Wolansky's shmaltz herrings. He reckoned that when the planes came over, Wolansky lifted the lids off the herring barrels, allowing the smell to waft into the air and into the cockpits. The pilots would throw up from the smell, causing them to veer off and crash a long way from the street. The wisest said it was luck, which it was; so luck and life went on hand-in-glove. The gloves coming from a Polish wheeler-dealer who lived somewhere near Brick Lane.

So this was Hessel Street, about three quarters of a mile along the Commercial Road from Aldgate East on the right hand side. If the bus had been going too fast you might have missed it, but you would probably have been able to smell it if the wind were blowing in the right direction.

By the time the Second World War ended, peace had broken out in the street. Well, a truce anyway. There were far more pressing things to worry about than arguing over the price of the Lithuanian's saucepans, even though they were, according to the Russian, far too expensive.

In 1948, there were two burning issues that occupied the good, great and not so great minds of the Jews of England. The first was the setting up of the state of Israel. "Next year in Jerusalem, please God, if I can find the money and the Arabs stop fighting us." At last, a home for all the Jews of the world. "But whatever you do, don't tell the Moldovans."

The other, a far more worrying matter for a significant few, was to send rabbis scurrying through ancient texts, Jewish laws and by-laws, teachings and commentaries, and all manner of learned works. The problem was the newly set up National Health Service and free teeth, free false teeth.

Young Rabbi Katz, into his third year as rabbi of Nelson Street shul, was walking home along the Whitechapel Road, having just purchased a tea strainer from Johnny's hardware stall, when he was stopped by Harry Greenberg.

"Excuse me rabbi, I'm sorry to bother you, but can I ask you a question?"

"Harry, it's nice to see you. Ask away."

"Are they kosher?"

"Are what kosher, Harry?" Rabbi Katz hadn't a clue as to what he was talking about.

"National Health false teeth."

"How am I supposed to know?"

"Because you're a rabbi."

"But I'm not a National Health rabbi," replied Rabbi Katz, trying to make light of the question.

"So what am I supposed to do?"

"What about?"

"About false teeth."

"Do you need false teeth?"

"Not at the moment."

"So what's the problem? Why are you asking me such a question?"

"Just in case I need some of my own taken out and I need false ones," replied a very worried looking Harry.

"Don't worry. By the time you need false teeth, Harry, National Health ones will be kosher, of that I'm certain." Which meant, of course, he wasn't certain at all. He was just trying to find a quick way out of the discussion he had been sucked into unwittingly.

"That means they're not kosher at the moment."

"At the moment I don't know. Remember, I've not been a rabbi that long. I still have lots of thing to learn."

Harry was driving the young rabbi mad. "At the moment you don't know if they have to be kosher or not. That I understand, but can they be koshered if necessary?"

"As I said, it might not be necessary to kosher false teeth, including National Health ones. To be honest, it's something I should know but I don't, so I'll try and find out the answer. I need to talk to other rabbunim, so it might take a little while. You know what it's like, one rabbi will say one thing and another one will say something else and a third will say something completely different, but in the end…" Poor Rabbi Katz, sighed, looked up, shook his head in resignation and thought of blaming God for creating the National Health Service.

"So what happens if I get hit in the face by a van tomorrow morning and lose all my teeth?"

"I'm sure God will give you an emergency medical exemption certificate," replied Rabbi Katz, hoping that it would be the last answer he would have to give. But Harry still had one final question to ask.

"What about having to kosher them for Pesach?"

That did it. Rabbi Katz had had enough. "Go away, Harry and stop driving me crazy. When I get an answer, you'll get an answer. That's if I see you in shul."

And so they both walked on, Harry one way, concerned that he might have to set foot in a shul, and Rabbi Katz the other, concerned that his hair might be on the verge of going grey and that he might be in need of an aspirin to kill the headache that had come on so quickly.

But in fairness to Harry, he had asked a good question and one that the rabbi would have to research. There would also need to be discussions with other, wiser and older rabbis. More arguments! Not just about National Health false teeth, but about false teeth in general.

And Harry didn't even keep a kosher home. So what was he going on about?

By the late forties some of the early Hessel Street settlers were dead, many, but certainly not all, taking their kosher, or not, false teeth with them. But Solly Bernstein, bachelor, aged 31, with a mouthful of his own teeth, was alive and well, but not necessarily well in the head. He was, however, well on the way to concocting yet another crazy scheme to make himself rich. His bank account had been haemorrhaging for months and it was time to stop the bleeding; putting a plaster on it was pointless. He needed real money to stop the flow.

His previous ideas of becoming the richest man in England had all failed spectacularly, leaving him to fall back on his meagre income as a cutter for Kestlebaum the tailor. It wasn't as if Kestlebaum paid poorly. It was more to do with the amount of work that Solly did for him. Not a lot. In fact, Kestlebaum was generous to a fault, allowing Solly time off whenever an idea struck, which was often, too often. It is possible that Kestlebaum's generosity was fuelled by the thought that Solly might, someday, strike oil, become a millionaire, and remember Kestlebaum kindly.

Of course, Kestlebaum, of course. And the Chief Rabbi's a Catholic.

One of Solly's previous ideas, a scheme of such simplicity whereby he found a way of bankrupting Hitler and destroying the German economy overnight, sadly never reached the powers that be at the War Office until 1946. He was convinced that his plan would have shortened the war by two years at the very least. The plan included, naturally, a commission of 2% on every pound saved by the Allies. How it got lost in a mound of paperwork at the War Office was anybody's guess. But in early 1947 he received a letter from them thanking him for his offer to supply sixty-five light bulbs and four dozen packets of hairnets, but they would not be needed. What light bulbs, what hairnets? thought Solly. There must be another Solly Bernstein.

He was, however, wise enough to keep a copy of his master plan just in case there was another war. All he needed to do was to scratch out 'Germany' and replace it with whatever country Great Britain was at war with. Next time, though, he would be ready and not allow the government to lose the paperwork or dismiss his idea out of hand, although he might consider dropping his commission to 1%.

A scheme to allow Jewish pensioners the right to their own permanent deckchair on the seafront at Westcliff for an upfront fee based on age and life expectancy failed to get off the ground, as did another plan to offer a free copy of the Jewish Chronicle with the purchase of a 1/6d plastic raincoat. The idea of selling water that came out of Rabbi Fishman's kitchen tap and marketing it in bottles as Genuine Kosher Drinking Water fell on deaf ears, so he decided to put a similar scheme forward to the local Catholic Church hierarchy and was surprised when, without giving any reason, they rejected out of hand the idea of Solly selling bottles of Father Patrick's Water.

Things were going from bad to worse. But he still had ideas; big ideas. He did, however, admit to himself that he needed help. It was all well and good coming up with great ideas and schemes, but it was difficult to do things on one's own. Okay, help might mean having to share the profits, but it would be better than having no profit at all. Sadly he knew nobody who had the same mindset, or understood the workings of a genius.

Then Solly met Harry.

And all because of a craving for viennas, Bloom's viennas.

A meeting made in heaven. A meeting of two like-minded lunatics. A meeting that took place in Hessel Street. A meeting of such disturbing proportions that, to this day, nobody knows how the two of them managed to avoid the men in white coats that weren't butchers.

It was by pure chance that they met. Harry lived in a flat in Brady Street, a million miles from Hessel Street, even as the crow flies, so he rarely went there - shame on him. And Solly lived in one of the flats in the street.

Both were in Joe Gorminsky's butcher shop to buy some Bloom's viennas. Every other butcher had sold out, which is why Harry was in Hessel Street. For some unknown reason there was a run on viennas. Maybe somebody from Bloom's was spreading a rumour that there was going to be a shortage and it was time to stock up. Maybe a lot of people just fancied viennas. It happens. Harry had got there first and asked Joe's son-in-law, Reuben, for two pounds. Reuben said Harry was in luck because that's all that was left. On overhearing this, Solly started to walk out. "Hold on a minute, Solly," called Reuben, "where are you going?"

"I just heard you say that you'd sold the last lot of viennas, and that's all I wanted. I'll come back tomorrow when you get some more in."

Harry interrupted. "Wait, wait, you can have half of mine. I only want a pound; the rest is for my mother. I'll tell her that everybody's run out. She won't know that I bought a pound for myself."

"Are you sure that's okay. I don't want to be the one who's responsible for upsetting your mum."

"Well, she's upset enough people, so don't worry about it."

"Okay, if you say so. Thank you. Sorry, I don't know your name."

"Harry, Harry Greenberg."

Solly tapped his forehead. "Of course it is. Harry, it's me Solly, Solly Bernstein."

"Solly, God, I didn't recognise you. I haven't seen you in years. It must be at least ten. Definitely before the war. The last time I heard about you was last year from a friend of mine. He told me the story about deckchairs for pensioners at Westcliff. I'm sorry you failed. Great idea, though."

"Thanks for reminding me," answered a somewhat forlorn looking Solly.

"Don't look so depressed. I'm sure it only failed because you didn't think wide enough. You only went for Jewish pensioners. You should have gone for all pensioners."

Nobody knew there were other pensioners in Westcliff and there were no records of anybody ever seeing a non-Jewish pensioner on the promenade at Westcliff.

Before they could continue, Reuben interrupted. "Excuse me, you two bigshot wheeler dealers, is there any chance you can pay up and go?" Reuben had separated the viennas into two bags. "Right, 1/9d each."

"What do you mean 1/9d? Everybody else is charging 1/6d a pound," protested Harry.

"Nobody's charging 1/6d because nobody else has got any. I'm the only one."

"Of course you're the only one. It's because you're charging more than everybody else."

What was the point of arguing? Every point. But they still paid 1/9d each.

As they left the shop, Solly asked Harry what he was doing for the next hour or so.

"Nothing much. I've just been to the dentist. I've had a terrible toothache for ages. He wants to take a couple of teeth out so I told him I'd think about it. In the meantime he told me to use oil of cloves; it might help kill the pain. Better it killed the cost. My dentist hasn't signed up for the National Health yet so I might have to change and find one that has, and get it done for free."

"And work?"

"Not much. I do three or four days a week on a stall down the Whitechapel Road for a friend of mine, and on Sundays I do the Lane for him."

"I can't believe it, all these years and I've never seen you around."

"I seem to do all the shlapping, whilst Jack does the selling, that's why. And you?"

"I'm working for Kestlebaum the tailor on and off, but to be honest, I'm bored. I need a challenge. I've got a few plans up my sleeve but nothing concrete." He paused then asked, "Married?"

"Why? Do you want to marry me?" he laughed. "No, I escaped just in the nick of time. But that's another story. And you?"

"No thank you very much. It's not for me," he lied. Then he dropped his voice to almost a whisper. "Listen, come back to my flat just up the street. I've got an idea that could make us both some money. And I've also got something for your toothache. Better than oil of cloves any day and it smells and tastes much better."

Harry shrugged his shoulders. "Sure, it's got to be better than going to see my mother and her having a go at me for not getting the viennas. I'll tell her later."

"So where're you living?"

"I'm still in Brady Street Mansions but on my own I'm pleased to say. My uncle owned a hardware shop in Hackney and when he died he left me a few bob. So I moved out from living with my parents. At the moment I'm okay, but if the rent goes up too much I might be in a bit of trouble."

"Well, let's hope both of us can make a fortune with what I've got in mind and then you won't have to worry. Brady Street Mansions will be history."

Solly lived at number 22 Morgan Houses. Morgan Houses was the block of flats that stretched almost the length of Hessel Street on the left-hand side if you're coming from Commercial Road. The name confused everybody, even those who lived there. Hessel Street used to be called Morgan Street for donkey's years until some clever so-and-so decided to change its name round the early 1900s, in honour of Phoebe Hessel, some crazy woman who dressed as a man so she could join the British army. But that was a hundred and fifty or so years ago. Why didn't they name it Hessel Street years earlier instead of waiting so long?

Solly's flat was spotless. If nothing else in his life he was meticulous to a fault when it came to cleanliness. The mahogany drawer leaf table and four chairs plus the sideboard in the lounge-cum-dining-room were all beautifully polished. Pictures of his parents and other members of his family recently and long gone from this world adorned the walls, and a few pieces of china that the family had collected over the years sat neatly on the mantelpiece.

The scullery comprised a sink, gas stove and small fridge - don't ask where that came from - with a small working surface above a bank of drawers. No bath. He would go twice a week to Betts Street Baths or the Turkish Baths in Poplar.

Solly's parents had died before the war. His father, who had married very late in life, died from a heart attack, and his mother died a couple of years later from what Solly believed to be a broken heart. The fact that she was hit on the head by a heavy block of wood that fell from a building site never altered his belief. As he often said, "If she wasn't so depressed she would never have gone that way; she would have taken a different short cut."

"Harry, take a seat." Solly opened the door of the sideboard and pulled out a full bottle of Johnny Walker Black Label whisky and two glasses."

Harry's eyes lit up. "My God, Heaven in a bottle! Where did you get it from?"

"It was my dad's and it's been sitting in the sideboard ever since he died waiting for the right moment to come along. And I'm certain this is that moment." He peeled off the seal, removed the cork and poured two ample portions. "I know this might be a delicate situation given your pain, but what do you know about false teeth?"

"Not much. But by the time the dentist's finished with me I could be an expert."

"By then it might be too late, but never mind. Stay there, I'll be back in a sec. Drink up. The pain will go quicker than you can say Johnny Walker."

Harry did exactly that. He picked up the glass, placed it just under his nose and sniffed. He then put it to his lips, opened his mouth and took a gentle sip. Nectar, nothing less than pure nectar. He swirled it around his mouth, took a deep breath through his nostrils and then swallowed. What pain? he thought to himself. Who needs a dentist and cloves when you've got whisky?

Solly returned carrying two very large carrier bags and emptied the contents onto the table. False teeth, dozens of them. Top teeth, bottom teeth, part sets, full sets. You name the combination, Solly had them.

Harry was lost for words, which was rare. He was never lost for words.

"How, what, where?"

"And there's plenty more,"

"Where did you get them all from?" asked an incredulous Harry.

"I know people at the London Jewish Hospital, and I also know a guy who works for a firm of undertakers, and sometimes things go sideways instead of down. There are a lot of people who don't want to be buried with their false teeth. It's something to do with false pride. 'I came into this world without teeth, and that's the way I'm going out.' At least that's what some of them say."

This cannot be a coincidence, thought Harry. There's a greater force at work here, somewhere.

"I know this might sound crazy, but why? Why have you got so many? They look disgusting. It's a mishegus."

"Harry, my new old friend, you never know when you're going to need false teeth. And we need them now, right now. And so do a lot of other people. In fact, they don't know it yet, but they're going to need them very soon."

Poor old Harry was confused. He always fancied the idea of getting his teeth into some scheme or other and make a few bob, but this? This was beyond even his understanding. And it shouldn't have been.

"So? Explain."

"Simple. It's coming up to Pesach and people are going to need Kosher for Pesach false teeth. That's it, that's all there is to it."

This is more than a coincidence, this is providence, Harry thought.

The moment he saw them, the penny should have dropped, especially as he had been talking to Rabbi Katz about the very same thing a few weeks earlier, which, in fairness, he had forgotten about. Surprisingly, the rabbi had never given him an answer. But then again, Harry hadn't gone to shul.

Solly continued, "Gunnuf companies and people make a lot money at Pesach. You tell Jews things have to be kosher for Pesach and they believe it and buy them, especially if you put the price up."

"It's got to be kosher for Pesach, look at the price."
"It's daylight robbery."

"True! But it's Kosher for Pesach daylight robbery."

"You're right, I never thought of it that way."

"Are you sure you have to have Kosher for Pesach dentures?" His memory of asking the rabbi the same question came straight back.

"There are lots of people selling false teeth, even Woolworths. And as you know you can now get them for nothing on the National Health."

"Very True, Harry, but not Kosher for Pesach false teeth. At least I don't think so. Anyway, it doesn't matter. People don't know if you can or you can't. And if they don't know, they'll buy them, just in case. Especially if you tell them they need to buy them. Remember, every Jew buys, just in case."

Harry sighed. "This is fantastic. I've never been able to come up with any good ideas, but I've always wanted to get involved and work hard with somebody who does, and I'm sure you're the right somebody, and this is the right time. I don't know why you haven't become a millionaire."

"Because I've always needed someone like you. A like-minded person who understands the workings of a genius. A man after my own heart. And I can see by the look on your face. It's changed from one of shock to one of 'we can make a lot of money here.'"

And Solly was right. Harry was just the perfect partner. "Okay, so far so good. It's one of the greatest ideas I've ever heard. But how are we going to sell them?" He should have known the answer straight away.

"That's where you come in. Where did you say you work? Down the Waste? Whitechapel Road? How many people walk down there every day? Dozens, hundreds, maybe more. And how many of them are Jewish and old? Loads of them, all looking to save a bit of money and, on Pesach especially, they definitely want to save a few bob. And we're going to help them with our cheap as chips dentures. And if they don't need the dentures for themselves, they'll know somebody who does need them - even if the somebody doesn't know they do. And they're all being taken for a ride by these gunnuf companies and sheisters charging a fortune. But we won't be charging a fortune. That's the difference. We'll be charging a fair price; no, a very fair price."

"So, you want us to take them for a fair ride by selling them Kosher for Pesach false teeth which they may or may not need. We should be ashamed of ourselves." He stopped talking, looked at the dentures, smiled, exposing the most perfect set of teeth possible and then shouted, "I love it. I love it. I love it. This year it's Whitechapel and next year it's going to be Golders Green and a semi-detached house." He then polished off the rest of the whisky in his glass in one victorious gulp.

He continued, "I've just thought of something. My friend, Jack, who runs the stall, is getting a consignment of Bonn's matzos in for Pesach, all genuine, but maybe a little older than they should be, maybe three or four years, give or take a year here or there. But they've all got Pesach labels on them. Jack bought thousands of them, not matzos, the sticky labels. If last year's anything to go by, he'll be sold out within three or four days, and we'll be able to use his stall. He doesn't like working harder than he has to. And, more importantly, we can buy a load of labels from him. We're going to need them. Solly, I wish I hadn't lost touch with you for so long."

"I'll drink to that," said Solly, filling the glasses with yet more nectar.

There was a pause in the discussion whilst they both took another sip of one of God's greatest creations. Then Solly said, "Mmmm, I've just thought. There might be a problem, which may or may not be a pleasant one."

"What's that?"

"What happens if we run out of dentures completely, even if I get a re-stock? People won't be happy if there's a long queue and we don't have any left. There could be a riot. They could be fighting tooth and nail over them. I can see the headlines in the East London Advertiser, 'Police Break up Kosher Denture Disorder.'"

Harry thought for a moment, beamed the beam of a man whose mind was on fire, and replied, "I've got it. Don't worry, Solly, I have the perfect answer. We'll sell them Kosher for Pesach denture vouchers they can redeem next year. Not only that, we can sell Kosher for Pesach denture gift tokens they can give to somebody else as a present."

Genius - pure genius.

It was a match made in Heaven. Two meshugenas waiting at the gates - to Colney Hatch Lunatic Asylum.

And so it came to pass. Over the two following weeks, Solly and Harry prepared their assault on the Jewish population of East London with their Kosher for Pesach false teeth. Harry knew a man who worked for Waterman's the box makers so he managed to get hold of more than enough gift boxes of various sizes and other wrapping material, just in case they ran out of their stock of dentures and needed to buy more from Solly's 'sources'. He also bought some small white cards and envelopes, as they might have to sell gift cards and vouchers.

You have to plan ahead.

And Solly even had a name for their business. "I've got a great name for us, Harry. We call the business Solhar Dentures. I've taken the first part of my name and the first part of yours and put them together. What do you reckon to that for a great idea?"

"Why can't the first part of my name be first?"

"I thought about it and came to the conclusion it wouldn't be a good idea. Just think about it."

It took Harry a few seconds before the obvious sunk in. "Now I understand. So Solhar it is."

They washed and cleaned the dentures, polished them as best as they could, packed them neatly and, using Harry's old, but never-before-used children's John Bull's printing set, printed Solhar Dentures, the details of the false teeth, and the price, on each box. And, most importantly, stuck on a Kosher for Pesach label on the underside of each one. They were works of art. Even Harrods would have been impressed. Not that Harrods sold dentures. Or did they? Even Harry's toothache had gone, and so had the whisky and most of their money.

But it didn't matter, they were going to make a small fortune. But how big a small fortune? That was the question.

The calculations were easy. Sale price minus costs. What could be more simple? Anything probably, considering neither had any financial or business sense.

Solly, more positive than he had been in years, was convinced that they could easily sell between four to five hundred sets of teeth without too much difficulty. So by adding all their outgoings together including the cost of the stall for a couple of days, and working on a 200% mark-up on each set - approximately, they would be into a very handsome profit of at least twenty pounds each. This figure, however, did not take into account any vouchers or tokens they might sell. That would be a bonus.

Considering the average wage for a worker in the East End was about four pounds a week, twenty pounds each wasn't bad at all for their first joint venture. In fact, it was a small fortune that they would put towards their next foray into the business world. That's if they sold every set, but not if they sold none or only some. Of course, that was the one thing that had never crossed their minds.

Pesach was getting closer and closer, and they were working harder than they had ever done before, but it had to be done under a veil of secrecy. Nobody was to know what they were up to. The last thing they needed was for somebody else to jump in and get the business and financial rewards Solly and Harry so richly deserved.

Solly told Kestlebaum that he needed more time off for some important research into his next scheme. Kestlebaum was a little relieved. Business was not that good, even coming up to Pesach, so if Solly wasn't working, he wouldn't be getting paid. It suited them both. Harry, when he wasn't shlapping for his friend, Jack, had nothing else to do but work towards his aim of becoming rich.

Then the time came. Jack had sold his consignment of Bonn's 'Kosher for Pesach' matzos in three days, just as Harry predicted. The stall was theirs. The denture venture adventure was about to begin.

A week to go before Pesach; prime selling time.

"Get a new smile for Pesach. Get your Kosher for Pesach dentures here. Buy while stocks last. When they've gone, they've gone. Be the envy of all your friends." Harry was working on his sales pitch. It had to be the performance of a lifetime.

He went over to Solly's flat early in the morning. Not a minute of selling time to be wasted. The plan was simple. Harry would go and set up the stall with as many dentures as he could possibly carry whilst Solly would go off to see Sideways Sid at the undertakers to see what other deals could be done on futures in dentures, just in case. He would meet Harry later in the day down the Waste with the rest of the dentures, count their takings and celebrate the good news with a bottle of the hard stuff.

Harry managed to load at least two hundred boxes into six large carrier bags, and carried three in each hand. He made his way down the steps of the block of flats and headed for Whitechapel Road and their fortune. He got to the top of Hessel Street, turned right and then waited at the traffic lights. He just had enough time to glance over his shoulder and look at Frumkins' wine shop at the corner of Cannon Street Road and Commercial Road. He was wondering how many bottles of Palwins wine or, better still, Johnny Walker he would be able to buy with his newly found wealth. The lights changed, Harry crossed over Commercial Road and made his way down New Road.

Then!

Harry's mind was so occupied with how rich he was going to become he forgot to stop when he reached Fieldgate Street and carried on walking. He didn't see the steam roller coming from his left, and the driver didn't see Harry. The collision was catastrophic. Harry was knocked flying in one direction, whilst the carrier bags containing the crown jewels went another, straight under the steam roller. The most crushing blow of all to Harry and Solly's well-planned and faultless scheme had just taken place.

Two hours later, a pained Harry found himself recovering in Casualty at the London Hospital, bruised, battered, bloodied and minus four teeth. The only good news for Harry was that two of the missing teeth were those that his dentist wanted to remove. As he was sitting waiting to be discharged, Rabbi Katz came by. "I'm sorry you're not too good, Harry. I just heard what happened so I thought I'd come straight away to see if you're okay. Please God you'll recover soon.

Oh, by the way. If it's any consolation, there's some good news for you on the teeth front. I'm pleased to tell you that after discussions between the rabbunim, we've all agreed you don't need to have kosher for Pesach dentures. But if you're really worried, boil them. That'll do, according to a couple of the older rabbis. There was an article about it in the Jewish Chronicle a couple of weeks ago. Maybe you read it. Anyway, I have to rush to the London Jewish Hospital now and see Mrs Silverman and her ingrowing toenail. Have a good Pesach, Harry, and I hope to see you in shul soon."

Hope away, rabbi, hope away.

For obvious reasons, Harry couldn't reply, but gently nodded his head in grateful acknowledgement. The pains got worse and Harry closed his eyes. Maybe if he died there and then, the aches, pains and distress would go away for all time.

If only Harry had gone to shul at least once in the past few weeks.

If only Harry had read the Jewish Chronicle.

If only Solly hadn't just agreed to buy two hundred sets of dentures at a shilling a set.

If only Solly had talked to Joseph the denture seller in Aldgate first.

If only there were no such things as Bloom's viennas.

If only Harry hadn't met Solly, again.

Letter from a Loser

It was the Hessel Street bachelors Monday night card school at
Norman Silver's flat. Once a fortnight, three of the most eligible
Jewish bachelors in the East End would meet to take money from
the most ineligible, Issy Fisher. Issy was, without doubt, the worst
card player in the history of card playing. It wasn't as if he didn't try
and learn, and it wasn't as if the others just thought it was a quick
and easy way to earn money. Issy refused to stop. Every time they
suggested he didn't join in, he insisted on joining in. So what could
they do? Take his money, that's what. But in fairness to the three of
them, they did, on more than one occasion, try to cheat so that he
could win but it was a pointless exercise. He still managed to lose.
That's how bad he was at cards.

But it wasn't only at cards that Issy lost. He lost at Ludo and darts
and draughts and chess and even Snakes and Ladders. It made
no difference what game he played, he lost. And what's more it
extended to team games. Even as a kid, nobody would pick him to
play in their street football team because they knew that there was
a very good chance that they'd lose, however good the team was.

They would rather have played with half a team than have Issy in their side. He was a human bad luck charm.

There were losers and losers in Hessel Street, including the great Solly Bernstein, but there was no doubting the sad and undeniable fact that Issy Fisher was the street's top ranking shlemiel.

He knew deep down, however, that one day things would turn in his favour and he would find a way of getting back the money he had lost playing cards with his friends. He was certain that one way or another, maybe not at cards, he would eventually turn a corner and be the success his parents had been praying for since the day he was born. He just needed time. But time and money were running out.

They had just finished playing yet another round of pontoon and Issy was banker; Issy lost four shillings and the other three had won four shillings between them.

"Just one more hand, please. Give me a chance to win some of it back," pleaded Issy.

"You've got a better chance of going out with Princess Margaret than winning tonight, or any night, Issy. Why don't you just realise that you're no good at any card game. You even lose at patience," said Sid Lever, who had probably taken more money from Issy than anybody else. Sid looked at Issy's desperate face, sighed and said, "Alright, but this is the last hand. Everybody in?" Everybody was in and Issy lost even more money.

Why didn't he just put money into three envelopes and hand them out every other Monday night? It would have saved a lot of time and misery.

Issy was 33 years old, weighed in the region of fifteen stone and was about 5' 7" in height. Add to this a nearly bald head, new wire framed National Health glasses and a set of prematurely browning teeth from smoking too many Woodbines and Capstans, Issy looked the part of a loser. That was until that crucial Monday night. The

Monday night that was to change his life forever.

Before then, everything he had touched turned to dust. He had even failed his medical to do his part in the war - much to his relief. Overweight, poor eyesight and the inability of not being able to run more than ten yards without stopping to catch his breath, were just a few of the reasons given. There were also unfounded rumours that he was turned down by the Armed Services because they were terrified that if Issy joined up there would be no chance of the Allies winning the war. But it was only a rumour.

And to cap it all, Issy was one of the few failures dealing on the Black Market during the war. The problem being that he was trying to sell things that nobody wanted, which is how he managed to buy them so cheaply - and not sell them.

"Get in touch with Issy, he'll buy them."

"But nobody wants them."

"But Issy doesn't know that nobody wants them, so he'll buy them."

"And when he finds out that nobody wants them?"

"Tell him they've gone out of fashion but one day they'll come back into fashion. All he has to do is to wait until the war's over."

So Issy bought them, whatever 'them' were, and the spare bedroom in his flat quickly became an overstocked stockroom. And as for 'them' coming back into fashion after the war; unfortunately, nobody told him what war.

He was on the slippery slope to financial oblivion. The only good thing was that his parents paid for his flat in Hessel Street. Things were bad enough without having Issy live with them. Good thinking, Mr and Mrs Fisher.

Job after job and good money after bad, and, understandably, not a love affair in sight. So that was Issy Fisher, a born loser.

> "A loser is a loser is a loser. Whatever he tries his hand at, he loses. It's just as well he hasn't found a woman who'll have him; he'll lose her as well. Probably on the way to the wedding. He'll get lost going to one shul and she'll be waiting for him at another one."

As Issy left the Norman's flat around midnight, he was certain that he had lost for the last time. It was Sid Lever's comment that Issy had a better chance of going out with Princess Margaret than winning at cards that gave him the idea. And what an idea! And one that he had to act upon straight away.

His present very part-time job behind the counter at Kossoff's the bakers allowed him the luxury of staying in bed until at least eleven in the morning. The next morning, however, was different. He was up and about by nine. Tea and a piece of toast by nine-thirty and he was all set. Pen in hand, clean paper and carbon paper for a copy in front of him. He was ready; ready to write the letter of a lifetime. Now, the one thing that God had blessed him with was beautiful handwriting which is why, in addition to everything else, there was no chance of him becoming a doctor.

And this is what he wrote:-

Princess Margaret   *42 Morgan Houses*
Buckingham Palace   *Hessel Street*
London   SW1   *London E1*
4th February 1951

Dear Princess Margaret,

I know you must be very busy at the moment what with having to look after and play with your new niece, Anne, and everybody in your family being busy with the Festival of Britain coming up and other royal stuff, but being a loyal servant and a great admirer, I am writing to ask you for your help.

My name is Israel, like the country, but everybody calls me Issy, Issy Fisher. I live in a place called Hessel Street, which you may or may not know is up the Commercial Road from Aldgate in East London. On second thoughts, I'm sure you have never heard of it but you never know. I work part-time for a local bakery that, by the way, sells very good bread, beigals, strudel and lots of other stuff your family might like. But, to be honest, I don't think my prospects at the bakery or anywhere else are very good, which is why I'm asking for your help.

I've been a failure all my life, not being able to keep a job or money, even my dole money. My mother and father have given up on me, and I've come to the conclusion that you are my last chance of succeeding in life. Don't worry, I'm not asking you to marry me. I know that you're not allowed to marry commoners such as myself. We Jews have the same problem - not about marrying commoners, we do that all the time. No, about marrying someone who is not Jewish. All I'm asking for you to do is to write to me saying you'd be pleased to come and have tea with me in Hessel Street. You won't have to turn up. You can cancel at the last moment saying that you've got a bad cold or something. I can then show the letter to everybody, and my standing in the street will go up and up. I will no longer be a failure.

If you're not allowed to write that sort of letter, just say you can't come, but can you make sure that the envelope is marked Buckingham Palace. At least that'll give everybody in the street something to talk about, especially the yachnas, sorry, gossips. For your information, a yachna is Yiddish for a gossip. Our postman has got a big mouth so I'm sure he'll tell as many people as possible that I've got a letter from Buckingham Palace. In fact, all he has to do is to tell one person, and that person, whose name I cannot divulge for reasons of national security, will tell everybody. Nobody around here can keep a secret, especially if you tell them not to tell anybody.

I hope you do not think I am taking a liberty writing this letter, and look forward to hearing from you very soon.

Please give my regards to the rest of the family.

Your obedient servant

Israel Fisher

Ps if you don't think it's right to write a letter, that's okay. All you need to do is to send me an envelope from Buckingham Palace and you can just put in a blank piece of paper. Nobody would dare open the envelope.

Issy

What a letter, he thought to himself. This is the best thing I've ever done.

At last he knew he was on to a winner. But only if...

As he finalised the letter, he started talking to himself out loud. "If she says she can come, I win, and if she says she can't come, I still win. As long as the envelope is marked Buckingham Palace. I just have to pray that she replies. Please, God, do me this one favour. That's all I'm asking. Thank you." Then he started to panic. What happens if she agrees to come? Where would he put all his stock? How would he be able to clean his flat up on his own? Where would they be able to park the royal car? They would have to close the street. How, what, where? A thousand problems to resolve and just as many questions. He then decided it was a pointless exercise worrying about any of it until he received a reply...if he received a reply.

He folded the letter and placed it into an envelope, addressed it, took a stroll to the post office in Philpott Street, along the Commercial Road - he couldn't trust the local post-box - purchased a first class stamp, kissed the envelope and posted his letter to Princess Margaret and success. He then went off to Kossoff's for an afternoon's stint.

Now all he had to do was to wait and pray. He was convinced that it was only a matter of time. And it was.

The reply came ten days later, and the envelope was marked 'Buckingham Palace'. The postman was about to the deliver the letter to Issy when he was waylaid, as usual, by Doris Feldman, the undisputed doyenne of East End yachnas.

"Anything of interest?" Doris had to know everything - first or, better still, before it happened.

"None of your business this time, Doris. This one's very special. It's for a Mr Israel Fisher."

"For Issy, Issy Fisher? Issy never gets letters, especially special ones. Let me look. No, better still, give it to me. I'll take it up to him. I was going that way anyway."

Of course you were, Doris, but you might take a detour to your flat and steam the letter open.

"No chance, Doris. This one's very important. I have to deliver it myself."

"Okay, so tell me what's so important about it."

"I can't say." He knew he would.

"I know secrets," whispered Doris.

"Okay, okay, but don't tell a soul I told you." He knew she would.

"As if I would do such a thing." As if she wouldn't.

"It's from Buckingham Palace," he whispered, "and it's marked private and confidential."

For a moment Doris was silent, but only for a moment. "From

where? Are you sure? How can that be? This is Issy we're talking about," said a stunned Doris.

"Don't ask me, Doris. All I do is to deliver letters, I don't write them."

"Let me just have a peep. That's all, a peep. I won't say a word."

The postman, holding the envelope close to his body, moved it slightly so that Doris could see the front. "That's it," he said, "that's all I'm showing you."

"Oivay, oigevalt, oivay. You're right. I've never seen anything like it in my life. I have to tell Hannah. No, I mean I'm going off not to tell her. Goodbye, goodbye. Thank you for not showing me." And off she went, wobbling and hobbling down the street, waving her hands in the air, mumbling to herself. As for the postman, it was the first time he had ever held an envelope that had come from Buckingham Palace so he had to make sure it was delivered by hand and not just pushed through the letter box. He had thought about wearing white gloves to handle it, but decided that that was going over the top, just a little.

He walked up the steps to Issy's front door, straightened his uniform, coughed and knocked on the door. Issy put on his glasses - he was already dressed - and opened the door.

"Mr Fisher?" He knew Issy but had to make the procedure sound formal.

"Yes."

"I have the greatest pleasure in handing you this letter that has come directly to you from Buckingham Palace. May you have a pleasant day. Good morning to you, sir." Sir? This was Issy he was talking to.

"And good morning to you, Mr Postman." He didn't know his name. Issy took the letter and closed the door behind him. He looked at it, put it to his nose and sniffed. The most beautiful perfume he had ever smelled, including the box of allegedly highly desirable, but completely unsaleable perfume that somebody had sold him during the war. He closed his eyes and sighed.

Please God, please God, he thought to himself. Please God, Doris has seen the letter. Sometimes, Issy, wishes come true. It worked. His plan had worked. It didn't matter what the letter said. In fact, he wasn't sure that he should even open it. If Doris knows all about it, that's all that matters. But he did open it, just in case Princess Margaret was coming to tea. It read as follows:-

Dear Mr Fisher

Her Royal Highness, Princess Margaret, has asked me to write to you on her behalf.

Regretfully, she is unable to accept your kind offer to entertain her for afternoon tea in Hessel Street, due to many prior commitments, but does thank you for your very kind offer and comments.

She does, by the way, remember her mother mentioning Hessel Street to her when she was young but cannot remember the context.

However, she would like to know a little more about the bakery where you work, as there are times when she fancies nothing more than a cream cheese or smoke salmon beigal, or just a piece of strudel. If you are in a position to supply the aforesaid items as and when, she would be most grateful. If by chance, you have a telephone, would you kindly forward the number as soon as possible. A smoked salmon beigal may be needed at any moment.

Her Highness will, of course, ask you to be discrete with regard to this matter as it is not something that she wishes to become public knowledge.

Her highness looks forward to your reply in the near future.

Penelope Middleton-Smythe.

Lady-in-Waiting

Ps Princess Margaret also wishes to know if the bakers make a good chola.

More than anything he could possibly have hoped for. And within minutes everyone in the street would know that he had received a letter from Buckingham Palace, and they would have to guess the contents. He, of course, would not say a word.

"It's a mistake. It's for another Issy Fisher."

"In another Hessel Street?"

"Is there another Hessel Street?"

"Maybe not, but I'm sure there must be another Issy Fisher."

"But not like this one."

"No other Issy Fisher is like this one."

"That's why Buckingham Palace has got the wrong one."

"How can Buckingham Palace be wrong?"

"When they're not right."

"Ah! Maybe it's a different Buckingham Palace."

"Do you know of another Buckingham Palace?"

"No. Do you know another Issy Fisher?"

"No."

"Then we're evens."

Now for part two of Issy's plan. Even though he wasn't sure that the first part of his plan would come off, when you need a part two, you need a part two to be in place, just in case.

Silence, whatever happens, silence. If anybody asks him what the letter was all about, he had to maintain a silence, a dignified silence. A silence befitting a man who had just received a private and confidential letter from Buckingham Palace.

"I'm sorry. I can't talk about it. I'm sworn to secrecy and silence."

When his mother asked him what was going on, Issy politely told her that he was not allowed to say a word, not even to his parents. Okay, so a little creativity was coming into play but things were moving in his direction. A little flexibility in the truth was not a bad thing under the circumstances.

His father, in a state of complete denial, turned to his wife and said, "Now I know he's gone potty. I don't know who he is any more, as if I did before. We need to have him certified. We need to have him locked up." With that he waved his arms in despair and walked off. His wife yelled at him as he disappeared into Commercial Road, "You know he takes after your side of the family, not mine. Just remember what happened to your uncle Hymie."

Not even Doris knew what had happened to his uncle Hymie.

It was pretty obvious that the number of people in Hessel Street who needed locking up for their own safety and the sanity of others, or the other way round, was increasing by the hour. No, by the minute. Somebody should have thought of turning the street into a private asylum catering specifically for the Jewish community.

Unfortunately, from a financial point of view, but fortunately, in this particular instance, for Issy, it was another day without work at Kossoff's. Now he had to put part two of his plan into action. It was time for him to walk from one end of the street to the other and back again, slowly. But this time it would be different. No hands in pockets and head hovering just above the ground. It was time for a straight back and a head held high, mighty and proud. This was the new Issy, no, Israel Fisher. He lost count of the number of people who stopped him. Everybody was given the same answer. "I can't talk about it. Not yet. All in good time." It was the 'not yet' that got tongues wagging.

"He's been given an award," said Hannah Woolf, Doris's best friend and another top-notch yachna.

"What for, losing? People don't get awards for losing," said Doris.

Are you sure, Doris?

"It's a fake. It's all a fake. Nobody in their right mind from Buckingham Palace would write to Issy. In fact, nobody in their right mind anywhere would write to Issy."

"Unless Issy wrote to himself."

"Then it would definitely be a fake."

"Where would he get a royal envelope from?"

"He made it himself."

Such creative thinking, Hannah, but Doris put paid to all that.

"Of course it's not a fake, Hannah. I saw the envelope with my own two eyes," said Doris. Not that she had ever seen a genuine one. "Don't worry. I'll find the truth out soon enough and then everybody will know." Not true, not true. Not this time.

That night, Issy went to sleep with the knowledge that his life had changed forever. But what next? The stage was set for part three.

Next morning, Issy was up bright and early, went to his wardrobe and took out his one and only suit, and pressed it as best as he could. He then found the cleanest shirt and tie which, again, he pressed to his own sense of perfection. He even polished his shoes. Next it was time to comb what was left of his hair, and scrub his hands and teeth. After an hour of preparation, it was time to look in the full length mirror on the wardrobe. A miracle! Even he was shocked by what he saw. He had to look again to make sure who he was looking at. Then it was time to do the most important thing of all - raid his piggy-bank. He had no idea how he had managed to have saved nearly ten pounds during the past six or so years, but he had. Or was it the fact that his mum would come in now and then and pop in a few bob?

The third and final part of The Plan was about to come into play. He knew the street would be busy around mid-day, so, on the stroke of twelve, he made his way down the steps of the flats and into the street, then headed towards Commercial Road, slowly, very slowly. There was no need to rush. It was as busy as he had expected. Heads turned, and heads turned again. The yachnas were out in force, waiting and waiting for something to happen, just like crazed newspaper reporters from the News of the World or some other Sunday newspaper. No-one was quite sure what, no, who they were looking at. Surely it couldn't be Issy. But it had to be. There was only one Issy Fisher in Hessel Street.

"Is that who I think it is?"

"Who do you think it is?"

"Somebody who looks like Issy Fisher."

"As long as it's someone who looks like him then it's okay."

"It *is* Issy. It *is* Issy. Where's he going dressed up to the nines like that?"

"He must be going to the Palace. Dressed like that he must be going somewhere posh. I've never seen him so clean."

"And there's nowhere posher than the Palace. So that's where he must be going."

"I can't believe with my own eyes what I'm seeing," said Doris to herself. "I've got to see what's in that letter." Which, much to her regret and shame, she never did. She was angry with herself. Angry that she had not been able to see the contents of the letter, and worried that she might be about to lose her standing as the leading yachna in the East End. Something she was always worrying about. Well, it was her own fault. There was nothing stopping her from getting hold of a small stick of dynamite, blowing a hole in Issy's front door, crawling through, finding and reading the letter and putting it back in place without anybody being the wiser. But it was an idea that hadn't even crossed her mind. Maybe she *was* slipping.

When Issy reached the top of the street, he paused, looked around and saw the admiring onlookers, well, the busybodies and yachnas. He turned his head back to the main road and smiled to himself. His next action took everybody by surprise. He hailed the first available taxi that came by. The taxi driver pulled over, wound down the window and asked, "Where do you want to go to, mate?" Issy thought he was lucky that it wasn't one of his cabby friends. Then again...

Issy opened the door and got in. "Anywhere you like, my friend, anywhere you like. Just drive somewhere nice and interesting."

"What about Buckingham Palace?"

"That'll do me just fine."

As the cab pulled away, Issy slumped back in the seat and thought about who he could write to next. The Prime Minister? The President of the United States? All the presidents and kings and queens in the world? All of them...and as many famous people as he could think of, as long as he could find their addresses. He just needed to make sure the reply envelopes had headings on them.

First thing next morning he would start making his list and then take a trip to the library to search for addresses. And he promised himself that he would never play cards again.

But whatever you do, Issy, don't forget to write to Princess Margaret as soon as possible; beigals and strudel could become your bread and butter, if not your fortune. And don't forget to mention that Kossoff's sell really good cholas.

Yoseler the Philosopher

You can forget Aristotle. You can forget Plato and discard Descartes. And as for Philo and Moses Mendelssohn, forget them both. And when you get to Voltaire, that anti-semitic good-for-nothing, forget him without giving it a second thought. And you can also add Mendoza and Nietzsche to the list. The greatest philosopher of all was, without question, Yosel Finklestein of Hessel Street. Better known as Yoseler the Philosopher by his acolytes, the Yoselites.

Now, the only thing we know about Yosel's early childhood is that he had one. Nothing special or, conversely, something very special when you lived in Hessel Street.

According to contemporary records, however, we do know that at the age of thirteen he started work at Mazin's the booksellers and publishers in the Whitechapel Road, so there's a very good chance that he was able to read and write, otherwise they would probably not have employed him. But you can never be sure.

"Ken you read and write English, young Master Finklestein?" asked the interviewer who could do neither and spoke in an accent that came from somewhere between Southend on Sea and the Black Sea.

"Yes, sir." Rare for someone so young.

"Can you read and write Hebrew?"

"Yes, sir." Not so rare.

"Very good. Ken you be understanding Yiddish?"

"Yes, sir. Of course." Naturally.

"You are obliviously a very bright young mench, so mazeltov, congratulations, you are now being the proud owner of a new job."

"Thank you, sir, thank you very much. But excuse me, sir, can I ask a question?"

"Is it to do mit de ridiculously low amount of money ve're going to pay you?"

"No, sir."

"Den ask away."

"Can I ask what the job is?"

"Of course. It's very important det you know vot job you're going to do. You are to be holding the very important job of senior...and junior tea maker."

"Thank you, sir, but can I ask you another question?"

"Is dis vun about how hoften ve're going to pay you not regularly?"

"No, sir."

"Den you can ask avay, but this has to be your last kvestion. I'm a very important and busy business man."

"Yes, sir. If I'm only making the tea, sir, why do I need to be able to read and write?"

"So you don't be making coffee by mistake."

This was, no doubt, Yosel's first brush with philosophy, albeit from a distance of at least two hundred miles.

When Yosel left Mazin's fifteen years later, older and wiser but just as poor, he went to work at the East London Advertiser in their advertising department. From there he went to the Jewish Chronicle doing a similar job but with more responsibility. During the blitz on London in 1940, Yosel was given an additional job but, sadly, without any increase in pay. He became the Jewish Chronicle Special War Correspondent for Hessel Street. A job he took most seriously, although, in truth, it involved almost nothing at the most. He was to give a full report every time a bomb hit the street and comprehensive details of any fatalities and casualties, excluding chickens and other livestock. Hessel Street's great escape meant that the total number of reports he submitted amounted to the grand total of zero. That was not the point. He was ready with notebook in pocket and pencil behind ear just in case a report was needed. Little did he know that the young tea boy at the Jewish Chronicle was the war correspondent for Cannon Street Road. It was only when the war finished that Yosel found out about the tea boy and resigned in indignation. How could they give a lowly tea boy the same responsibility as a seasoned advertising man? He should have stayed on. A few years later, the tea boy became a Jewish Chronicle war correspondent covering the Suez crisis.

After working in various semi-interesting and not so interesting jobs for the next couple of years, Yosel had had enough. Getting up every morning and doing similar mundane things day in, day out was becoming a chore. It was time to stop, consider his future, and do something different; something completely different. Something that would give him a new lease of life. But what? Some people join friendship clubs and play cards or lotto every afternoon. But that was for the elderly, which he certainly was not. The lazy take up the exhausting pastime of doing nothing and others just sit around waiting to die. A few, more adventurous ones, take up hobbies such as doing 5000 piece jig-saw puzzles and, without question, every one of these jig-saw puzzlers, if that's what they're called, complaining that there were only 4999 pieces in the box.

> "Why is there always one piece missing and it's always the sky?"

> "It's not missing. You're just not looking properly."

> "I've looked everywhere."

> "But you haven't looked where it is."

> "Listen, if I knew where it was I wouldn't have been wasting my time looking where it wasn't."

> "But you don't know where it is or isn't, but I do."

> "Where's that?"

> "In the box with the other bits you haven't used yet. Look, here it is."

> "You just put it back in there."

> "Why would I want to put it back in the box?"

> "To drive me mad, that's why."

Jig-saws, shmig-saws, lotto, shmotto. Yosel wasn't interested. He had to do something different. He had to do something that nobody else in the street or even the East End had ever done. But what was he to do? After considering and contemplating endless possibilities, and, at the same time, driving his wife round the bend for weeks, he finally came up with the answer. And it was an answer that would shake the very foundations of Hessel Street.

"Miriam, I've made a decision about my future. I'm going to become a philosopher."

"Well done; congratulations. At last, a decision. Good for you. How much does it pay?"

"Nothing."

"Well at least it's not going to cost us anything. When do you start?"

"As soon as I grow a beard and my hair gets longer."

But why become a philosopher? Better still, ask why not. Not only that, you need to ask what a philosopher does and how you go about becoming one. The simple answer to this most complex of questions is to ask a philosopher. And if you don't get an answer you can understand, which is understandable, or, far more likely, can't find a philosopher, ask yourself, but don't expect a straightforward response.

So Yosel became a philosopher, but nobody, including Yosel, was sure how it happened. One thing is certain, though. He did not have a piece of paper confirming his qualifications.

But regardless as to how it came about, within a short period of time, people from all over the East End were flocking to his front door at 68 Morgan Houses in Hessel Street, seeking guidance and to hear his words of wisdom. After years of being a nobody with a small 'n', he was now a Somebody with a capital 'S'. How word got around nobody knows but there's a good chance that a couple of yachnas were involved. And maybe one of them was a little hard of hearing.

"Have you heard about Yosel Finklestein?"

"No."

"Apparently he gave somebody some very good advice by mistake, and all of a sudden everybody wants to talk to him and hear what things he has to say. And now, according to someone whose name I don't want to mention, he's thinking of hiring a shul hall and spouting out his words of wisdom. It's not normal."

"Norman Wisdom's hiring a shul hall?"

"Yosel Finkelstein not Norman Wisdom. All of a sudden he's a somebody, a so-called wise man. I tell you it's gone to his head. It must be all that long hair and the crazy beard he's grown."

"Norman Wisdom's grown a beard?"

"I don't know why I bother. I'm not talking about Norman Wisdom. I'm talking about Yosel Finklestein."

Why didn't you say so in the first place? What about him?"

"He's become a philosopher, that's what."

"That's nice for him. I hope he'll be very happy. By the way, what's a philosopher?"

"Who knows? Let's go get some cold drinks."

"Good, I need to go to Goldrings for some bread. It's cheaper than Kossoffs."

Yosel was now Hessel Street's and possibly the East End's foremost philosopher and agony uncle. There was nothing he didn't know and nothing he couldn't talk about or give advice on. Whether people understood what he was talking about or not was not the issue. Whether he understood what he was talking about or not was not the issue either. Words of so-called wisdom would flow from his tongue as smoothly as advocaat found its way down a bar mitzvah boy's throat. Yosel, now Yoseler the Philosopher, believed he had an innate understanding of human nature and how humans could, without any logical explanation, behave in a way that was not necessarily intended by the instigator or understood by the victim, even if it were self-inflicted. Thinking is one thing, knowing is something else. As Yoseler once said, "The barrel of knowledge can never be filled by herrings alone."

He had a philosophical saying or proverb or a word of comfort for every situation or problem. Not that the saying or proverb necessarily had anything to do with the situation or the problem, but he had one, nevertheless.

"Remember, my friends, the truth can only be found in the ripening of a prune," said Yoseler at the first gathering of Yoselites.

"What's he talking about?"

"How should I know?"

"Because you know about these things."

"What things?"

"The things he's talking about."

"If I knew what he was talking about, I'd be up there, not him."

Of course, nobody bothered to ask Yoseler if he knew what he was talking about.

But according to at least two people, he did know what he was talking about even if they didn't. Here indeed was re-born a wise man. If they didn't understand what he was talking about he was either wise or mad, and as they couldn't prove he was mad, he had to be wise. Thus, standing before them then was Yoseler the Wise, Yoseler the Philosopher.

A few years ago there was a rumour that English Heritage was considering putting a blue plaque up to commemorate where Yoseler had lived. Of course it never happened. It was just a rumour. Anyway, it didn't help that the block of flats no longer existed.

But Yoseler, if he had still been alive, would have had a saying on learning of their fate, *"It's better to knock down a rumour than a block of flats."* True, but only if you took Langdale Mansions, another blot on the landscape, and Morgan Houses out of the equation.

But way before the flats were converted – tastefully - into a pile of rubble, when Hessel Street was in the latter years of its prime, a young newly-wed housewife, Sadie Glickstein, not the Sadie Glickstein with the Blackwall Tunnel for a mouth, the other one, went to Yoseler the Philosopher with a problem. A problem she had been harbouring for days.

"Mr Yoseler, sir, my name is Sadie, Sadie Glickstein. I'm sorry to bother you but may I have a few words?" She was pale and looked old beyond her years, however old she was.

Yoseler beckoned her in. "Come in, come in and you don't have to call me mister, Yoseler will do."

"Thank you, Mr Yoseler. I'm sorry to bother you but I have a problem and I've been told that you might be able to help."

"If I can then of course I will. Please, take a seat. Where have you come from, you look exhausted?"

"I've walked all the way from Chicksand Street just off Brick Lane."

Ah! I know it well. Now I can see why you're so tired. That's a long way to walk. Please, have a little of Miriam's honey cake, it'll give you your strength back, or maybe some lemon tea." Yoseler's wife,

Miriam, was in the 'kitchen' cooking. The smell was wonderful which, as it turned out might not have helped matters. But how was Yoseler to know?

"No thank you. I can't stay very long. My new husband will be wondering where I've got to." She looked a very worried young woman, and only just married. Yoseler considered the possibility that if she was newly married and had a problem, he might have to call on Miriam's for advice. But not yet.

"So how can I help?"

"This is very personal. So personal I can't even talk to my mother about it because she's responsible for the problem. Which is why I've come to you."

A Jewish mother responsible for a problem? Surely not? But it was a perfect situation for a philosopher to get involved, and a Jewish one at that.

"Can I ask what your mother's name is? Maybe I know her because I'm sorry to say I don't recognise you from the street or from around here."

"I'd rather not say if that's okay with you, Mr Yoseler."

"It's fine by me. Whatever you don't want me to know is fine and whatever you do is also fine. So tell me. Anything you say will be in confidence. It will be confidential just between the two of us. Nothing you tell me will ever be disclosed to anybody else, including my wife." And it would always stay confidential. If Yoseler the Philosopher said it would stay confidential, that's what it would stay. But if he didn't mention the word 'confidential', well, let's say it might not stay confidential. "What's this problem that's worrying you so much?"

Sadie cleared her throat and, taking a deep breath, said, "It's chicken soup with lokshen."

"Chicken soup with lokshen is the problem? Explain." Even Yoseler was taken aback. Maybe he did need Miriam's help. But not yet.

"It's the only thing I can make properly, so I don't make anything else and I have a terrible feeling that my husband might soon get fed up with it." Tears started to well up in her eyes. Yoseler handed her a page from the Jewish Chronicle so she could wipe her eyes and blow her nose.

"Thank you, you're so kind," she said. "Are you sure you can spare it?"

He nodded and smiled. "Don't worry, there's plenty more from where that came." He paused, and then asked, "How long have you been married?"

"Sixteen days, this very day."

"And how many times have you made him chicken soup with lokshen?"

"Fourteen."

"And always with lokshen?"

"Always."

"Fourteen out of sixteen, mmm. And the other days?"

"It was our honeymoon. We could only afford two nights away. But the place we stayed at served chicken soup with lokshen both days." Sixteen out of sixteen was definitely a world record.

"So why can't you talk to your mother about it?"

"Because it's her fault. She's a terrible cook. The only thing she's good at making is chicken soup. She ruins everything else, even the chicken, which she manages to overcook almost every time. Oh, and toast, and then she sometimes burns it."

"Toast? She sometimes burns toast?" This problem went far deeper than he had first thought.

"Yes, toast. She taught me how to put a piece of bread onto the end of a toasting fork and stick it in front of the open fire. It took me a while but I managed to do it in the end. Then she taught me how to make the soup. It was difficult at first but after a couple of years I became very good at it. But she couldn't teach me how to make anything else properly." Poor Sadie, a Jewish daughter and not being able to cook. Miriam's help was definitely needed, but not yet. She continued, "Can I tell you something else, Mr Yoseler?"

"Of course you can. Tell away."

"My mother always thought my father loved her soup, but to be honest, he hated it after having it day in day out for so many years. That's why, on lots of evenings, after work at Wickham's the department store, he would go to Johnny Isaacs chip shop in Whitechapel for a bag of chips and some fish or to Bloom's for a salt beef sandwich. He always saved a little for me, so when my mother was in another room I would eat it and then pretend to go for a walk so I could throw the paper away."

"And your mother has never found out over all these years?"

"No, never." A Jewish wife and mother not finding out about something to do with her husband or daughter? Impossible! And what's more, not normal. She definitely needs my help as well, thought Yoseler. "And she always wondered why we had so little money. Please Mr Yoseler, please don't say a word to anybody, please. I don't want to get my father into trouble. I'm also very worried my husband will do the same thing and eat somewhere else." As if he hadn't already.

"To keep one's words to oneself at a moment like this is an honour. Silence is the foundation of all generosity and understanding," said

Yoseler off the top of his head and through his mouth or somewhere else. There was no doubting the fact that he had a silver tongue to match his fine head of silver hair and matching beard.

Sadie looked clueless, but gave a gentle smile of gratitude.

Yoseler the Philosopher shook his head and leaned back in his chair. "Mmmm. This is indeed a situation that does need a little contemplation, and one that I can understand for you is most delicate." And, gently wagging a forefinger, said, "Remember what Samuel Johnson once said, 'when a man tires of his wife's lokshen soup, he soon tires of his wife'. We must resolve this problem as soon as possible. But have no fear, it will be resolved."

Who knew that Samuel Johnson was Jewish? Ah! His first name, Samuel, Shmuel; that gave the game away. Well, according to Yoseler it did. Another secret, and the only person who knew was Yoseler. But where did he find out about the real, Jewish, Samuel Johnson?

Suddenly, the poor young girl burst into uncontrollable tears. But Yoseler's philosophy on tears was very simple. It's better to have them crying first and then laughing rather than the other way round. He handed her another page from the Jewish Chronicle.

Yoseler knew that he would have to think of a comforting and satisfying answer without delay. Poor Sadie, just married and the marriage was going to end quickly, and all because of chicken soup with lokshen. Suggesting that she left out the lokshen, or maybe replace it with kreplach would definitely not help because there was no chance that she would be able make kreplach, or anything else you could put in soup. And anyway, it was the chicken soup that was the problem. So after giving it his careful consideration, he decided not to mention it.

As young Sadie wiped her eyes, cheeks and nose, and tried to compose herself, without much success, it has to be said, Yoseler took a little time out to consider the past.

The eighteenth century Jewish philosopher, sage and onion seller, Shlomo Schon von Bonn definitely got it wrong when he addressed a large gathering of his followers in his home town and said, "A man can never have enough chicken soup, especially with lokshen."

Within years, hundreds of men had died overdosing on chicken soup or choking on lokshen. Yoseler did not want Sadie's husband dying so young from an overdose of chicken soup or choking on lokshen. Nor did young Sadie. As hard as she tried she found it impossible to control the torrent of tears that continued to pour down her cheeks and soak the page from the Jewish Chronicle.

Even Yoseler hadn't seen so many tears. "There, there, don't worry, don't worry. Calm yourself. The fact that you have come to me is good because whilst you have been crying and drying your face, I have been thinking. And because I have been thinking I think I have the answer to your problem." And it involved Miriam.

Young Sadie, sniffing and wiping her nose on the sodden page, which unfortunately happened to contain an article entitled 'Kosher Cooking for the Modern Jewish Housewife' looked up and asked, "What's that Mr Yoseler, what's that?" Her eyes pleading for help.

"**Borsht**," came the resounding answer from Yoseler the Philosopher. "Make him borsht. My wife's got a very nice recipe which she will give you, and she will teach you how to make it. At the same time it will keep your husband very happy. You will come here once a week for the next ten weeks and my wife will also teach you how to cook other things that will keep your husband even happier. Remember, my wife is the real, no, only breadwinner in this family. She works for various kosher catering companies, cooking and preparing for weddings, bar mitzvahs and lots of other functions. She just loves cooking. But don't worry, she won't say a word. It'll be our secret. Just the three of us."

Before the secret was only between Sadie and Yoseler. Now he's added somebody else. Mmmm!

"Oh, thank you Mr Yoseler, thank you. But are you sure that your wife won't mind?"

"Listen, Miriam is the kindest person in the world and when I tell her the problem she will be only too pleased to help. She's in the kitchen cooking at this very moment as I am sure you can smell . . . wait, wait, please don't start crying again. It will not help, but with Miriam's help all will be resolved."

Young Sadie stopped crying and sniffling. "Thank you. I don't know what to say. Thank you and thank your wife even though she doesn't know what she's let herself in for." Really? Miriam had learned the art of cooking and listening to a conversation in the kitchen many years ago.

"How can I repay your kindness?" She gave him a quick kiss on the cheek. The tears had dried up and a smile returned to her face.

"By inviting me and my wife to your first anniversary party," he answered with a red face and a smile that matched Sadie's.

Sadly, the anniversary never happened. The following evening, as he was leaving Johnny Isaacs, Sadie's husband slipped on a pickled cucumber that had fallen out of somebody's bag, cracked his head on the pavement and died on the spot.

However, there was good news. After the mourning period was over, Sadie started visiting Yoseler's wife for cookery lessons and three years later won the prestigious East London Jewish Cook of the Year award. She was lauded for her wonderful cooking and invited to go to America on a lecture tour. Whilst there, she met and married a multi-millionaire Jewish restaurateur, and never looked back. And all because Sadie went to see Yoseler the Philospher.

Would Aristotle have been able to resolve such a life challenging problem? Definitely not. And Plato? Would he have had the intellect to understand the meaning of Jewish life without chicken soup? Without question, no. And what of Philo and Moses Mendelssohn?

Here the situation is somewhat different. What makes a good chicken soup is a question that Jewish philosophers throughout history have tried to answer and have always failed. Jewish mothers, however, have always known the answer.

But arguments about soup in the Jewish home have raged on for centuries. Chicken soup, again according to Shlomo Schon von Bonn, with lokshen, transcends life itself. It is the substance that holds the universe together and without it there is nothing. Another meshugena who would certainly have been at home in Hessel Street. His Jewish contemporary and bitter rival, however, and Yoseler's hero, Moshe die Mench von Munchen, argued differently. He posited the notion in his seminal work 'The Borsht Is Yet To Come', that borsht was much better for the human soul given its richness of flavour and colour but, conversely, chicken soup had the potential to wipe out every Jew in the world. "Logic has it that if we keep killing chickens at this rate, eventually there'll be no more chickens and if there are no more chickens, there'll be no more chicken soup, and if there is no chicken soup there is no Jewish life. But you can always grow beetroot."

And Yoseler the Philospher understood and agreed with this notion. So when he stood up in front of seventy five Yoselites, at a meeting at the Grand Palais in Commercial Road, two hundred or so years later, he supported the argument that borsht was far better and healthier for Jews than chicken soup. He even coined one of the twentieth century's greatest slogans, 'Borsht is Best'.

But there were others, the non-followers, the Anti-Yoselites, who thought that what Yoseler was saying to his followers was utter nonsense, especially when it came to the meaning of soup in the Jewish home. As far as they were concerned he was a fake philosopher, a false prophet, a con man, a charlatan, a man with a silver beard and long hair who knew nothing but said a lot, just like a barrow boy. If that were the case, then, how did he know so much about the secret life of Shmuel Johnson, and the life, works and times of Shlomo Schon and Moshe die Mench? To this day, nobody has found out.

But the detractors didn't care. They were convinced, without an iota of proof, that Yoseler was earning a fortune out of what they thought was a very clever way of making money, philosophy, whatever that was. To them it was irrelevant that Yoseler only charged when he had to cover the cost of hiring a hall. He was out to make money, a lot of it, and that was that.

One brave soul even had the temerity to stand up in a meeting and shout out, "How can you call yourself a philosopher when you talk so much rubbish?"

Exactly! You've answered your own question. You should have become a philosopher.

Unfortunately, at the same meeting, one of Yoseler's female followers, who was a little hard of hearing, and maybe misheard what he had said about borsht, took part in the following conversation many years later.

"I'm sure he said breast."

"No, definitely borsht. He definitely said without doubt that borsht was best. I was there in the front row, all those years ago, when he said it."

"So was I."

"In the front row?"

"No, the back. But he definitely said breast."

"Why would he say breast?"

"Because he's a man."

"But it was in a shul hall."

"So why should that make a difference? A breast is a breast, even in a shul hall."

"But this is Yoseler the Philosopher we're talking about, not just any man. He was a mench. He would never say breast."

"Maybe you're right. Maybe he did say borsht is best and not breast. But it's too late, I've told everybody"

And so she had.

Warts – The Problem

Sid Abrahams and Abe Rosen, now both retired, were, as usual on a Tuesday afternoon, downstairs at Joe Lyons tea rooms in the Whitechapel Road - by the side of the station. They could have gone to the one in Aldgate, but it was too far to walk because, according to Sid, the one in Whitechapel was nearer to Hessel Street, and as they were walking from Hessel Street it stood to reason that the one in the Whitechapel Road was nearer. Whether it was or not was an argument for another day. It would have to be measured inch by inch, on foot. That day, however, might be a long way off.

Anyway, the one in Aldgate wasn't private enough to talk about something that Sid said was very private.

As they walked into Lyon's, Sid asked whose turn it was to pay.

"Who paid last time?" replied Abe.

"I can't remember."

"Then it's yours."

"Are you sure"

"No. But does it matter?

"No."

"So if it doesn't matter, it's your turn."

So Sid paid, and Abe would pay the following week, only if they could remember who paid this time.

Sid, who had lost the toss and was paying, stood in the queue waiting to be served, cafeteria style, whilst Abe walked downstairs and found the most private table, in the corner, near the emergency exit. Emergency, shmergency. The door was bolted and chained anyway. Somebody had forgotten to unlock it. Sir Joseph Lyons, may he rest in peace, would have turned in his gravy. If there were to be a real emergency, however, almost everybody downstairs would be in mortal danger, depending, of course, on the emergency. If it wasn't a life threatening emergency, it wasn't really an emergency, it was just called an emergency but was, in truth, just a problem, so nobody would die. Admittedly it could be a big problem but a problem nevertheless and not an emergency. However, the fact that Sid and Abe were seated at a four-seater table was, in due course, to become a problem, as there were only two of them.

A couple of minutes later, Sid came downstairs with the two drinks and took a seat opposite Abe.

"So what do you want to talk about that's so private?" asked Abe.

Sid looked around to make sure no-one was listening. "Warts," he whispered in reply.

"Shwartz?" asked a confused Abe.

"Not Shwartz, warts."

"I'm sure you said Shwartz." Abe was convinced that Sid had said Shwartz.

"No. You might have thought I said Shwartz, but I said warts." Sid was absolutely certain that he had said warts.

"Maybe it's your pronunciation."

"Maybe it's your hearing."

"There's nothing wrong with my hearing."

"There's nothing wrong with my pronunciation."

"According to you."

So, before they could discuss the matter that was so private, the matter regarding Shwartz or warts had to be resolved.

"You might have thought you said warts but said Shwartz instead. It can happen to anybody, especially you."

"But I don't know anybody called Shwartz."

"Just because you don't know anybody called Shwartz, doesn't mean to say you didn't say it. You don't know Winston Churchill but you've said his name."

With a resigned shake of his head, Sid picked up the sugar sifter and poured two helpings into the best milk and a dash that somebody else's money could buy. Unfortunately, this time it was his money. One day, he thought to himself, this milky coffee is going to make somebody a fortune, all it needed was a change of name and someone to sell it to the world. He never said it or did anything about it. So Sid remained poor.

"What are you doing?"

"Changing the subject."

"But putting sugar into a milk and a dash isn't changing the subject."

"Yes it is. This is my physical way of changing the subject." A good reply; and one he hadn't thought of before.

"Anyway, how can you put so much sugar in?" asked Abe with a look of utter disgust. He always asked the same question and always got the same reply.

"By doing this." Sid lifted the sifter again and pretended to pour more sugar into his drink. "I just like my milk and a dash sweet."

"But you won't be able to taste the coffee."

"What coffee? For the amount they put in they might as well wave a bean at it. Anyway, it still tastes wonderful. Don't ask me how they do it. I don't know. And as for the sugar, so what! You're not drinking it, I am. If you don't want to put sugar in yours, that's fine by me, but for me this is the best way to drink it."

"Too much sugar is bad for you."

"Too much of everything is bad for you."

"Not money."

"True."

Not that either of them knew.

"So what do you want to talk about that's so private?"

"Warts, definitely warts. Not Shwartz," answered Sid as clearly as he could.

"Now you're making yourself clear. This time I definitely heard you say warts. What about them?"

Then Sid beckoned Abe a little nearer.

"Come closer, I don't want to have to shout." In the end, they were so close they could have touched foreheads.

"It's Issy. He's got warts."

"Which Issy?"

"Issy the Stick."

Issy Steingold, Issy the Stick, was given his name because of his diminutive size. An emaciated kosher chicken wouldn't have wanted to be seen dead with legs like Issy's. Sometimes, when he stood sideways and the sun shone in the wrong direction, he was almost invisible. He would have made a perfect foil for a magician who wanted to make somebody disappear on stage. All that was needed was some clever lighting and Issy stripped to the waist. People would have come from miles around just to see him disappear before their very eyes. "And they didn't even use smoke or mirrors. It was magic, a miracle."

But back to the problems.

Abe raised his voice a little. "Issy the Stick's got warts?"

Sid placed his forefinger to his mouth. "Sshh, keep your voice down. Do you want everyone in the place to know what's wrong with him?" Abe shook his head and signalled an apology with his hands.

And now it was time for the other problem. Not an emergency, just another problem.

An old lady they thought they might have known from somewhere a long time ago placed her tray on the edge of the table. Both Abe and

Sid gave her a look.

"Can't you see we're having a private conversation? Can't you please find another table?" asked Abe politely. There must have been at least five empty tables, two-seaters and four-seaters. No, of all the tables in the place, she has to sit next to us, he thought.

"But I always sit at this table, and there are only two of you. And anyway, you can't have a private conversation in a public place," she complained.

"And another anyway, we're waiting for somebody else," replied Sid

That didn't help, and the old lady placed her tray, with a plate of beans on toast and a mug of tea on it, further along the table.

"If you're waiting for somebody else, that'll only make three. In the meantime there's still room for one more, my friend, who's on the way and will be here in a couple of minutes. And when your friend turns up, if he turns up, you can all move." This was a problem that had to be sorted - quickly.

Sid asked her to come closer. As she bent down to hear what he had to say, he whispered, "I'm only asking you not to sit here for your own benefit and safety. My friend here is suffering from something downstairs. If he explodes, we could all be in trouble, and the emergency door is locked."

"I think I'll find another table." She picked up the tray and moved away as fast as her endangered legs could take her, but not before taking a chance with her life and whispering to everybody else downstairs. She then made her way upstairs to relative safety.

The smiles on Abe and Sid's faces said it all.

"So where are the warts?"

"He won't say. But if the Stick says he's got them and they're not on his hands, he must have them somewhere that he doesn't want to mention, which can only mean one place, and he must be worried."

"Could they be down there?" asked Abe, pointing with his index finger to an area just below his waist, hoping that nobody else in the place would see.

"They could be anywhere, but if he doesn't want to tell me where they are, I'm sure they must be down there, although he hasn't said so, so it's not certain."

"Why doesn't he go to the doctor? He'll give him something."
They both took another sip from their tall glasses, and both made 'this is good' faces at each other.

"Would you go to the doctor with them down there?"

"You just said they weren't down there."

"No, I said I wasn't certain. They could be."

Sid took a final mouthful of his milk and a dash. "I knew I shouldn't have ordered this. It's my own fault. Once I drink one, I always want to have another one." As he said it, he looked around and noticed that everyone else in the place had disappeared. The so-called smell that wasn't a smell had just become a great big stink. But the good news was that they had more privacy and could talk a little louder.

"So, tell me, would you go to your doctor?"

"You're right. I don't think I would. People would only talk. You know what doctors are like. They're the biggest unwitting big mouths going. As you leave the surgery, they always shout out as loud as they can; something like, 'Don't forget to rub the cream in properly, and come back next week if the rash doesn't clear up.' That's all I need, a doctor with a mouth the size of Wales."

"So what does the Stick want you to do?" asked Abe

"Help him cure his warts without him having to go to a doctor."

"What do you know about curing warts? Have you become some sort of miracle worker all of a sudden?"

"Of course I've not. I'm not going to cure him, but I have to help him find someone who can. There's got to be somebody out there who isn't a doctor but an expert on warts, especially down there."

Abe scratched his almost hairless head and then rubbed the back of his neck. It gave him time to think.

"Somebody once told me that if you stick a wart in vinegar it helps. Something to do with the acid. I don't know. Maybe it's an old wives' tale."

"And if the warts are down there?"

Abe was trying to be as helpful as possible. "Beggars can't be choosers. If it works, it works. It might just take a little bit more vinegar."

"And if it doesn't?"

"Try some more."

"And what happens if it still doesn't work?"

"Then your crotch will smell like a chip shop."

News of Abe's 'so-called problem' had obviously reached all four corners of Lyons'. One of the counter staff came downstairs, took a very deep breath, walked past them as fast as she could, unlocked the emergency exit and opened the door.

Health and safety first. Or was it fresh air?

"After what you said to that woman about me, I'm not sure we're going to be welcomed back. On the way out, we're going to have to tell them at the counter upstairs what we were talking about. Not the truth, of course. We'll make up another story."

"Agreed. But you can't help me with my problem?"

"I have been. Anyway, I thought it was Issy's problem."

"It is, but it's also mine, and now because you know, it's yours as well."

A problem shared, as they say, is a problem to pass on for somebody else to worry about.

"Duct tape. That's another way you can get rid of them. You wrap duct tape round the wart and after a while it'll go. Or that's what I've heard."

"Again, what happens if he's got them down there?"

"Look at the size of Issy, he's not going to need much duct tape. And if that doesn't work I think you can even get rid of them with matches. Light the match, blow it out and then rub the wart with the end of the match or something like that. I think it's all to do with the sulphur. Maybe you don't light the match. But I'm not sure I'd want to do it down there either way."

Who comes up with all these crazy ideas?

Sid waved a hand of dismissal. Why did I have to get involved with this? he thought to himself. There was too much thinking and not enough thought going into resolving the problem.

They had finished their drinks and were about to leave when Abe clicked his fingers and exclaimed, "I've just remembered something, and somebody who could help." They got comfortable again. Sid thought about having another milk and a dash but changed his mind, worried about *his* problem below the belt. If he had another one he could be pishing all night.

"There's a woman who comes to Hessel Street and cleans for Joe Gorminsky." Only Joe in the street could afford to have someone clean for him. "Anyway, she's supposed to be a gypsy and is always talking about spells and cures and how she can magic away anything. I'm sure she once told someone before the war she cured an old German guy who had a ring of warts round his neck. One week they were there and the next, gone."

"Pity the German didn't go and the warts stay."

The war was long over, but there was still a bitter hatred towards the Germans. Good or bad, dead or alive, what was the difference? Only the Jewish Germans, good or bad, were saved from the opprobrium.

"So how can we find her?"

"We go to Hessel Street and ask Joe Gorminsky."

There was a problem.

"What happens if he asks why we want to talk to her?"

"We'll tell him we know somebody who's looking for a cleaner."

There was another problem.

"Joe won't believe us. He knows we don't know anybody who can afford a cleaner."

Abe had the answer. "We'll tell him we're looking for a cure for a friend who's got a really bad rash, the doctors can't do anything for him and maybe she can concoct a cream he could rub in that would help or she could magic up a spell."

Sid nodded in agreement and gave a satisfied smile. "Not bad, not bad at all - for you." Then he thought of another problem "Wait a minute, if she comes up with cream or a spell for a rash, how's that going to help with his warts?"

"Good question with a simple answer. We tell him that when we get the cream we need to see her to thank her personally and pay her. Then we tell her the truth."

"Not bad. Not good, but not bad, apart from the fact that we would have wasted money on rash cream and not warts cream."

"Not necessarily. If one of us gets a rash we can use it."

"But what happens if she doesn't want to be paid, and she's just doing it out the goodness of her heart."

"Don't worry about it. We'll cross that bridge roll when we come to it."

The woman who had opened the emergency door came back, took a deep breath and cleared the two glasses and placed them on a tray. She looked at Sid and Abe with what could only be called disgust. "If you two have finished could you please vacate the table as we have lots of clients waiting to sit down."

They looked around at the empty tables. What clients? Everybody had gone upstairs for what they thought was their own safety. The place was deserted.

Abe stood up and said, "We were leaving anyway. And don't believe anything that old woman says. She's a number one trouble maker, *and* she's got bad ears. My friend said that I've got problems with the gas downstairs in my house not my ar..." he paused before continuing, "and some blokes are coming to check if the pipes are faulty somewhere."

The woman apologised. "I'm sorry, fellas, I'm new here. I should never have listened to her. She's obviously loopy going around telling everybody a crazy story. Look, don't worry. I'll go and sort it out, and next time you come in, the coffees are on me."

Mr Lyons, you mean. It didn't matter; good customer service was good customer service. And that's what you got at Lyons; especially at their posh Corner Houses. Not that either of them had ever eaten in one of them. But they had heard. One day they would go and find out for themselves.

They left Lyons and made their way to Hessel Street via New Road. It was the quickest way - possibly. Maybe if they had cut round the back of the London Hospital, it would have been quicker.

"Are you sure this Lyons is nearer to Hessel Street than the one in Aldgate?"

You can only ask the same question a finite number of times, or maybe not.

"Does it matter?

"Only if you need to save time."

Both Sid and Abe had plenty of time on their hands and neither needed to save time. And neither needed or wanted to be at home. Their wives were busy in their flats in Hessel Street doing things that only busy women do. Whatever that was. And if they weren't there being busy, they would be in each others flats busying and nosying themselves with other people's business.

"Did you hear what happened to Sadie Goldblum?"

"No, what?

"I can't say. I'm sworn to secrecy. I'm not one of those yachnas, you know."

"Of course you're not. So, tell me. Who am I going to tell?"

"Who knows? So sshh, come closer, but keep it to yourself."

The walk to Hessel Street took them longer than expected. And they had only walked it a thousand times before. They should have known how long it took. But that was then and this was now, even though the 'then' was only a few days ago. They walked down Hessel Street and reached number 35, where Joe Gorminsky had his butcher's shop. Joe was standing outside smoking his at least fortieth cigarette of the day.

"Joe, how are you?" asked Sid, as calmly as he could, given the circumstances.

"I can't complain." But he always did. "What can I do for you? Do you want some mince? Reuben's just made some fresh." Reuben was Joe's son-in-law, who supposedly worked in the shop. In fact, if Reuben had worked as hard as Joe smoked, they would have both been millionaires. As it was, most of Joe's money had gone up in smoke or at the dogs, and plenty of what was left went on Reuben's addiction to cherry brandy.

Sid, who could never afford Joe's meat, replied as politely as possible. "No thanks, Joe, we don't need any for the moment."

"Fine, but if you do, let me know, I'll knock a bit off the price."

"Thank you, Joe, that's very kind. Anyway, we wondered if you could help. We're looking for the lady who cleans for you."

"Jeanie? Why?"

"We need her help with a certain matter."

Joe discarded the fag end of his cigarette, removed a Senior Service packet from his jacket pocket and took out another cigarette. He then fumbled about for his box of matches, which he found in his apron, and lit his at least forty-first. He then blew out the match and threw it on the pavement next to the fag end. He would sweep both up when they closed the shop for the night.

"So what's the problem?"

They had to get their story right. It wouldn't do to confuse the situation. They had to be clear and not contradict each other. And they had to keep Issy the Stick's name out of it. It might have been better if they had used duct tape over their mouths and mimed.

"It's a friend of ours," said Sid, taking courage in both hands.

"Who?"

"We'd rather not say. He wants to keep it private," answered Abe.

"Anyway, he's got a problem with a really bad rash on his back that the doctors can't cure, so we wondered if...er... whatshername. . . Jeanie, could possibly concoct a cream that he could rub in or do something that might help."

"Well, I know she cured a German who had warts, but I don't know if she can cure a bad rash if the doctors can't do anything," replied Joe through a fog of cigarette smoke.

"No, no, this friend definitely does not have warts, only a rash," stuttered Sid, worried that he might say the wrong thing.

"Who said anything about warts?" said Abe trying hard to back up Sid's story. "We're talking about a bad rash, only a bad rash, that's all. Nobody mentioned warts." They were both struggling to keep their story together.

Joe took another deep breath of poison.

"Well, she'll be here this afternoon. She's on her way to see Issy the Stick, who definitely does have warts or whatever they call them, on his feet, or so he thinks," said Joe. "When she gets here, I'll tell her the problem. Come back at about five and I'll let you know if she can help. Warts I know she can do, but a bad rash, that's another matter."

Sid and Abe thanked Joe, shook his hand and promised to return later, then hurried away as slowly as they had no choice but to do, towards Commercial Road.

Now everyone knew about Issy the Stick's problem. They might as well have written about it in the Jewish Chronicle - with photographs.

"And you said it was private. The whole world knows. Issy must have said something to somebody else and that's how Joe knows. And Joe told Jeannie the gypsy out of the goodness of his heart, and she contacted Issy and told him that she could help," said Abe.

"But Issy told me that I was the only one he told."

"And you believe everything that people tell you?"

"I believed Issy."

"And if somebody told you that Fred Astaire was Jewish, you'd believe them. *And* you said he had them down there."

"I told you I didn't know for sure where they were. But they were down there, way down there."

"But they weren't where you suggested they were."

"Ah! Not necessarily. That's only according to Joe. He could have known the truth and was keeping it a secret so as not to embarrass Issy."

If Joe had told them what he really knew they might have, inadvertently, told their wives and in a very short time everybody would know.

But Abe and Sid knew something else. They knew that their badly concocted plan might land them with a concoction that neither of them needed.

By the time they reached Commercial Road, the conversation had taken another turn, and it was Sid who started the ball rolling down Memory Lane.

"You know something? I've just remembered. I did know someone called Schwartz - Judah Schwartz. Just before the war he changed his name to Anthony Curtis and opened a menswear shop in Hackney somewhere."

Of course Abe had to put him right. "No, you're thinking of Bernard Schwartz that rhymes with warts. He was the one who changed his name to Anthony Curtis and opened a shop in Hackney, not Judah Schwartz that rhymes with carts. Judah Schwartz changed his name to Ivor Short and opened the bakery up in Stoke Newington. It was definitely Bernard Schwartz who changed his name to Anthony Curtis. Where he came up with such a name is anybody's guess. Maybe he didn't want his new name to sound too Jewish." Abe was certain of his facts. Not that either of them had a great memory for certain facts.

"Are you sure?" questioned Sid, certainly not sure that Abe was sure.

"As sure as I'm standing here."

The fact that they were walking made no difference.

"And another thing I want to ask you if you're so clever. How is it possible for two people with the same surname to pronounce it differently?"

"Countries, that's how. They come from different countries or regions in the country so they pronounce it differently. I'll give you a for instance. We pronounce Paris Paris but the French pronounce it Paree. We say London but the French call it Launderer or something like that. It's simple."

Sid was really impressed with Abe's knowledge, but had no intention of telling him.

As they got to the top of Hessel Street, Abe suddenly stopped. "You know something? On second thoughts I think you're right. It's all coming back to me after all these years. Judah Schwartz that rhymes with carts was the Jewish Austrian who didn't, to my knowledge, have warts. Bernard Schwartz was the one whose name rhymes with warts and, if I remember correctly, was the Schwartz that liked playing darts. But I could be wrong." But he wasn't wrong because Sid had been right all along.

It was time for another milk and a dash. But this time they fancied going to Joe Lyons in Aldgate and, to save time, they would take a bus there and back so they could talk to Joe at five o'clock.

"Look, quick," said Sid. Of course, Abe had no idea what Sid was talking about.

"What quick? What?"

"Look, there's a bus coming. Let's run and we can catch it."

The last thing that either of them wanted to do was to run for a bus. It was a good idea in theory but one they had no chance of putting into action. "Are you crazy or something, Sid? Run? My nose has got a better chance of running than my legs. Don't worry. We'll wait and get the next one."

"But by the time another one comes, which could be ages, we could have walked to Whitechapel."

"That's very true. But what happens if it starts to get late to get back in time to see Joe?"

"Easy, we take a bus from the London Hospital to Aldgate and then we get another one up the Commercial Road."

"Obviously."

So a decision was made there and then to walk back to Joe Lyons in Whitechapel. This time, however, they would go by the quickest route, which was via . . .

But on the way, Abe had a problem. Half way down New Road, and out of the blue, he got a sharp pain on the sole of his right foot and had to stop. He was in agony.

"What's wrong?" Sid was most concerned. They knew they had to get to Whitechapel and back by five or, worse still, not go at all.

"I'm not sure, Sid, but can I ask you a question that may or may not be relevant to our situation?"

"What is it?"

"Can you catch warts by just talking about them?"

What a Swell Party This Is

The army of anti-Semitic rain clouds that had been pouring wrath upon the citizens of Hessel Street for three unholy days decided enough was enough. It was time to move up the Commercial Road and give as much grief as possible to the unsuspecting populace of Essex. Why should Hessel Street always get the brunt of bad weather?

So, with the rain clouds gone and the sun cherishing a rare moment of triumph, things were looking a little brighter along the lower reaches of Commercial Road. But in Hessel Street, in particular, there was a double triumph.

Not only was the sun shining but there was real gossip in the air. It was time to roll out the red carpet, crack open a bottle of highly suspect kosher champagne and rejoice at the news.

It wasn't as if there had been no gossip about, but it was all run-of-the-mill stuff and nothing to get really excited about. It needed

something extra special to stir the army of yachnas into action.
And this was something more than extra special. At last, the waiting
for real gossip was over. Mazeltov!

There were pregnancies and pregnancies. Some planned and some
brought about by an error of judgement or timing. And every now
and then somebody thought an immaculate conception had taken
place. But as far as Hessel Street was concerned, this pregnancy was
different. This one had no marriage attached to it.

As usual it was Doris Feldman that started the ball rolling. She was
walking along Hessel Street with Hannah Woolf, another member of
the yachnas' first team.

"Don't say a word to anyone if you can help it, Hannah. You know
what it's like round here. One mouth leads to another and before you
can say there's a beigal in the oven, everyone will know."

"Doris, I don't know what you're talking about. Know what?"

Doris looked around to make sure everybody nearby was listening.
"Ssshh, you want everyone to know that Rivka Rubinstein is
pregnant?"

"Well, I didn't know. Nobody told me," said a surprised Hannah.

"I just told you."

"But I didn't know before. Now I know, thank you. But who told
you?"

"I can't tell you, they want to remain unanimous, but whatever you
do, don't say a word to anybody."

"Doris, My lips are sealed," lied Hannah.

"Pity Rivka's legs weren't," said a disgusted looking Doris, with
more than just a hint of mischief in her eyes. "I knew it would happen

one day, the way she carries on with this one and that one. She has no class. It's like I've always said, you can take a fish out of water but you can't force it to become smoked salmon. So remember, a fish is a fish is a fish and silence is silence, so we say nothing to nobody because there's nothing to say."

Well, that's clear.

So when Hannah told Annie Harris not to tell anyone about Rivka's condition, it came as no surprise to Doris when Millie Bloom told her not to say anything about Rivka being pregnant because Millie had been sworn to secrecy by Annie Harris.

So yet another way of keeping a secret in Hessel Street is to tell somebody that it's not a secret. Simple, if it's not a secret, what's the point of telling anybody? So it stands to reason, therefore, that if you want nobody to know the secret, tell everyone.

Now to the facts about the pregnancy that nobody knew about.

Fact one: according to Doris, Rivka was pregnant.

Fact two: there must be a father.

Fact three: what fact three? Numbers one and two are enough. What other facts do we need?

"So who's the father?" asked Hannah.

"Who isn't the father?" Doris replied with yet another question.

"You know what she's like, one man here, another one there, here a man, there a man, everywhere another man."

"Well, if it's a man, at least I can count my Norman out."

"Listen, for all I know it could be the iceman that comes around every week."

"But the iceman's not Jewish, he's a g . . ." shouted a shocked Hannah.

"Sshh! How many times do I have to tell you to keep your voice down? I didn't say it was the iceman, who for all we know might be Jewish. I said it could be. It could be the coalman or the dustman. It could be a butcher or a baker. The only thing I'm sure of, it's not Yitsak the beigal seller."

Yitsak the beigal seller, well into his seventies, had enough trouble lifting his beigals let alone anything else. Of course, Doris had to explain to Hannah in graphic details the problems that Yitsak might have. On hearing about the possible problem, Hannah's imagination went into overdrive.

"Yitsak the beigal seller's dead."

"Really? What happened? Did he die of a heart attack?"

"Possibly."

"What do you mean 'possibly'?"

"He was caught in a compromising position."

"What, with his beigals?"

"Not with his beigals, with Rivka Rubenstein. Now she's pregnant. The time of miracles has returned."

But at least Yitsak had been taken off the list of potential fathers - for now.

Doris continued, "Until we know for sure who the father is or isn't, it's nobody. And in the meantime we don't even know she's pregnant, so we say nothing, not even to each other. Agreed?"

"Agreed. But if we don't know, how did we find out?"

"From somebody else who doesn't know what we don't know because we haven't been told," answered Doris.

Well that was as clear as a bowl of barley soup to Hannah, who by now was so confused she was in need of refreshment. "Come, let's go and get a drink from the Ashkenazi brothers before I go dizzy."

The Ashkenazi brothers had a hole in the wall shop at the top of Cannon Street Road, where everything legal and illegal could be bought. From fruit and vegetables to sweets and chocolates and from soap and washing powder to light bulbs and plugs, from soft drinks to hard ones, and if they didn't have it, "Come back in half-an-hour." How they got so much stuff into such a small space defied physics. They were definitely the forerunners of all night shopping. They would open late morning and close around four or five the following morning. This was, naturally, a great help to the ladies of the night who, when short of a packet of three or six or twelve could count on the brothers to come up with the goods. Time was money for both parties. It was a pity that Rivka hadn't taken advantage of what the brothers were selling. Maybe she had asked them but on this fateful occasion they might have run out - a rarity. But it can happen.

Doris and Hannah, certainly not ladies of the night, ordered two glasses of sarsaparilla at 2d a time and continued to discuss Rivka's pregnancy which, they had both agreed, they would not talk about.

"I think it's very sad," slurped Hannah. "She's a good looking girl. She could have had anybody."

"She did," replied a smiling Doris.

"Not like that. I mean for a husband."

"Each to his own. You got married and I didn't. Maybe she doesn't want to. Maybe it's more exciting for her this way. Who knows?" Before Hannah could reply, Doris continued, "Look, the sun's shining. Let's go for a walk to Watney Street market."

Doris obviously didn't want to talk about her marriage-less life.

It was now Tuesday and at least four people knew about Rivka's condition. If Rivka knew, which, according to Hannah, wasn't certain, it would make at least five. By Thursday at the latest, everybody in Hessel Street, if not the whole of East London, would know, and by Friday at least a dozen men would be working on their alibis.

But, of course, Rivka did know she was pregnant, and she was sitting in her flat in Hessel Street wondering, as if she didn't know, how she managed, at the ripe old age of twenty-four and unmarried, to get herself into such a mess. Her body had been host to many a weak man in the street and, as she had never charged, this was the time for cashing in; this was the time for blackmail. This was the time for revenge on all those who, to the outside world, were pillars of Jewish society, doting family men and wonderful fathers. But, when it came to matters of flesh and lust, were unable to keep their private parts private.

Rivka took a pencil and a piece of paper from the sideboard, sat at her table and began to compile a list. Name, time and place. It was lucky that she had a fantastic memory, and a very creative one at that. She took the calendar from the wall and started to work backwards. It didn't take her long to work out who the father was, but it was pointless blackmailing someone who had very little money. No, it would be better to play around with a couple of dates and names and find somebody worth blackmailing.

It was the moment for the trusty pin. She wrote down the names of the four wealthiest men in the street - men she had known, in the biblical sense, at round about the right time. All married, of course, and highly respectable, or so it seemed to the outside world. She closed her eyes and placed the pin fairly and squarely on…. Sol Liberman's name. Aha! Of course Sol was the father. Who else? There was no doubt in her mind. "I can remember as if it was yesterday."

Next she had to decide how, when and where to break the bad news to him. She would also tell him how much it was going to cost for her to keep quiet. For him to deny it would be futile. Rivka had a great memory for anatomy. "Listen, Liberman. How many people know about your birth mark apart from your wife?" Game set and match! Now it was a question of how much.

Then she thought about it a little more. The consequences! It wouldn't be right for a family to be destroyed because of a father's wandering eye, hand and . . . No. Liberman was off the list. In fact, everybody was off the list, except the real father. But was she about to tell the world his name? Was she about to tell the father? No. It took two or three or four or more to tango, so, no, she would keep the father's name a secret, for now and maybe forever.

By Sunday morning, everybody in the street knew that Rivka was pregnant, but nobody knew that she had decided to keep the father's name a secret. This, of course, led to an outbreak of premature speculation amongst the virtuous men of Hessel Street.

"It couldn't have been me. I was looking after my booba every night for weeks," said the first.

Sure, nobody looks after their booba for weeks.

"I was in Cliftonville on holiday so count me out, but I've got an idea who it might be," said the second.

"Who?"

"I don't want to say, just in case I'm wrong."

"I had a sprained ankle for weeks," said the third.

"You know who I haven't seen for a while? Maybe he's the fath….," said the fourth.

Then Doris, who just happened to be in the street at the time, butted in on the four-way conversation.

"You should all be ashamed of yourselves, speculating all over the place." Pots and kettles came to mind to at least one of them. "None of you know, or all of you know, or one of you knows, so say nothing till everybody knows."

A look of collective innocence came over the four of them, which to Doris could only mean one thing; they were all guilty - of something. The group broke up as the men went to their respective homes to finalise their alibis, and Doris went to Hannah's flat contemplating whether or not to tell her that she had heard four men talking about the thing she and Hannah said they wouldn't talk about, but as it was now public knowledge, they could talk about it.

"We need to find out who the father is," said a determined Doris.

"I've got an idea," replied Hannah. "We put an ad in the Jewish Chronicle asking for the father to come forward. If he's an honourable man, he'll do the right thing."

"What happens if he's not Jewish?"

"We put the same ad in the East London Advertiser."

Whilst Doris and Hannah continued to talk utter nonsense, Rivka took courage in her hands and went to see her mother, Ada, in Langdale Mansions, to break the news to her. But, strange as it may seem, things were not as bad as Rivka thought they were going to be.

"Oi! How could you do this to me, your only mother? Oi! I might as well be dead from the inside upwards. Oivay! I need smelling salts." It could have been much worse. Rivka's mother could have already committed suicide. "Oi! How could my only daughter do this and not tell me she's with child? I had to find out from a yachna, a big-mouth. Oi! If only your father was still here."

"What are you talking about? You threw him out because you thought he was a good-for-nothing and we haven't seen him since. He doesn't want to know about us."

"What's that got to do with it? He's still not here." Her mother started rocking back and forth in her armchair, wrapping her arms around her body. "Oivay! I need to lie down in a dark room. How can I face my friends ever again? You've brought shame on the family. What are your booba and zayda going to say?"

"What are you going on about? Booba died years ago."

"So what? Just because she's dead doesn't mean to say she's not going to find out. News gets around." And how!

"And zayda? He's been in a home for years and hasn't a clue what's going on so don't bring him into this. Anyway, you don't visit him very often so he won't find out."

"Stop changing the subject. And what about your uncle Lionel from Hendon? Oi! I'm going to be the new black sheep of the family. I'm going to have to move to the North Pole. It's the only place where nobody knows me." Things were looking up for Rivka. "And I bet the father's one of your low-life men friends of the opposite sex. Oi! Now I'm having trouble breathing." It could have been much worse. She could have already stopped breathing. And as for uncle Lionel, Rivka's favourite relative, well, he'd been married three times before he had reached the age of fifty and was infamous for having, according to legend, fathered more children out of marriage than in, so he was no paragon of virtue. But maybe, he would be the one person to understand her and be sympathetic.

"Mum, I'm sorry but it's not the end of the world."

"Oi! It might as well be. Oivay! All I see around me is darkness and it's the middle of the day."

"Look, it's happened and I'm very sorry. I made a terrible mistake.

What else can I say?"

"You can say you're not preg...Oi! I can't even say the word." It could have become much worse. She could have said the word, fallen over and cracked her head on the fire surround.

Rivka rushed into the kitchen and got her mother a glass of water. "Here, drink this. It'll make you feel much better."

"Oi! The only thing that would make me feel better is strychnine. I think there's some in the top drawer in the kitchen." She continued to shake back and forth and, for good measure, from side to side.

Ada's Oscar winning performance cut no ice with Rivka. Enough was enough. Rivka had had her fill of her mother wallowing in false self-pity. It was time to fight back. "Right, listen to me. You're not having the baby, I am." Her mother interrupted with another 'oi!' and a wave of her hand in front of her face. "And I'm fed up with your dramatic ois and oivays. You're a drama queen. You should be on the stage at the Grand Palais doing Yiddish theatre." Ada gave Rivka one of those looks that only a Jewish mother can give to a daughter. "Good, have you recovered from considering suicide? Thank you. Just remember who's having the baby. And don't worry about me, I'll get along fine." Which she knew she wouldn't be able to do without her mother's help. "But if you want to help me get through this then that's fine with me as well."

Ada was well on the way to recovering from her near-death experience. "So, you didn't want my help when you were getting pregnant, and now all of a sudden you want my help when it's too late. Typical!"

Of course, what Ada had said made no sense at all, but Rivka decided not to push the matter further. It was time for a little humility. "I'm very sorry you didn't hear it from me first but I hadn't realised that the news would travel so fast. I wanted to be the one to tell you."

"You live in Hessel Street. What did you expect, an oath of silence?

Anyway, how did somebody, and I can guess who, find out?"

"I don't know. The only one who knew was Doctor Levy and he wouldn't say a thing; he's a doctor."

"Do you know how thin those walls are in his surgery? They're thinner than a piece of San Izal lavatory paper. Everybody sitting in the waiting room can hear what's going on. And I bet a pound to a penny that one of those yachnas was sitting there." The fact that Ada was a top class yachna was irrelevant. This was her daughter they were yachnaring about.

Things were slowly moving in Rivka's direction, albeit very slowly. At least Ada had stopped oiying and oivayzmeering. It was a start.

But in Hessel Street the starting gun had gone off ages ago. Hour after hour, day after day, gossip was on the rampage. From ear to mouth and from mouth to ear, and from here to there and from there onwards to everywhere where there was an ear and a mouth. But it was time for someone to call proceedings to a halt. And there was only one person capable - the rabbi. Rabbi Fishman of Cannon Street Road shul.

The rabbi did not look happy at all as he walked along Hessel Street and spotted Doris walking away from him. "Doris, a minute of your time, please."

Doris quickly turned round. "Ah! rabbi, it's nice to see you. I'm sorry, I was in a hurry. What can I do for you?"

The rabbi was not one to mince his words. When strong words were needed, the rabbi was the man. "Doris, you have to stop gossiping."

Doris feigned complete innocence. "Rabbi, I don't know what you're talking about." Doris, enough; this is the rabbi you're talking to, not one of your yachnaring friends.

"You know very well. Talking about Rivka the way you're doing.

You and your friends have to stop, Doris. Gossiping is bad enough but spreading gossip about a woman in her situation is not right. You should know better. Anyway, I will be saying a few words in shul on shobbus about the situation and I hope you'll be there with your friends. And one thing more. If you want to tell everybody that I'll be saying something please feel free to do so."

Doris had never felt so embarrassed in her life. "Yes, rabbi, I'll do my best to tell everyone I know and everybody I don't know. Please give my regards to your wife, and I'm sorry if I upset you. From now on I won't say another word about it." Doris, how could you lie to a rabbi?

Ten minutes later Doris met up with Hannah. "I've just come from a very important meeting with Rabbi Fishman. He's going to say a few words on shobbus about you know what with Rivka and we have to tell everybody to be there to hear him. It seems people have been yachnaring away and he doesn't like it. I don't know who he's talking about and I don't want to know. But whoever they are should be ashamed of themselves."

Quite right, Doris, quite right, taking the moral high ground. She had decided that the rabbi was not a man to be messed with. One word from him to you know who up there could find Doris talking to you know who down there.

"And here's another thing. I've worked out that whoever's missing on shobbus is the guilty one."

"What, even a woman?"

"Hannah, I sometimes worry about you. Whatever men are missing could be the father. And if they're all there, look for someone with a red face. It means they're guilty."

"But it's quite warm; lots of people will have red faces."

"Then we look for the man who's sweating the most. Remember, guilt brings out the sweats like nothing else."

"Does that mean we say nothing?"

"No, this time we do have to say something - to everybody." But, did everybody include Rivka and her mother? Probably not. So it didn't include everybody but most people. However, if somebody else mentioned it to either of them, that would be different. Now all Doris had to do was to find somebody who would tell Rivka or her mother what the rabbi was going to do. And the simplest way of doing that was to tell one of her yachna friends not to say a word to either of them, especially Ada. Then they would definitely find out.

And Doris's plan worked a treat. Doris told somebody who told somebody else to tell somebody, which is how Ada found out.

"Now look what's happened, the rabbi's got involved. That's all I need. Soon it'll be the whole royal family." It didn't stop there. "I'm sure I've got some smelling salts in the kitchen cupboard." And, "I must have a false beard and moustache somewhere so I can go out and do a bit of shopping before I starve to death." What, after one day? In Rivka's absence, Ada was wandering around her flat talking to herself. Not that it would have made much difference had Rivka been there, she probably wouldn't have been listening.

As it so happens, whilst Ada was talking to herself, Rivka was in Hendon talking to her uncle Lionel. She needed an honest and sympathetic ear and uncle Lionel was just the person to talk to. She had been on the phone to him earlier that day to tell him the news but it was too late. He already knew. But how did he find out so fast? Gossiping carrier pigeons was the only answer she could come up with. That, and the fact that Hendon was obviously full of yachnas, middle class yachnas, but yachnas nevertheless.

As she made her way to Hendon - not as far as Hotzeplotz, but pretty close - she considered how lucky uncle Lionel was, getting out of the East End. There was no doubting the fact that he was the brains in the family. After leaving school and working the street markets for a couple of years, he managed to get himself a job in a firm of accountants, qualify, and after ten or so years they made him a partner. On the way, and after two disastrous marriages and many infidelities, he had the good fortune to marry Yetta Marks, daughter of one of the senior partners. So why couldn't she, Rivka Rubinstein, have married an accountant; after all, she *was* Jewish?

Once the usual pleasantries were over and auntie Yetta had given Rivka a comforting and reassuring hug, uncle Lionel got straight down to business. "Don't you worry about your mother, she'll come round in the end. She'll have no choice. The last thing she needs is for me to remind her of what she did when she was young, younger than you. Remember, I knew her before she became a virgin."

"Lionel, stop being so disgusting. This is your niece you're talking to, not one of your dozens of ex fancy women, that's if they are ex."

"Of course they're ex. They became ex when I married you, my darling."

Ah! When you married me, not when you met me. I see!"

"I meant when I met you. It was a slip of the tongue. Can't a man make a mistake?"

"If you're anything to go by, more than one." She walked over to where uncle Lionel was comfortably seated, gave him the look of death, then a smile and kissed him on the forehead. "I'll be in the kitchen. And don't think I won't be able to hear you."

Ah! Family secrets. It seems that uncle Lionel might have had more ex's than on a football pools coupon. And what had her mother done all those years ago that had been kept under wraps for so long? Was Rivka a bast....? Not a chance. No, that couldn't be the answer. She had seen her mother's wedding certificate and her own birth certificate. So what could it be?

"After the look your aunt just gave me I'm not saying another word," said uncle Lionel with just a hint of a smile, "but if your mother wants to talk to you about her and Joey Rabinowitz, it's up to her."

Who the hell was Joey Rabinowitz? Surely Rivka wasn't the outcome of a highly secret illicit affair that everybody knew about. "Uncle Lionel, are you trying to tell me that my mother and this Rabinowitz were having an. . ..a…a and I'm the product of. . ."

Uncle Lionel had to butt in. "I told you I wasn't going to say another word and I meant it. But no, definitely no. Well, not to my knowledge. Anyway, you look just like your dad, but better looking by far."

"So?" Rivka wanted to hear more, but uncle Lionel had realised that he had already said too much. But was that going to stop him?

"That's it. There's no more to be said about what I've just told you and why your dad walked out on your mother and ended up dead in Spain."

Another bombshell! Uncle Lionel would, without question, have been at home in Doris's company.

"What are you talking about? Mum said she threw him out because he was a good-for-nothing." She paused for a moment. "And he's dead?" This was, without doubt, the biggest shock of all to Rivka.

"She told me he left the country to go and live in Australia and didn't want to have anything to do with us. And I believed her."

"Well, it's not quite true, Rivka. I'm sorry but in fact it's not true at all, and your dad definitely did not go to Australia. He might have been a good-for-nothing as far as your mother was concerned, but he was a good and kind man. He was only a good-for-nothing in her eyes and your grandparents' eyes because he didn't want to work any more than he had to, which wasn't very much in the first place. He was too busy with the Communist party to make much of a financial contribution to the family."

At that moment auntie Yetta came back into the lounge from the kitchen, carrying a large carving knife "That's enough, Lionel, you've said enough. What she doesn't know she doesn't need to hear about after all these years. Some things are best not said." Another one who knew but kept silent. How could so many people keep such a secret for so many years, especially with all those yachnas about?

This time, however, uncle Lionel was having none of Yetta's interference. There and then he made a decision. It was time to be open and honest. Why keep a secret secret from the one person who needed to know the truth. "Yetta, first of all, put down that knife before you do somebody some damage, including yourself, and second, keep out of this; this is my side of the family. It's time Rivka was told the truth, however painful."

"Fine," said Yetta, waving the knife in front of her face and then pointing it at uncle Lionel, "but if Ada finds out you're going to be in big trouble, mark my words. And don't blame me. I've warned you."

"Yetta, I have officially noted your concern regarding my welfare and hereby declare that you will in no way be held responsible for my premature departure from this world at the hands of my sister, Ada. My niece, Rivka, will now bear witness. Hold up your right hand."

Rivka agreed and said that she would be prepared to stand in front of uncle Lionel and defend him to within a whisker of her own life should her mother lunge at him with an axe or any other instrument that could kill, including her mouth. Auntie Yetta, who knew better than to get into an argument with her husband when he was in such a belligerent mood, looked at the two lunatics - fortunately not on her side of the family - stopped waving the knife and went back into the kitchen to prepare dinner. The dead chicken was about to get the brunt of her wrath.

"So, uncle, tell me the truth. I'm not a kid any more. And after what you've already said, nothing will surprise me."

"Okay. But remember one thing. Whatever's happened or happens, your mother still loves you and will do her best for you, whatever she says to the contrary. Now, what do you want to know about first?"

"How come my father died in Spain?"

"Before we come on to that you need to know something else."

So what was the point of uncle Lionel asking her what she wanted to know first?

"First of all you need to know about Joey Rabinowitz."

"So, tell me."

"Joey Rabinowitz was a good friend of your dad's and the local Communist party secretary. But. . ." Uncle Lionel paused for a moment to consider whether he should continue, which, of course, he did, "when your dad was out on the streets rallying the hoards and trying to persuade them to buy the Daily Worker, support the Communist party and become members, Joey was only interested in one member, if you get my meaning."

Rivka got his meaning all right. Her mother was having an affair with the local secretary of the Communist party who was one of her dad's best friends. She was certain that that wasn't allowed for in the manifesto, not that she'd ever read it.

"And my dad?"

"Ah! Now we come to the sad bit. This was in late 1935 and you were about three years or so old. Your dad found out about the affair when he went into the bedroom one evening and found Rabinowitz's Communist party membership card on the floor by the bed. It must have fallen out when he…never mind. Your mum tried to deny the affair but it was no use. Anyway, your dad walked out on her but knew that you would be better off staying with your mum because he didn't have a regular job and he wouldn't be able to look after you. Then a few months later the civil war broke out in Spain and he decided, along with a lot of other Jewish communists, to join up and fight the fascists. What a mishegus! Then it all gets a bit complicated." As if it wasn't already. "There are no official records of your dad dying in the fighting or even fighting, but word got back to us that he got drunk one night and was knocked over and killed by a truck whilst he was riding a bike. Now, we don't know much more than that. They decided to bury his body in Spain for some reason and they gave him a good Jewish burial. Your mother was beside herself with grief that she had caused his death by having the affair with Rabinowitz. Not that that was the first one."

Wait a minute though, thought Rivka. Why didn't they bring the body back to England? Why did her dad think it was a good idea to go and fight in another country when he had a daughter to consider, even though she wasn't living with him? Why didn't her dad go and find Rabinowitz and kick him as hard as he could - between the legs? Maybe he did but uncle Lionel didn't want to say. And what was her dad doing riding a bike in Spain when he was drunk, anyway? That's if he had been drunk. That's if he had been in Spain. Mmmm! Something wasn't quite right. Maybe uncle Lionel might not be telling the whole truth or anywhere near the truth after all. But why would he lie? It was all getting very confusing. Maybe auntie Yetta was right and he shouldn't have said anything to her even though she wanted to know. There were too many maybes to think about. But all these questions and other questions about her mother's multitude of affairs would have to wait for another day. Whatever the truth, she had ammunition, lots of it and, according to uncle Lionel, plenty more locked away in a storage facility somewhere at the back of his brain.

What Doris would only have given to be listening in on this conversation.

But there was one other thing that Rivka did want to know. "What happened to the low-life Joey Rabinowitz? Did *he* go and die in Spain?"

"Joey fight? You're joking. Moved to Bournemouth with a nineteen-year old from Stoke Newington and became very rich as a property dealer. So much for the Communist party!"

"I think the wrong man went to Spain."

"You could be right. Let's forget it for the time being. Now to another, far more important matter. The past can't be changed but your future can be, okay? So, if you need any help with money when the time comes you have to let us know. We can help."

"That's very kind of you, uncle Lionel, I'm sure I'll manage, but I promise to let you know if things get tough."

"Okay, but don't be proud. I have some money put away for a rainy day." He lowered his voice. "And anything unusual that might crop up in respect of my past life." He placed a forefinger to his lips. "But don't tell your aunt Yetta." As if she didn't know. After all, she was a Jewish accountant's daughter. "Now, will you stay for dinner?"

"I can't, thank you, uncle, I need to get back by tube and it's getting late."

"Don't worry. I'll drive you back home after dinner. The Bentley needs a bit of a runabout." Well, that summed up her life in a nutshell. Her mother had had affairs with a bunch of communists. Her father had been killed, supposedly, drunk in charge of a bike somewhere in Spain. She was unmarried and pregnant, and her uncle Lionel, the ex black sheep of the family, was driving her back to the East End in some swanky car.

Uncle Lionel called into the kitchen, "Yetta, Rivka's staying for dinner. We have to lay another place." What's with the 'we'? Uncle Lionel wasn't going to lay the table. Lay a bet on the dogs, maybe, but the table? Not a chance. "Rivka, you're staying for dinner. You can do without Hessel Street for a few more hours."

That was certainly true. But Hessel Street couldn't do without

Rivka, and Doris's mouth. She had already broken her promise to the rabbi on at least a dozen occasions but, according to her own moral standards and guidelines, as everybody in the world knew, it didn't count. By Thursday morning she and her cohorts had run out of people to tell and had no choice but to start relating the same story to each other again, but every time there was a slight alteration and exaggeration to the known facts.

"You know Rivka's having twins."

"How do you know?"

"By the way she walks."

"How does she walk?"

"I don't know, I haven't seen her walk, but I know somebody who has."

"And what did they say?"

"They said she walks like she's having twins."

"Then you have to believe it."

"Of course. If somebody who knows tells you something like that, you have to believe it. And wait a minute, don't they say that twins run in the family? If that's the case, we have to find a man who's a twin or has twin sisters or a mother with a twin sister or a father with a twin brother. Do you know anybody?"

"No."

"Much help you are."

But, as unlikely as it may seem given the situation, nobody suggested Rivka was having triplets only because none of them had seen anyone walking as if they were having triplets. That shouldn't have stopped them. It certainly didn't stop the person who, allegedly, saw Rivka walking as if she were having twins.

Now they would all just have to wait until Shobbus and listen to what the rabbi had to say. Maybe he knew if she was having twins.

Shobbus came in on time as usual on Friday evening, but what was not usual was the number of people in shul on the Saturday morning. It was full. It was full of the innocent and the guilty, the rich and the poor, the good, the not-so-good and the good-for-nothings of Hessel Street and surrounds. Even the sick turned up, just in case.

Just in case what?

Just in case tongues started to wag and word got out that they weren't really sick but were pretending to be sick to hide their guilt. That's what.

The men were seated downstairs and the women - second-class citizens - were seated upstairs in the gallery - out of the way. Of course, two women were well out of the way; namely Rivka and her mother, Ada. This was not the time or the place to be seen. Anyway, Ada was far too busy trying to stave off questions about her affair with Joey Rabinowitz and, for all Rivka knew, every member of the Communist Party of Great Britain.

But the two prime yachnas, Doris and Hannah, were in shul, naturally, and had even put on their best yomtov clothes. This was an occasion not to be missed and so one had to be dressed in one's best. They had a perfect view from their front row seats and could see the men joining in the service, and singing and davening like never before. Even the chazan, Jacob Cohen, sang as though he were auditioning for the Royal Opera House. It was as if their very lives depended on God's forgiveness for sins, real or imaginary, committed. But God knew what each had done during every second of every day, whether good or bad, legal or illegal. And he had, of course, arranged for these actions to be fully documented and placed in a large filing cabinet that stood by the side of his bed, marked 'pending'. He was just waiting for another top-notch Jewish accountant to die so the books could be checked and balanced.

Knowing she wasn't allowed to carry on Shobbus, Doris had sneaked into the shul the day before and hidden a pair of small opera glasses under one of the seats. Why didn't she just hang them round her neck? That would have done. It never occurred to her, that's why and anyway, it was far more exciting doing it this way. The fact that she and almost all the women were carrying handbags to shul made the whole exercise pointless.

So why did she need the binoculars? She needed them to get a close-up look at the men's faces. She needed them to see red faces. She needed them to see the level of sweat pouring out of each one. And, most important of all, she needed them to pick out the guilty party. That's why. But if Rabbi Fishman were to ask her what she was using them for, she would tell him that it was the only way she could read the prayer book because the print was so small. Only Doris!

It was time for Rabbi Fishman to say whatever he was going to say. Doris had looked around carefully and was certain that everybody who was supposed to be there, plus a few that she didn't expect to be there, were, and although there was lots of fidgeting and whispering and tutting, fake coughing and blowing of noses, there was no sweating. Not a wet face to be seen. Not a bead of sweat. Not even a red face. Something was not quite right, but Doris couldn't put her finger on it, not just yet.

Then Rabbi Fishman started. "My dear friends…" He looked around the packed shul very slowly, which raised the tension to fever pitch, and then continued, "it's good to see so many of you in shul today. It is a great pity that not more of you turn up on a regular basis rather than just on yomtovim. But it's good that you are here, even if it is for a particular reason. As I am sure you all know by now, I have a few words to say about a situation that happens to be causing great concern to many of you and the subject of gossip and intrigue to others." Doris looked at Hannah as if to say, 'Who's he talking about?' "But I shall keep what I have to say to as few words as possible. In fact, I will keep it to a minimum." He paused, looked up at the women's gallery and stared straight at Doris who, even without the aid of her binoculars, could see the clear look of disapproval on the rabbi's face. Hell, here I come, she thought to herself, the rabbi's had words.

The rabbi then looked straight ahead. "All I ask, my friends, is that we remember God's commandments."

Which ones, rabbi, which ones? Everybody wanted to know which ones.

"Thou shall not bear false witness against thy neighbour."

And? He said 'commandments, not commandment.'

And; **"Thou shall not commit adultery."**

With those words, the rabbi removed his tallis, wrapped it over his arm, and walked out of the shul.

Feinstein's Theory of Relatives

Downstairs, as ever, at Joe Lyons in the Whitechapel Road on a dire, dreary, Saturday afternoon in the middle of November, Abe and Sid each sipping a glass of salvation, a milk and a dash. And the misery of the day was about to be compounded by the arrival of the most miserable person in the East End of London; Ben Feinstein. The permanent hangdog expression on his face made a bloodhound look positively joyful. It was even said that he looked miserable on his wedding day, but when you consider who he married, Doreen Kaplovitch, that wouldn't have been surprising. Sadly, Feinstein had the unhappy knack of depressing everybody he came in contact with. It was even said by an unkind soul that Feinstein could make the Laughing Cavalier cry in despair. Not that the unkind soul had ever seen a picture of the Laughing Cavalier or, more likely, had any idea what it was.

"Can I sit with you for a few minutes, boys? I need to talk something over with you." Did Abe and Sid have a choice?

Abe stood up, pushed his milk and a dash across the table, walked round and sat next to Sid. The situation needed a two-man defence. Feinstein placed his mug of tea on the table and proceeded to top it up with four helpings of sugar from the sifter - and Abe thought that Sid had a sweet tooth; Feinstein beat him hands down.

"What's wrong, Feinstein?" asked Sid in mock concern. "You look worse than normal."

"I take that as a compliment," he answered, stirring the tea vigorously.

"How come?" asked Sid, looking quite bemused.

"Well, it means that sometimes I must look better than this."

Neither Sid nor Abe could argue with his logic. "Come on, out with it. What's up?" asked Abe.

"It's my son, Gerald."

"Gerald with the crazy wife, Sybil, from Southend?"

"How many sons called Gerald do I have, Sid? Of course Gerald with the crazy wife." He paused to sift another couple of helpings of sugar into his tea and then started to stir again. "Why can't they make sweet tea?" Something else to complain about! "It would save a fortune on sugar. Anyway, she's pregnant."

"Mazeltov," said Sid, with a beaming smile on his face, and trying to sound more cheerful and positive.

"Don't mazeltov me, it's not funny."

Sid's smile disappeared as fast as it came.

"What are you talking about, it's not funny?" said Abe, "You're going to be a grandfather, a zayda."

"It's not funny, Abe, because they've decided that if it's a boy they're going to call him Jesus."

"Christ! You're right, it's not funny," said Abe, trying hard not to burst into fits of laughter. "How did they come up with that crazy idea?"

"I'll tell you how," he replied, tapping a forefinger to his temple. "She's meshuga and her madness has rubbed off on Gerald. Now he's as loopy as she is. They might as well call him Loopy Gerald. It seems that she met a Spanish geezer a few years ago called Jesus but pronounced Haysuz or something like that, but spelt Jesus, and she liked the sound of the name. Better she should have liked the Spaniard and run off with him than marry my son and drive him crazy. Jesus Feinstein! They both need locking up, or I do for my own well-being."

"And what about Doreen? What does she reckon?" asked Sid.

"Who knows what she reckons? I never get any sense out of her at the best of times. But whatever it is you can rest assured it's not going to be good news for anybody, especially me. Can you imagine her looking at the baby saying, 'Cootchie cootchie coo. Come to booba, baby Jesus.'? And then there's the moyel and the bris. The more I think about it, the worse I feel. The whole idea is enough to make me throw up."

After managing to contain his laughter, Abe asked an interesting question, well, interesting for Abe. "Hold on a minute, if you're Jewish, can you call your son Jesus?" Even Sid was impressed, and it nearly, only nearly, brought a smile to Feinstein's face. "We might have to ask a rabbi," he continued. "You never know, it might not be allowed."

"Listen, just because it might not be allowed, doesn't mean to say they won't do it. Both of them are round the bend."

Sid decided to get in on the lunacy. "I've just thought of something that could be an even bigger problem."

Feinstein had to ask the question even though he was dreading the answer. "What now? As if I haven't got enough to worry about."

"What happens if the Jewish Chronicle accepts a small ad in the births column? Something like: 'To Gerald and Sybil Feinstein - a son - Jesus Israel Solomon. Mazeltov from all the boys in the manger.'"

Unfortunately, Feinstein had a mouthful of tea when Sid put forward the question. He choked, spluttered and sent a shower of tea across the table. Fortunately, both Sid and Abe saw it coming and, like the parting of the Red Sea, moved quickly to the sides of the table, allowing the offending tea to land safely on the floor between them.

"Sorry, Feinstein. I didn't mean for you to choke."

"Don't worry, choking to death could cure all my problems." And not even an apology for nearly drowning the two of them.

"Wait a minute; dying is the last thing we want you to do. Let's just pray it's a girl, and if it is, you won't have any problems," said Abe, trying to put a more positive slant on the proceedings. What a complete waste of time. He looked around and couldn't see anybody smiling. All he could see through the haze of cigarette smoke was a sea of miserable, downright unhappy faces. God, he thought to himself, Feinstein's Depression must be contagious. Or was it just the lousy weather? He chose Feinstein's Depression which, when he thought about it a little more, made the American Depression look somewhat of a jolly affair.

"I don't think praying's going to help. I've got this theory that God's definitely got it in for me. You can see that by looking at my family. Even the one I chose, Doreen, I got wrong. Or maybe God chose her for me without getting my permission. You know, I must have done some awful things in a previous life for God to take his revenge on me in such a terrible way, sending me all these diabolical relatives to torture me."

Abe was trying as hard as possible to lighten Feinstein's mood. "Listen, Feinstein, everybody who's having a lousy time with relatives says the same thing. And, anyway, you have to believe in reincarnation and all that nonsense, which I'm sure you don't, unless you do. You read in the papers about all those people who say that in a previous life they were a lady-in-waiting to some queen of England or was a butler for this famous person or a maid to that famous person, or they were a general in an army somewhere. Or these people always seem to be involved in some important moment in history. You never hear of anybody just being a caveman or a beigal maker or a kosher butcher in a previous life. Anyway, take it from me, if God wanted you to have a really bad time, he'd have made you a Leyton Orient supporter."

Even that didn't bring a smile to Feinstein's face. Not that he was really listening to what Abe had been saying. "Anyway," said Feinstein, "if they have a girl I'm sure they'll call her Mary Magdalene or some other meshugena name. You know something, boys, I've decided I hate everybody in my family. My son, my wife, my brother in Bournemouth, his wife and kid - who I don't really know that well - my mother, may she never rest in peace even though she's not dead, my father, for marrying her in the first place, and most of all, I hate myself for hating all of *them*."

"But your brother's a nice guy. How can you hate him?" asked Sid.

"For being my best man, that's why. If he had said no when I asked him to be best man, I might not have married Doreen. But, no, he had to be nice and say yes."

"So you hate him for being nice?"

"No, I hate him for not telling me not to marry Doreen."

"But we all have a choice, we all have free will. You didn't have to marry Doreen. Nobody forced you."

"Really? Tell that to God." By this time, Feinstein was stirring an empty mug.

It seemed that nothing either of them could say would ease Feinstein's grief and utter misery. They sat there in morbid silence for the next twenty seconds or so - it seemed a lifetime - Sid worrying, sighing and stirring another empty glass, Abe tapping his fingers on the table to the tune of Chopin's funeral march and Feinstein contemplating suicide or murder or both.

This was serious stuff. In contrast, Sid and Abe's lives seemed positively rosy. Feinstein was in a bad way; far worse than they had ever seen him. Both of them had known him most of their lives. He was four or five years behind them at school, so never really socialised as kids. His parents had lived in Hessel Street, in one of the flats. His father worked as a salesman for Sapphire's the fruit and veg wholesalers in Spitalfields and his mother was a professional make-up artist and nail refiner, spending most of the day making herself up and refining her nails.

Ben, however, was a fairly intelligent boy and managed to get a job as an accounts clerk at the Sussex Laundry at the corner of Commercial Road and New Road. He never made it to the top of the department but had a reasonable enough income by the time he married to be able to move out of the street and live in Arbour Square, a little way up the Commercial Road. And, as a bonus, all his laundry was done for free. Now that was worth a few bob on its own. If truth be told, however, Doreen could have bankrupted the company single-handed by the amount of laundry she had done each week for nothing. But nothing, it would seem, could change Feinstein's mood.

Then Sid broke the ice. "I've got an idea. Why don't you change your name?"

"What are you talking about, change my name? How's that going to help? Anyway, there's nothing wrong with the name Ben."

"Not your first name, shmendrick. Your surname, Feinstein. Then nobody will know you're related to the relatives you don't want to be related to."

"What are you going on about? What's the point? I'll still know, everybody I know will know I've changed my name, and I'll still have the same trouble from the same crazy bunch of relatives."

"But people you haven't met yet won't know, and a new name can give you a new lease of life - a fresh start. Lots of people do it. Look, Yitzak Shmidt changed his name to Ivan Smith, Monty Bloch changed his to Michael Black and even David Kaminsky changed his name. He changed it to Danny Kaye. And what about that newcomer film star Kirk Douglas? His real name is longer than the Commercial Road. Do you think they would have made it if they had stuck to their old names? And then, of course, there's Gerry Van."

"Gerry Van? What's he got to do with all this?" asked Feinstein.

"His grandfather, Solly, wasn't even Jewish. He converted. He was a Catholic called Michael Sullivan. He went the other way. He thought that if he converted and changed his name to Solly, Solly Van Damm, and said that he came from an old Jewish family from Holland, business would improve. So he converted and it did. He didn't really need to convert but he decided to go the whole hog, as the expression goes."

How did Sid know all this stuff?

"So why don't you change *your* name?" asked Ben.

"I don't want to or need to, but you do," answered Sid.

"No I don't, I need to change my relatives."

"Listen, Feinstein, there are some lonely people out there who would love to have relatives."

"Good, they can have mine with pleasure, for free, for gornisht. In fact I might even pay people to take them off my hands." Feinstein was getting more fretful by the minute.

"No, now you're getting carried away. You need to calm down. Take a deep breath." Which Feinstein did. "Hold it … good … now breathe out. Good. Well done." All of a sudden, Sid had become an expert in calming people down. Another hidden talent.

"Okay, I'm calm. What now?"

Abe looked at Sid as if to say 'what now?'

"What now is simple. All you have to do is to escape. You have to divorce Doreen, change your surname, move away and Bob's your uncle - there you have it, a new life."

Feinstein's problem had now been solved by a genius. "All you need now is a really good new surname. You need something different, something that doesn't link you to the name Feinstein, so Fine and Stein are out. It needs to be something you can be proud of; a strong, courageous name, something like errm errm, Marciano. Ben Marciano. There you go. All sorted. . . No, on second thoughts it sounds a bit too Italian, and people would only ask if you're Rocky's brother." He paused for a few seconds and then continued. "I've got it. How about something even stronger than Rocky Marciano? What about a tank? That's it, a tank. You can't get much stronger than a tank. Why don't you change your surname to Sherman, after the tank? Ben Sherman. There you go, it sounds perfect."

By now, both Feinstein and Abe were thinking to themselves that Sid had been taking drugs that may or may not have been legal.

"So, what you're trying to say is, divorce Doreen, which will take ages or she won't agree to anyway, move out of the East End and then change my name by deed poll to Ben Sherman. Let me tell you something, before I even pack my bags she'll have the shirt off my back and I'll be living on the streets."

"Could be worse, you could still be living with Doreen and still be related to your relatives."

This was getting them nowhere and Sid's humour was falling on deaf ears. Feinstein was desperate and neither of the 'boys' could help. It was time for more tea. "I'm just going to go up and get another cup, do you fancy another one?"

Sid and Abe looked at each other and nodded in agreement. In for a pound…and the weather was lousy. "Same again, Feinstein, thank you," said Abe. Strange, they never called him Ben.

As Feinstein reached the top of the stairs, Abe and Sid heard a peculiar noise. It was the sound of laughter coming from a corner table. An old man had started to laugh and as he did so, others nearby followed. Something very odd was happening. The mood had lightened. Feinstein's Depression had gone, along with Feinstein and, even stranger, the cigarette smoke. But he would be back within minutes. Would the mood change again? Would the cigarette smoke return? They would just have to wait and see.

In the meantime, it was time for questions. "How come you came up with such a crazy idea suggesting he change his surname?" asked Abe.

"I thought it might cheer him up. It was just for a bit of fun."

"And Marciano? What sort of name is that for a Jewish boy?"

"What sort of name is Kirk Douglas or Jeff Chandler for a Jewish boy?"

"Okay, Mr Clever, then what about Solly Rabinovitch?"

What about it? It's a Jewish name."

"Not according to your ideas. If Kirk Douglas and Jeff Chandler are Jewish names, then Solly Rabinovitch is a Catholic name."

"Now you're being silly."

"I'm being silly! And you want Feinstein to change his name to Sherman, after a tank?"

"Well, it was off the cuff and it still sounded a bit Jewish. I still think it's a great name and I bet that one day it'll mean something."

"Talking about something, we have to do something about Feinstein before he depresses the whole country."

"I don't think anything we say is going to help. He's got this crazy idea that God's got it in for him, so what can we do? I'm not going to have a row with God."

"So we do nothing, that's what we do. We've tried our best. He's going to have to sort it out himself. He's going to have to talk to Gerald and the Southend meshugena wife and persuade them to change their ideas."

"Have you met his wife?"

"No."

"Neither have I but I've heard on the grapevine that she comes from a crazy family. It seems that her mother holds the record for the fastest Jew to swim to the end of Southend Pier and back again without stopping, and her father holds the Jewish all-comers record for holding his breath under water for the longest possible time without dying."

"What's with the 'all-comers' bit?"

"I think it means that anybody who's Jewish from anywhere can go for the record, not just from Southend."

"Well, Jews are used to holding their breath so they should be world record holders. It's a pity they don't have an all-comers competition for Miserable Person of the Year. Feinstein would win hands down - every year, and we could be his agents. As for the daughter-in-law, at least we now know where her mishegus comes from. It runs in the family so she's got an excuse. But I suppose they'll support her and Gerald."

"I'm afraid not. They're both dead. Legend has it that her dad died trying to do some underwater Houdini trick and got stung by a thousand jellyfish, and her mum died when a fisherman hooked her round the neck when he was fishing from the end of the pier."

"You see, that's the way to go. Doing what you love the best." Which meant that both Abe and Sid would die drinking very milky coffee in Joe Lyons.

Then they saw Feinstein at the top of the stairs. In one hand he was balancing a tray with two glasses and a mug on it, and in the other hand he held a glass of water. He walked down the stairs carefully, making sure that nothing would spill. By the time he reached the bottom step the laughter that had started when he was on the way up was nowhere to be heard. And the cigarette smoke? It was on the way back with a vengeance. So it was Feinstein that had caused the depression. He made his way over to the table and placed the tray down.

Abe had to ask, and the answer was simple. "This is an ice cold glass of water and I didn't want it warmed up by the hot drinks."

There, what could be more obvious? And Feinstein thought his daughter-in-law and son were meshugenas?

"Milk and a dash for you, Sid. Another one for you, Abe, and a mug of tea for me."

"Thank you, Feinstein," said Abe, "it's very kind of you." Sid nodded in agreement."

"It's the least I could do." Not really. He could have added a couple of pieces of Battenberg cake; that would have added to the gratitude.

"So where were we?" asked Feinstein.

"In the middle of changing your name," answered Sid.

"Forget it, it's not going to happen. Anyway, all the good names have been taken by film stars."

"Okay, have it your way. We were just trying to help. So what are you going to do?"

"First of all, I'm going to drink this glass of cold water. Drinking cold water always makes me think better." He picked up the glass and with one violent swig finished the lot. "Now I feel better. I still don't know what to do, but I feel better."

"Good, I'm pleased. Now I've got another idea," said Sid.

"If it's as bad as the other one don't bother to tell me."

"No, this is really good, but you might not like what you have to do."

Feinstein picked up the sifter and started pouring sugar into his mug of tea. It would have been quicker to pour the tea into the sifter. "Let's hear it. It can't be worse than the last one."

There's gratitude for you, thought Sid, and all we're trying to do is to help. "This is what you do. You go home to Doreen and tell her that you've had second thoughts and now you love the idea that Gerald and Sybil are going to call their kid Jesus if it's a boy. Well, according to you, she never agrees with anything you say or do, so she'll go potty and think to herself that if you like the idea it must be wrong. Then she'll get in touch with the kids and bully them into changing their minds. You'll be seen as the hero by them for giving them support and she'll be seen as the villain."

"But what happens if they don't change their minds?"

"That's the joy of my plan. Doreen gets the blame either way."

Abe was staggered by the beauty of Sid's cunning, and if Abe was staggered then Sid was even more staggered by his own cunning. And as for Feinstein, he was also staggered, but wasn't sure why. "I don't understand," he said.

"It's simple. If they're forced to change their minds, they'll blame Doreen for bullying all three of you, and if they don't change their minds, they'll thank you for supporting them and facing up to Doreen. Okay, so Doreen will hate you even more one way or the other. Whatever happens, you can't lose. Of course, there could be a bonus in it for you."

"Which is?"

"She might want to divorce *you*."

All Abe could do was to watch in admiration at his friend's dedication to the cause. He was too awestruck to say a word.

Feinstein shrugged his shoulders, nodded his head and tapped his fingers on the table. "Mmmm, not bad, not bad at all. I told you that drinking cold water always makes me feel better and think clearer. This is the basis of a very good plan, Sid, thank you. All I have to do is to refine it a bit and it may just do the trick."

"It's a pleasure, Feinstein, I'm pleased I could help you think it out for yourself."

Feinstein managed to finish his tea in a couple of gulps despite it almost burning his mouth. "Thank you, boys, thank you. I'm going to have to go straight away. Strike whilst the iron's hot as they say and I still have the courage. I'll let you know what happens…but if you never hear from me again…" With those parting words he got up from his seat and made his way up the stairs and into possible oblivion. As Feinstein got to the top, Abe and Sid heard the sound of laughter all around. They looked at each other in silence before finishing their drinks.

"Where the hell did you come up with that idea? It was a stroke of genius."

"Believe me, Abe, it was luck. I made it up as I was going along. Let's hope it works. I couldn't cope with months of this."

They didn't have to wait months at all for the result. A week, that's all it took. The following Saturday, as they were having their usual at their usual, Feinstein came rushing down the stairs, wafted away the cigarette smoke, put down his mug of tea and sat at their table.

He still looked as miserable as ever, but said, "Boys, I knew I'd find you down here. There's good news." Not that you would be able to notice it was good news by the look on his face. "Well. I think it's good news." Ah! So it might not be.

"Well then, out with it. Did you put the plan into action?" asked Sid. He and Abe were desperate to know the latest.

"I didn't have to. They changed their minds anyway."

"How come?" asked a somewhat surprised Abe.

"How come? Who knows? Who cares? All I know is that they came to their senses and decided after all that it wouldn't be right to call a Jewish son Jesus."

Sid gave a wry smile and said, "I'm pleased for you, Feinstein. At least you won't have to change your surname to Sherman. So, what are they going to call it if it is a boy?"

"I don't know. I tried to speak to Gerald on the phone about it last night, but his crazy wife, told me he was too busy reading to talk to me at that moment, but she would get him to ring me back, which he never did. My son, Gerald, reading a book? I couldn't believe it, so I had to ask her what he was reading."

"And the answer?" asked Sid.

"She said he was reading something called the Koran."

Have a Rest, Yoseler

There are many different ways of keeping a secret in Hessel Street, but one of the best and simplest ways is to talk about it in public. And if you want to keep it top secret, talk about it at the top of your voice.

> "How can it be that important or secret if they're talking about it out in the open?"

> "True. Let's go see if we can hear somebody whispering. "

But two people did have a secret that was so secret that one of them didn't want to talk about it at all. Not even to the other person who shared the secret.

"We've been working back at Bloom's for more than a year now and we still haven't decided what we're going to do," said Little Cohen.

"But I still don't want to talk about it," replied Big Cohen.

Which, of course, meant he did want to talk about it, but not then, and not to Little Cohen. Little Cohen had been driving him mad since their return into making a decision.

"But we need to make a decision before it's too late."

"The only time it's going to be too late is when we're dead, so do we really have to make a decision right now, right this minute?" According to Little Cohen, the minute had been going on for far too long. It was now officially the longest minute in history. "Anyway," Big Cohen continued, "I'm too tired to think about it at the moment."

"You've been too tired ever since we got back. How long can a man take to recover? I recovered ages ago, but even if you are tired that shouldn't stop you from stopping us."

"You're fitter than me. That's why you've recovered and I haven't. I just need a little longer to think about it. When I get my strength back I'll talk about it."

"When will that be?"

"When? When? When? That's all you ever do, ask questions. When will be when, whenever that is. I can't give you an exact time to the minute… exactly."

The Cohens were sitting downstairs at Joe Lyons in the Whitechapel Road on a late Wednesday afternoon in August after finishing their long mid-day stint in the kitchen at Bloom's. And it was somewhat ironic that here were two Jews who worked at the most famous kosher restaurant in England, sitting in a non-kosher tea room whose founders were Jewish, as was the present chairman, Major Montague Gluckstein, with an OBE after his name.

Big Mo Cohen and Little Mo Cohen were having their weekly one-way discussion over making a decision. *The* decision! Two mugs of tea and a couple of rounds of toast each. That they could decide on. That was an easy decision to make. That was never going to change their lives. But the other decision they had to resolve was another matter altogether. Talking about it to anybody else, even one person, especially if a yachna was in earshot, could, no, would change their lives for ever. The change could be for the good or for bad. Neither knew. The difference, however, between the two of them was simple. Little Cohen wanted to know and Big Cohen wasn't sure he wanted to know, even though he did, but didn't know he did. They were the best of friends, but even the best of friends could disagree. And disagree they did. It wasn't an argument, it was just a disagreement. Everybody has a right to disagree. One thing was certain though, one of them was right or wrong or the other way around.

Then, out of the blue and without warning, Little Cohen slammed his hand on the table. He had decided the time had come. "I've made up my mind." A startled Big Cohen looked up from staring at an empty plate. "We have to talk to somebody about it within the next week or otherwise it'll be too late. And if you don't want to talk about it, then I'll do it on my own."

Having recovered from the shock, Big Cohen took a deep breath, leant back on the chair, rubbed his eyes and sighed in resignation. "You're right, you're right. Okay, you're right. Satisfied? I give in. We have to do it as you said. If we put it off any longer we'll never do it and then we'll regret it, even though we might regret doing it, anyway. Which we definitely will."

Well, that wasn't difficult. Little Cohen should have forced the issue ages ago, but he didn't want to upset his best friend, especially after what they had gone through. "I'm sorry, Big Mo, but it's for the best. The quicker we get it over with, the quicker we can get on with our normal lives. Keeping this secret to ourselves every day is making us ill. You never know, the person we talk to about it might say that the best thing to do is not to talk about it to anyone. Of course, by then it will be too late because we would have…never mind. Anyway, whatever will be, will be."

How many times had that old saying been churned out? But now it was time to consider a serious problem. Who could they talk to about the thing Big Cohen hadn't wanted to talk about for so long? "Whatever happens, I don't want to talk to anybody in my family about it," he replied. They hadn't said anything to anyone in either family as to where they had been and what they had done. They had even put their passports in a safe deposit box at the bank so that nobody could find out where they had been from looking at the stamps. So why start talking to someone in the family now?

"Agreed. Families are definitely out. So are friends, whatever friends we've got left," replied Little Cohen, reinvigorated by his friend's sudden change of heart.

"Agreed."

"So who's left?"

"Ah! There's the big question. Any ideas?"

Little Cohen sat for a while in silence, making a mental list of anybody he thought could help, and discarding them as fast as they came into his head. Big Cohen was doing the same but without the list. Then, in a moment of inspiration, Little Cohen came up with the answer. "Only one person, Big Mo, there's only one person we can trust and will be honest and open with us."

"Who?"

"Yoseler the Philosopher, Yosel Finklestein," answered a triumphant Little Cohen.

A big grin came over Big Cohen's face - at last, a smile, after all this time, a smile. Or was it a grin? Whatever you wanted to call it, it was better than the long miserable expression that had been hanging about his face for ages. "Agreed…again. Well done. Yoseler the Philosopher is the perfect person to help us - we hope." Big Cohen clapped his hands in satisfaction. "But what happens if he doesn't believe us?"

"Why do you have to be so negative? Believe me, he'll believe us. Why wouldn't he? It's so unbelievable, nobody would believe we would lie. Why would we make up such a story?"

Another question!

Little Cohen said that on their way back to their flats in Hessel Street, he would knock on Yoseler's door and arrange for a meeting, but would not tell him what they wanted to talk about. It was only fair that the two of them were present just in case one of them said something that might not have been right, even in good faith.

The two Mo Cohens, both in their early-thirties and, as luck or bad luck would have it, still unmarried, lived in the flats in the market. Living in Hessel Street in itself was fine, but being unmarried at their age was something else and caused concern for two people, or was it one?

"There must be something wrong with them, not being married at their age. It's not natural."

"What's not natural is you driving me mad all the time, so gay avek and drive somebody else potty."

"Alright, I'm sorry I spoke. I was just making a supposition."

Anyway, it was just as well that Big Cohen had always been much bigger than Little Cohen otherwise confusion would have reigned and arguments broken out as to who was who and who said what to who about you know who and what. It wasn't as if there weren't more Mo Cohens in Hessel Street. If anything, there were more Cohens per square inch in Hessel Street than anywhere else in East London, depending, of course, who you talked to, especially whatshername with a foghorn for a mouth, from the Lane, who says she knows every Morris Cohen in the East End. But most of the other Cohens in Hessel Street were older, and were normally referred to in different ways, such as Cohen the tailor or Cohen the fishmonger or Mr Morris *the* Hairdresser of London - what was he doing still living in Hessel Street? - or Cohen the baker or chazan Cohen or Cohen the good-for-nothing lowlife mumza who nobody had a good word to say about. But nobody had a bad word to say about Big or Little Cohen, except on the odd occasion, their parents. But they were family, and for that reason alone it didn't count.

So Little Cohen went to see Yoseler the Philosopher and told him that he and Big Cohen would like to talk something over with him and get some advice. Little Cohen said no more and Yoseler agreed to see them that very evening about eight. His wife had gone to stay with her sister for a couple of days, leaving him enough food for a month, so he could relax and talk to them. Little did he realise that he was not in for a relaxing evening at all. This was to be one of his most exciting evenings and leave him with one of his most taxing problems.

Luckily for the Cohens no yachnas or busybodies were in the street when they met up to go and see Yoseler. Even Doris wasn't looking out of her window. She was probably rummaging through back copies of the East London Advertiser to see if she had missed anything unimportant - to others.

"Are you okay?" asked Little Cohen.

"As okay as I'm ever going to be."

"Good. Quick, keep close to the wall. Let's get into his flat before anybody sees us."

Little Cohen knocked on Yoseler's door and within seconds it was open. "Come in, come in. It's good to see you both. Take your jackets off, it's still summer. And sit down on the couch." Yoseler took their jackets and hung them on the hook behind the front door.

"A little home-made honey cake and maybe a lemon tea?"

Big Cohen cleared his throat and answered, "I think maybe we'll need something stronger."

"Fine, I'll put two slices of lemon in the tea. No, no, I'm only joking. How about a little whisky?"

Big Cohen smiled and nodded in approval. "Thank you, Mr Yoseler; that will do fine for both of us." He looked at Little Cohen, who also smiled in agreement and appreciation.

"I'll be back in a minute." And Yoseler went into the kitchen to get the cake and glasses.

Big Cohen nudged Little Cohen and whispered, "Are you sure we're doing the right thing?"

"It's better than doing the wrong thing."

"This could be the wrong thing."

"You're right, but you could be wrong, so let's hope you are."

Yoseler returned in no time with a tray of honey cake, plates and glasses, opened a door to the sideboard and pulled out a bottle of Dimple Haig whisky "You know my wife cooks at so many functions that she keeps being given bottles of all sorts of drink. Look, I've got wine and whisky and kummel and gin and vodka and cherry brandy and advocaat and sherry and port. You name it I've got it. I could open up a shop to rival Frumkin's." Yoseler pulled out a small table from beside the sideboard and placed it in front of the two Cohens. "Eat and drink up. There's plenty more."

"Thank you, Mr Yoseler, you're very kind," said Big Cohen.

Yoseler sat opposite them in his new green upholstered Parker Knoll armchair - a birthday present from his wife and two children. After a couple of minutes chatting about the fact that Yoseler had not seen either of the Cohens' parents for a while and hoped they were well, he got down to the nitty gritty. "So, where do you want to start? You went off for months without saying anything to anybody, even your family and friends, apart from saying you were going away to do something important for some bigshot and that Bloom gave you time off. There must have been something in it for him, letting you go just like that. No doubt you'll tell me more. But now you're back, how have things been going?"

"To be honest, Mr Yoseler, we're bored working for Bloom's. We've been there a few years – apart from the time off - and we've had enough, even with the move to the Whitechapel Road, although it's a much better and nicer place. In fact, Big Mo and I are considering going into business on our own. Since we've been away we've been able to save a few bob so we're thinking about it."

"Really, and that's what you want to talk to me about?" asked a disappointed Yoseler.

"No. Maybe that'll be for another time. It's about what happened when we were away that we need to talk to you about. To be honest, Big Mo didn't really want to talk about it at all, but in the end I persuaded him."

"Ah! So there is a mystery. Excellent. Do you know, not even Doris knew where you were going. It must have been some big deal." True. If Doris didn't know where they had been, nobody knew. It had to be a big deal.

"So?"

Little Cohen looked at Big Cohen for approval. Big Cohen said, "Tell him. Tell him everything from the beginning. If you leave anything out, I'll give you a nudge or butt in."

"Thank you, Big Mo." Little Cohen gestured towards the whisky bottle. Yoseler lifted the bottle and poured Little Cohen a triple shot and the same for Big Cohen. "Don't worry," said Yoseler, "there's plenty more." There was always plenty more.

Little Cohen began. "I hope you've got lots of time, Mr Yoseler. It's a long story."

"Don't worry. We have all night and a lot of whisky. It's not often I get to drink without my wife giving me looks that could kill. I wouldn't mind, if she didn't keep bringing these bottles back, I wouldn't drink so much. Anyway, let's drink away. And remember, anything you tell me will be in strict confidence unless you tell me to say something to someone else."

Little Cohen continued, "Thank you. Well, it all started the year before last, just before Channukah, when a man - not Jewish - came into Bloom's and asked if he could hire a couple of top class Jewish cooks for a few months. It seems that Bloom wanted to know why - not unreasonable - but this man or should I say gentleman who, by the way, was very well spoken and well-dressed, said it was top secret. However, he was prepared to pay not only the cooks' salaries whilst they were away but pay Bloom a handsome sum for the privilege - all this we found out later. It was also on the understanding that they would get their jobs back when they returned. Well, as you may or may not know, Big Mo and I are not the greatest of cooks even though we work in the kitchen, but we can do a bit. Anyway, Bloom decided that the two of us would be ideal for the job, not even knowing what the job was. He didn't care. He gets paid whilst he doesn't have to pay us. And, of course, we weren't the best cooks, but how was this man to know? He took Bloom's word for it. Bloom couldn't lose."

Little Cohen looked at Big Cohen. "How am I doing so far?"

"You're doing very well."

"Thank you. Anyway, we're called out of the kitchen and introduced to this man who still hadn't given his name. We sit down at a table at the back and he starts talking. 'I understand that you are two of the best cooks in this place.' Well, we didn't want to disappoint him, so we nodded in agreement. 'Good. Now, before we go any further, I need to know a few things first. Number one, are you both fit?' Of course we're both fit, I told him. Big Mo did weight lifting and a bit of running, and I played football every week at Hackney Marshes. Even though we're in our early thirties we both keep very fit. He then asked if we had passports. Now, strange as this may seem, the year before last year, both of us applied for passports. We were doing the pools and thought that if we won we could go on holiday abroad. As it happened, we didn't win the pools, but here was a man asking if we had passports. Why would he ask if he didn't want us to go abroad?"

Yoseler replied, "That's a good question. To which there must be a good answer." This was getting better than a Dick Barton episode. Intrigue upon intrigue, he thought to himself.

"Big Mo wanted to know what it was all about, naturally. So did I. So we asked him. All he could say was that if we were interested, we would be going on an adventure of a lifetime but we would be away for months or even a year. He told us that we would be paid more than Bloom was paying us, whatever that was. Then Big Mo asked him why he needed Jewish cooks, which for Big Mo was a fair enough question."

"And the answer?" inquired Yoseler pouring himself just a little more whisky and beckoning them to have a piece of his wife's honey cake. "All he could say was that Jewish food was perfect for what they were going to do and that Jewish cooks were the best people to make Jewish food. Who could argue with that logic? It transpired that years earlier, by chance he read Florry Greenberg's cookery book and was convinced that Jewish food was perfect for their purposes."

Yoseler thought how good a cook his wife was and why she couldn't have gone to wherever they had been. However, having thought that, it was just as well she hadn't. Yoseler would have starved to death.

Then Little Cohen turned to Big Cohen. "Have I left anything out so far?"

"You're doing very well. Your memory is better than mine. But you haven't mentioned the camping."

"I was just coming to that. He then asked if we had ever been camping. To which I answered 'yes'. We had done a lot of camping with the Brady Boys Club when we were kids so we were used to it. In fact, we really enjoyed it. It was perfect for us; escaping from Hessel Street. Then he asked another very strange question."

"Which was what?" asked Yoseler

"Did we mind the very hot and the very cold?"

Big Cohen decided to butt in. "Did we mind the hot and the cold? What a question. If you had spent as much time as we did going in and out of freezer rooms and the kitchen, you get used to both. It wasn't a question of did we mind. We were at home in the cold and the hot. Cold fridges, hot kitchen, freezing storage room, hot kitchen. So we told him it wasn't a problem."

Little Cohen continued, "Big Mo's right. We didn't mind. He then told us that we needed to have medicals to check if we were healthy enough, and that we also needed to talk it over with our families before deciding, but we couldn't tell them where we were going. Well, as we didn't know at the time what we were supposed to be talking over, we both agreed. We told him that neither of us were married, which pleased him, but we would still tell our families that we were going away for a while but not tell them where. Then he told us what they were prepared to pay us. It was a handsome sum compared to what we were being paid by Bloom's so we shook on it - subject to the medicals and fitness tests. We also made sure that he got Bloom to sign a piece of paper guaranteeing our jobs back. We must have been crazy. A man we didn't know coming into Bloom's asking us to go somewhere to do something for months on end. For all we knew he could have been a gunnuf or worse wanting us to do some terrible thing like cook for a bunch of gangsters. But to be honest, we were fed up and needed a change. This sounded like the opportunity of a lifetime and a bit of excitement." Little Cohen looked at Big Cohen, who was just finishing a mouthful of honey cake. "Am I still doing okay?"

"You're doing very well. I couldn't do it better myself."

"True, but make sure I don't leave anything out." Little Cohen looked at the whisky bottle. Yoseler saw the look and topped up all three glasses.

The time was right for Yoseler to ask the question. "So where did he want you to go?"

The two Cohens looked at each other. "Tell him," said Big Cohen.

Little Cohen took another sip of whisky and a deep breath before giving the answer. "Everest, Mr Yoseler." Little Cohen paused for a moment before continuing. "Everest."

"I don't need a rest, go on."

"No, no. I didn't say have a rest. I said Everest. He wanted us to go on the next Everest expedition." Phew! Finally, it was out. After all this time, the secret was out. The two Mo Cohens had been on the latest Everest expedition. Two Jews from Hessel Street had been on the Everest expedition and nobody knew. Not even Doris.

Yoseler didn't move an inch for about ten seconds. Then it was time for another whisky. "Are you trying to tell me that the two of you have been to the Himalayas and up..? I don't believe it."

"There you are," said Big Cohen. "I told you he wouldn't believe us."

"No, no. I don't mean it like that. Of course I believe you. Who would want to make up a story like that? It's fantastic. Go on, please go on, I need to know more. This is a time for celebration."

Little Cohen looked a little more sombre than he had done all evening. Either that or the whisky was taking its toll. "It might not be. That's why we're here. You need to know the full story. You might change your mind."

"Please let me be the judge."

"Okay, but I have to tell you something first."

Big Cohen gave Little Cohen one of those 'are you sure?' looks. Little Cohen nodded back with an 'I'm sure' look in return.

"Well, as I told you before, we're not the greatest of cooks, so we needed to get some help before we went off."

"So why didn't you ask my wife?"

Little Cohen paused for a moment before answering. "We did. And she helped. She helped a lot."

Having asked a simple straightforward question, Yoseler was taken aback by the answer.

"Wait a minute. Are you telling me that my wife helped teach you to cook and she didn't say a word to me, her husband?"

"We asked her to promise not to say a word to anybody, and she kept her promise. But we didn't tell her where we were going. There was a month or so to go before leaving Bloom's, so whenever we saw her in Whitechapel or when she was on the way to the Lane we'd ask her a few questions. Just advice, that's all we asked her for. She thought we wanted to get on at Bloom's and she was happy to help. We asked her not to say anything and she hasn't."

"You know, my wife is the perfect person to tell a secret to, apart from me, that is. I'm very proud of her, even though she didn't tell me." Yoseler gave a smile of satisfaction and pride. "So, why can't we celebrate? You two will become the joint second most famous Jewish mountain climbers in history."

"What do you mean by joint second? Who's top?" asked Little Cohen, looking and feeling a little aggrieved.

The answer should have been obvious to both Cohens.

Yoseler lifted his shoulders and put both hands out in front. "Moses of course. Moses was the greatest Jewish climber ever. Mount Sinai. He climbed Mount Sinai."

Little Cohen said, "But he might only have gone half way up. He might not have gone right to the top."

Yoseler gave Little Cohen a look of disbelief. "What are you talking about, halfway up? Do you think God came down and said, 'take it easy, Moishe, I don't want you to wear yourself out because you've got a lot of shlapping to do later.'? Of course he went to the top."

"Okay, but Mount Sinai isn't as high as Mount Everest," said Big Cohen. Having not wanting to talk about it for ages, all of a sudden, he didn't want to be left out of the conversation.

"This has nothing to do with high a mountain is. This is to do with importance. Without him going up there, you wouldn't have been able to go where you went. It's time to celebrate. It's time to tell the whole world, well, Hessel Street at least and then the whole world will know, anyway." Yoseler was ready to polish off the whisky and even crack open a bottle of vodka.

"We can't," said Big Cohen. "That's why we've come to you for advice. It's not as simple as that."

"Of course it's simple. Unless you did something terrible, like poison someone with your food."

"No, nothing like that. In fact they loved our cooking. And to be honest the main food we served up was chicken, chicken soup, chopped liver, latkas and egg and onions. They loved it. The man who came to Bloom's was right. It was the perfect diet. They took tins of this and packets of that and in the end it came down to good old Jewish cooking. Without it the expedition would not have been a success." said Big Cohen.

"Then what's the problem?"

Little Cohen got the nod from Big Cohen to continue. "It's more complicated than you'd ever believe. First of all, we had to make a promise not to tell a soul where we were going and what we were doing."

Yoseler, looking more and more confused, said, "I'm sorry but I don't understand. Why?"

"At the time we weren't quite sure, then we realised. It wouldn't do to have had two nobodies from the East End, without any knowledge or history of climbing mountains, being part of the greatest expedition of all time. It would have been unheard of. Everybody else was trained in climbing and carrying in dangerous and freezing conditions and at altitude - they were all experts. Then all of a sudden we turn up - admittedly we were asked to go - and the strange thing is that we didn't have any real problems. Okay, we suffered from the cold and had breathing difficulties now and then, and sometimes we felt dizzy and sick from being so high. But we were fit so we survived. We had months of training with the team, and at the same time we were perfecting our cooking and teaching the others."

"Are you sure they didn't want you to say anything because you were Jewish?"

"Definitely not. Most of them didn't know. Anyway, by the time it was all over, everybody wanted our recipes, even the shlapper, sorry, the sherpas. In fact, one of the sherpas was thinking of giving up sherping - if that's the word - and opening up a chicken soup kitchen in Nepal. Everybody was happy with us."

Yoseler decided it was time to stop drinking. He needed his brain to be clear. "But I've seen photographs and film of the expedition and there's not a sight of you anywhere."

Little Cohen had the answer. "To be honest, we spent most of the time cooking. We didn't have a moment to stop and have our photos taken. We were too busy."

Yoseler thought this a very reasonable answer, but needed to ask more questions. "So why did you promise not to say a word? I'm sure nobody else had to promise."

It was Big Cohen's turn to answer. "Maybe it had to do with the fact that it might have diminished the achievement. These were great men, great climbers and we were nobodies from Hessel Street. And anyway, we wouldn't have wanted to take anything away from them."

"But surely the opposite would be true. It shows that everybody and anybody from whatever background can do fantastic things in the right circumstances. You don't need to be rich or come from a privileged background. You just have to have the will. And you had the will. In fact, you had more. You had courage. You two could go down as two of the greatest Jewish adventurers of all time. You should be proud of yourselves instead of hiding the truth from the world."

The two Cohens looked at each other and then at Yoseler, who knew there and then that he had not been told the whole truth. "So what is it that you're not telling me?"

"What we really came to talk to you about," admitted Big Cohen.

"Which is?"

Little Mo put his hands to his face, scratched an imaginary itch in his hair, took a deep breath, sat upright and exhaled. "Not believing everything you hear and see."

"Explain!"

Little Cohen took another deep breath. "Hillary and Tensing weren't the first people to conquer Mount Everest."

Then came the longest pause of the evening followed by Yoseler's next question.

"What do you mean, they weren't the first?"

"Exactly that. Exactly what Little Mo said."

"So, if they weren't the first, who were?"

An even longer pause.

Yoseler didn't need to repeat the question. "Are you trying to tell me that you two were the f…?" He paused, but before he could continue, Little Cohen and Big Cohen nodded their heads. There was no need to say anything.

Yoseler couldn't believe what he had just heard, and was seriously considering the possibility of downing not only the rest of the whisky and vodka but getting on to the kummel and brandy as well. "So you need to explain to me how this came about."

"It's very simple," said Big Cohen, whose tongue had no doubt been loosened by the whisky.

Simple? Nothing is simple with regard to this story, thought Yoseler.

Big Cohen continued, "We only wanted to help out as much as possible, We were worried that Hillary, who, by the way, we thought was a woman before we started out, and Tensing would be hungry and freezing cold by the time they got to the top. So Little Mo and I thought we'd go ahead and leave some food for them. Some hot chicken soup in a flask, which, to be honest, might not even have been warm by the time they had it, and some latkas and chopped liver, wrapped up to make sure they wouldn't freeze. And that's it. That's what we did. All we wanted to do was to help."

"But the others must have wondered where you'd got to."

Little Cohen gave the answer. "Not really. We told everybody that we needed a few days rest after all the cooking we'd done and that we'd be in our tent if we were needed. Our tent was right at the edge of the camp so nobody worried if they didn't see us for a while. We had taken enough food and water, and a Primus stove, so we told them we'd be fine."

"So what would have happened if you had got killed on the way up or down?"

"We didn't even think about it," replied Big Cohen. "But if it had happened, then you could imagine the headlines in all the papers, especially the JC. Not that we would have known anything about it."

Yoseler had been listening to the most remarkable story he had ever heard, but knew there was more to be told. "Wait, wait, wait. What about Hillary and Tensing? Surely they must have said something about the food."

Little Cohen, holding an empty glass and feeling the worst for wear, shook his head and replied, "That's another story altogether. They never said a word. Nothing, gornisht. They didn't even notice us when they were making their way up. We tucked ourselves away for a couple of hours rest before making our way back, so they might not have seen us."

"Maybe they didn't find the flask, latkas and chopped liver."

"Impossible," replied Big Cohen, "I saw the flask sticking out from Hillary's rucksack when they got back."

At last, after a year of not wanting to do or say anything, Big Cohen, with tears welling up in his eyes, slotted in the final piece of the jig-saw.

Unbelievable, thought Yoseler, nobody could make up a story like this. It must be true. They definitely needed his help. He looked at the empty whisky bottle and three empty glasses, stood up and staggered to the sideboard. He pulled out a bottle of unopened vodka and made his way back to his armchair. He sat down, placed the bottle on the table, closed his eyes before rubbing them and then stroked his grey beard. It was going to be a long night. He looked up at the two Cohens and said "Big Mo, Little Mo, we have a problem. But whilst you two have been talking and drinking, I have been drinking and thinking. . .and I have come up with the solution."

"Which is?" asked Little Cohen, desperate for the answer.

"It's simple. We finish this bottle and then, maybe, another one and say nothing...to anybody. . .ever. This conversation never took place."

Where Have All The Slotkins Gone?

The November fog that had blanketed Hessel Street for the four previous days had finally lifted, allowing its inhabitants the privilege of breathing what was laughingly called fresh air once more. But the mood of the members of HESTA had certainly not lifted. In fact, it had deepened. It had deepened so much that the fog that they had been cursing for so many days had become an irrelevant footnote when compared to the anger felt by the forty or so members of the Hessel Street Traders' Association. They had been summoned to an extraordinary emergency meeting by Joe Gorminsky, the chairman.

"How did Joe Gorminsky become chairman of HESTA and president of the shul at the same time?"

"Because he's a gantse macher, a bigshot, that's how. That's what bigshots do. They become chairmen and presidents. But give credit where credit's due; he does a good job, whatever job it is that chairmen and presidents do."

"Which is?"

"I'm not sure but I think it's called calling the shots."

"Which means?"

"Telling everybody else what to do."

"I think I'll apply for the job."

But why call an extraordinary emergency meeting? Because money was missing. And so was Slotkin the treasurer. That's why.

"What sort of name is Slotkin, anyway? I've heard of Zlotkin and Robotkin, but never Slotkin."

"Maybe it used to be Zlotkin and the family changed it to sound more English."

"Meshugena! Zlotkin, Slotkin. What's the difference? One doesn't sound any more English than the other."

"But to Zlotkin, Slotkin might."

"True. Why didn't I think of that?"

The meeting was held on the last Wednesday evening in November, in the hall attached to Cannon Street Road Synagogue. It was an open meeting so anybody could attend but only members could participate. Fat chance of that happening!

The hall was almost packed to the non-existent rafters. In fact, there were nearly as many non-members as members. And amongst them, notable and not so notable dignitaries. Doris and Hannah, highly notable yachnas; Sid and Abe, notable nobodies but friends with everybody; Mickey Strong, definitely a notable nobody, whose name used to be Monty Steingold, and who worked for Leo Silver the fruit wholesaler in Spitalfields. He had to be there. In fact he had to be anywhere there was a chance of an argument. Lew 'Lefty' Lefkovitch the curtain maker and very amateur boxer from Christian Street had made himself comfortable, sprawled across two chairs. He was a semi-notable only because he participated in the fastest knockout in amateur boxing history – his. The first punch, after two seconds, from Kid Rabin sent Lefty sprawling across the ring and into the record books - plus a trip to the London Hospital. Of course, the most notable of all notables was also in attendance, namely Yoseler the Philosopher. He would sit, listen and consider.

Amongst the members seated in the hall were Mendel from the sweet shop, Morry Gold from one of the fruit and veg stalls, Arnie Lissack, who owned the shoe shop, Lipman, one of the four thousand butchers in the street, Alan Jacobs from the bakers, but nobody from Kossoff's or Goldring's. Lennie Lazarus the grocer, Wolansky minus his herrings, but not the smell, Ronnie Flaxman from the fruit shop at the top of the street and Alf Silver, the egg and cheese man. Gross, Robotkin and Goldberg, not a firm of Jewish solicitors, but three more butchers and poulterers, sat next to each other whingeing on about the lack of business and how expensive the price of wholesale kosher meat was. Yetta Levine, the fishmonger, sat beside Hetty the haberdasher and moaned about everything, from the cost of wholesale fish to the crazy rents they were being asked to pay. It was a miracle that so many butchers and fishmongers or anybody else that had a shop or stall made a living in such a small market.

Two other members of note were also present, Solly 'Bananas' Barron and his brother Lazar, both concerned that this was going to be the second meeting in the course of a few days where money was going in the wrong direction. The other meeting being at Hackney Wick on Saturday, where every dog they had placed a bet on decided to take the night off.

The miserable looking bunch of members sat in the front eight rows and the non-members at the back. To make sure that nobody who wasn't a member of the association could intervene, there was an eight foot gap between the two groups. It wouldn't do to have someone who was not a member getting involved. As if anybody was going to stop them.

"What happens if you want to say something?" asked Hannah.

"So I'll say it," replied Doris.

"But you're not supposed to."

"Has that ever stopped me before?"

"No."

"So why should they start stopping me now?"

"You're right. So say something."

"I've got nothing to say…for the moment. And, anyway, the meeting hasn't started yet."

Joe Gorminsky - the bigshot - sat facing the crowd, behind a large oak trestle table. To his right sat Sol Zimmerman, vice-chairman, and to his far right sat Manny Levine - no relation to Yetta - who, as secretary, would take the minutes. The chair between Joe and Manny was vacant. It's where Slotkin the Thief, the no-good, lousy stinking good-for-nothing low-life, may he rot in hell, treasurer should have been sitting.

Joe called the meeting to order by slamming his gavel on the table. "Quiet please, everybody, quiet . . . Thank you. I'm sorry to have had to call this emergency meeting but, as many, if not all of you, may know by now, we have a problem, a big problem. A problem we have never faced before so I won't beat about the bush." Joe cleared his throat and continued solemnly, "Friends, almost all the money we have paid into the association over the past year has gone….. And so has Dave Slotkin."

Uproar!

Morry Gold was the first to stand up. "Where is the bastard? If I get my hands on him he'll be in for a second circumcision." There was a chorus of approval for Morry's legitimate outburst. Joe slammed the gavel down again.

"Morry, calm down, and everybody else, please. And can you not use language like that in a shul hall." Morry waved his hand and nodded his head in apology. "We mustn't jump to conclusions. Just because the money has gone and so has Slotkin doesn't mean to say he's stolen it. It could just be a coincidence," said Joe.

Lennie Lazarus was the next to stand up and stick his oar in. "Coincidence my tuchas, excuse the language. Since when does one and one not make two? The mumza has stolen our money. We need to call the police and have him strung up. I can put up with a heat-wave or snow or sleet or fog or any rubbish weather or even a thief taking from my shop but to have a so-called friend steal from me; that I can't put up with. Remember, when the hole in the beigal is bigger than the beigal, start asking questions."

Sol Zimmerman butted in, "Wait, Lennie, I understand what you're saying." He was the only one. "But Joe's right. We have to take one thing at a time. We can't just call the police without making sure we have all the facts."

Lennie, hitting the palm of one hand with the other to emphasise his points, replied, "What facts? Is the money missing? Answer: Yes. Is Slotkin missing? Answer: Yes. Are they all the facts we need? Answer: Yes. Thank you. I rest my case. Call the police. Better he gets arrested before we get done for murder." He sat down looking around for nods and mumblings of agreement and approval, which he duly got. Even Kopel Rosenberg, the shika - the street drunkard, was nodding and he hadn't a clue as to what was going on.

Before Joe could reply, Lissack from the shoe shop wanted information. "Excuse me, but do we know how much he's stolen?"

Joe replied, "If, and it's still a big if, he's stolen it, to the nearest penny it comes to most of it."

"Which is?" asked a frustrated Lissack.

Joe looked down at the sheet of paper in front of him. "£325 exactly. There's still £15/6/11d in the account. But it could be a bit more because that's only what I've worked out from the last bank statement. It doesn't include the latest interest."

Morry Gold was back on his feet. "Big deal, a bit more. The only thing I have any interest in is getting my, sorry, our, money back. This man," he paused to remove a piece of paper from his jacket pocket, and read, "has impugned the integrity of the association and needs to be dealt with in a manner befitting such an august body."

A resounding "hear, hear," came the call from everyone there even though most of them hadn't a clue as to what he was talking about.

"What does 'impugned the integrity' mean, Doris?" asked Hannah.

"No idea. He must have read it somewhere today, found out what it meant and wrote it down."

"And what's an august body?"

"Somebody who got sunburnt. How do I know? Now sshh, let's listen to what they have to say."

"I am shushing."

"No you're not, you're talking. I'm the one doing the shushing."

Doris and Hannah had been sitting at the back of the hall with the rest of the non-members, listening to the commotion. They obviously wanted and needed to know what was going on. This was not an opportunity not to be missed. This was gold dust. This was perfection. This was where yachnas' dreams come true. This is why they needed to keep their ears in full working order and their mouths shut.

Levitas, yet another fishmonger, was the next member to vent his wrath. "You can't trust these foreigners anymore. They come here and take everything from us, and give nothing back to the community. They should be excommunicated back to their own countries."

It was Manny Levine's turn. "What are you talking about, shmendrik? You're a foreigner in this country. We're all foreigners."

Levitas replied with enough venom to make a snake feel impotent. "But we didn't all come from Moldova."

Ah!

It was lucky that nobody else in the hall had come from Moldova, otherwise a riot would have ensued and another world war started.

As it was, the mood was becoming uglier.

"Anyway, guntsa mucha Levine, who are you calling a foreigner? I've been here since before the first world war," a voice yelled from the back of the hall. The first non-participant to participate, but probably not the last.

Levine replied. "Listen, Strong. I'm calling all of us foreigners. That's what we are. And we'll be foreigners until we die."

"Talk for yourself. I've got a British passport."

You might have a British passport, but it's a foreign British passport. When your great-grandchildren get their passports, they'll be true Britishers. Until then we're all foreigners. British foreigners. Anyway, you shouldn't be talking, you're not a member."

Strong started to make his way forward for a serious confrontation with Levine when Kopel the shika, who had been having trouble staying awake, managed to stagger to his feet. "What's this got to do with Slotkin?" he asked.

Strong stopped dead in his tracks. Silence. Kopel had made sense. When did he sober up? Had he sobered up? The trouble with Kopel was that nobody knew when he was sober or not, so it made little difference.

Kopel flopped back onto his chair and promptly fell asleep, and Strong retreated sheepishly to the back of the hall. Joe thanked Kopel for his input and said, "Now we've all calmed down, can we talk about this in a rational and intelligent manner. If we keep shouting at each other, we'll get nowhere."

"Hear, hear," came another response from all, save for Levitas, who was still mumbling under his breath, "Moldovan mumza. Wait till I get my hands round his throat. He'll wish he was a chicken waiting for the shochet."

Joe continued, "Now, nobody has seen Slotkin or his wife, Rene, since Sunday, which was the last time he was at his fruit stall. By chance I had to go to the bank this morning, and that was when I found out about the missing money. The manager said that Slotkin had gone in on Monday morning, written out a cheque there and then, withdrew the money and left. He didn't think any more of it until this morning when I told him that nobody had seen Slotkin since. As you know, we only take out a lot of money when it comes to yomtovs like Purim and we buy food and things for people who don't have much. And, of course Chanukah is coming up and that costs us a few bob for Chanukah gelt. But it was only when I got home that the penny, if you'll pardon the pun, dropped."

"First impugned and now pun. Where do they keep getting all these posh words from, Doris?" asked Hannah

"I've no idea. Maybe they've been going to evening classes. Remember, if you're a guntsa mucha or president of something, you've got to sound as if you know what you're talking about."

"Since when?"

"True. Now can we listen without you keeping interrupting?"

Lissack thought it strange that Slotkin had left some money in the account. Why not take it all? "I can only imagine that he didn't want to be seen acting suspiciously. Remember, he's always putting money in and taking some out. If he had taken all of it out, someone might have got suspicious," answered Joe. "He had to leave some in there."

Lissack said it was a fair enough answer but said he wasn't happy that the bank hadn't asked Slotkin what he was going to do with the money.

"Why should they?" replied Joe. "They know him well enough not to ask such questions."

Doris and Hannah were in their element. Doris was in heaven - and next to a shul. A month's worth of gossip in one evening.

"He's got a woman somewhere, definitely a woman," whispered Hannah to Doris.

"Slotkin, a woman? Are you crazy? His wife would kill him if she found out."

"Ah! *If* she found out."

"True."

Sid and Abe, who were sitting just in front of Doris and Hannah, were also deep in whispered conversation.

"Aren't we lucky that it wasn't our money he stole," said Abe.

"That's if he stole it. We still don't know," replied Sid. "Maybe he just borrowed it for a few days. He might have needed it for an emergency."

"Such as?"

"An emergency. It doesn't have to be a specific emergency, just an emergency."

"Can you lend me a couple of quid?"

"What for?"

"I can't tell you. All I can say is that it's for an emergency."

Doris tapped Abe on the shoulder. "Can you keep your voices down a bit, we're trying to hear what's going on." A terrified Abe slid a little further down on his chair.

And Yoseler the Philosopher just sat and listened. He would consider the situation and come to his own conclusion later.

Joe continued, "Now you know our position, we have to decide what to do. Some of you want to call the police straight away, which I can understand. But consider this: do we really want to tell the police that a Jew has stolen money? Especially when he's stolen money from other Jews. They would love it, and so would the local papers. Think of the headlines."

"True, very true. Joe's talking sense. Maybe we should hold back for a couple of days. Let's try and find out a bit more and see if we can solve it ourselves, and if by the end of the week we don't have any luck, then we'll tell the police." Zimmerman, as calm as ever, had made perfect sense. Even Levitas agreed.

Then Hetty stood up. "Listen, everybody. I agree with Joe and Sol. I've known Dave all my life and so have most of you. He's a good man. Never been in trouble with anybody. He's your friend. Not one of you has ever said a bad word against him until now. All of a sudden you're up in arms and want to kill him. Believe me, there's more to this than meets the eye. Something's not right."

Morry stood up yet again. "I'll tell you what's not right. He's never stolen from us before."

"You don't know he has now, do you?" replied Hetty. "You just assume he has. Now, be sensible and don't behave like a mob crying for blood. Let's try and find out more."

A round of applause from most of those in the hall, including the non-members. Even a very reluctant Levitas clapped. The only two that didn't were Morry Gold and Kopel the shika. Kopel was too busy snoring and Gold was too busy being angry.

"Thank you, Hetty," said Joe. "Now I think we should take a vote on it. As you know, we need a two-thirds majority to pass a motion. So, I put forward that we wait until Friday to see if we can sort out what's happened. If we don't find out by then, we'll call the police."

Zimmerman seconded the motion.

"All those in favour please raise their hands," said Joe.

There was no need to count. Only three members opposed the motion. Even Kopel, still seemingly asleep, raised his hand in approval.

"Thank you for your confidence. I think that Sol here should do a bit of investigating if that's okay with everybody." There were nods of approval from almost everybody. "If anybody has any ideas, including the non-members at the back, please let him know. If nothing comes up by Friday lunchtime, we'll go the police. Okay? Good. Now, does anybody else have anything to say before I bring this meeting to a close?"

A voice from the doorway replied.

"I do."

Heads turned to see who was talking.

It was Slotkin. "Joe, why have you called this meeting without letting me know? I'm the treasurer. I should have been told." There was a shocked silence in the hall as Slotkin walked in with his wife, Rene.

For once, Joe was almost lost for words, but gathered his thoughts in time for a reasonable answer. "Errm, errm. Dave, errm, it's, it's good to see you. We wondered where you were. I called the meeting because it seems that somebody has, we think, stolen money from the association."

"What?. . . Stolen money? . . .How? . . . When?. . . Who would do such a thing?"

"You, Slotkin, you. You stole the money, you good-for-nothing lowlife," spewed Morry Gold.

"You've got a chutzpah coming back here after what you've done," shouted Levitas.

Shouting, yelling, finger-pointing, verbal abuse, and all of it aimed at Slotkin. Poor Rene was terrified and retreated behind her husband for protection. Doris - obviously - stood up and came to Rene's defence. "Come, sit with me and Hannah until they sort it out. Hannah move up a bit, Rene can sit between us."

"Thank you, Doris, you're very kind," replied Rene.

Doris…kind?

It was Joe who brought the meeting to order. The gavel came down three times. Each time louder than the previous. "Silence, all of you, please. This is a shul hall. Behave yourselves. You're not at a football match. Thank you. Now let's hear what Dave has to say for himself." Joe waited for silence and then asked, "Dave, what have you got to say for yourself?"

"What do you mean, what's there to say? There's nothing to say. How could you even think I would steal money from anybody, let alone my friends? I'm very hurt. I've never done anything dishonest in my life and all of sudden I'm accused of stealing. I've never even stolen a penny let alone a pound."

"Until now," interrupted Morry Gold. "You've stolen our money and we want it back…straight away."

More waving of fists, more shouting, more finger pointing.

Joe slammed the gavel down again. "Shut up, all of you. I'm chairman of this committee and I expect you all to behave. Thank you. Dave, this is very embarrassing for all of us. So, please, tell us why did you, if you did, take the money?"

Slotkin, burning with anger, replied, "I have no idea what you're talking about. I've been away for a couple of days buying a car. I went to the bank on Monday morning, took out some money from my account and went off to Brighton with Rene to see my brother. He had a friend who was selling a car and wanted to be paid in cash. I don't know anything about missing money."

"Can I ask how much you took out?"

"Of course. £325. Here, look. Here's my cheque book." Slotkin put his hand into his breast pocket and pulled out…the wrong cheque book. "Oivay. Oh, my God. What have I done? I must have picked up the wrong cheque book at home. I was in a hurry to get a train to Brighton. I never bothered to look. I just wrote out the cheque, signed it and handed it over to the cashier. He never said anything, gave me the money in an envelope, and I left. That's it. How could I have made such a terrible mistake? I'll put the money back first thing in the morning. I'm really sorry. I know how it must have looked. But at the same time you should all have known better. You should all be ashamed of yourselves. And you frightened Rene. That makes it even worse."

Red face after red face. Heads disappearing into laps. Embarrassed coughs, bottoms wriggling on chairs and Hetty looking smug and angry at the same time. Kopel was snoring heavily and missed the commotion. Morry kept mumbling to himself that it was Joe's fault. If he hadn't called an emergency meeting nobody would have been the wiser and Slotkin wouldn't have been a wanted man with a price on his head. And Doris? Doris was Doris, soaking up the gossip with relish. "I knew it, I knew it, I knew it all along."

"So why didn't you say something?" asked Hannah.

"Sometimes it's best not to interfere. Especially as we're not members of HESTA."

"True."

An embarrassed and uncomfortable looking Joe knew he had to say something. He was the president and it was he who had called the meeting. "I don't know what to say, Dave. I, we, we're all very sorry. We shouldn't have doubted you ever. But we did, to our everlasting shame. I shouldn't have called the meeting so quickly. I should have done some more checking before saying anything, but I was so worried I jumped to a terrible conclusion trying to protect the association's money. All we can do is apologise and ask for your forgiveness."

More "hear hears" and cries of grovelling approval.

"Joe, you've known me a long time and you know I'm not a man to hold a grudge, but this is something completely different. I never believed that my friends would shout and scream at me this way. I'm going to have to think about it all. I'm going home with Rene and I'll talk to you tomorrow, Joe. Come Rene, let's go home."

Rene stood, kissed Doris on the cheek and thanked her for her help. Doris gave her an 'it's nothing' look in reply.

Not one member of HESTA could look Slotkin in the face as he and

Rene made their way out of the hall.

"Lucky we didn't call the police," said Zimmerman.

"Lucky indeed," replied Joe, who immediately called the meeting to a close. Not even a cup of tea and a biscuit for the crowd. Frayed tempers had calmed. Strong was still keen to have a confrontation with Levine, but every time he made his way towards him, Lefkovitch blocked his way.

"Go home, Strong, go home. Haven't we had enough trouble for one night?"

Strong thought, I could knock you out with one punch, and then thought again, what happens if I miss? He decided to go home.

Thursday morning and the Slotkins were nowhere to be seen. Nor on Friday. Zimmerman knocked on the door to their flat. No reply. And where was the car they were supposed to have gone to Brighton to buy? Joe and Zimmerman were worried. At lunchtime on Friday Joe went to see the bank manager. The good news was that no more money had been taken out. The bad, no money had been paid in.

"If they don't show up by tomorrow, we'll have to call the police," said Joe to Zimmerman in shul on Saturday morning.

"I have a terrible feeling that's what we're going to have to do."

Joe nodded in agreement and looked down at his prayer book. He would have to pray harder than he had ever done before, but he knew deep down that God would have far more important things to worry about.

At the same time as Joe and Zimmerman were doing their best in shul, Morry Gold was sitting at home sharpening a knife on a leather strop, Levitas was trying to find out what "mumza" was in Moldovan and Yoseler the Philosopher was still considering the situation. Doris and Hannah were planning their assault on the ears of the East End, even though Doris wasn't quite right when she said she knew what was going on all along, and Sid and Abe were wondering where they could go for an emergency loan.

And by Sunday morning, after the police had been called, there were plenty of questions to be asked and not an answer in sight except for…

"Why did Slotkin and Rene come back?" asked Hannah.

"You obviously do not understand the workings of the criminal mind," replied Doris.

"And I suppose you do."

"When you've read as many true life crime magazines as I have you get a good idea of what's going on."

"So you know what's going on?"

"Of course. It's very simple. They've left the country. The only problem they had was that they'd forgotten their passports. That's why they had to come back, and everything they did in the shul hall was for show. They should be given Oscars. And we got taken in, even me."

Hannah was taken aback by the idea that Doris had been fooled. This was a shocking and unheard of situation. "So how did you find out?"

"I didn't, but last night I remembered reading about a couple before the war who did almost exactly the same thing and I don't think they ever got caught. The Slotkins must have read the same story and thought they might as well give it a go."

"But stealing from friends isn't right. I could understand it if a low-life like Mishkin wanted a bit of the high-life and did something like this, but the Slotkins?"

Doris shrugged her shoulders. "That's what happens when you change your name. It changes your personality."

"I didn't know that," replied Hannah.

Neither did anybody else.

And there were more questions to be answered.

Why was it that nobody bothered to ask how Slotkin managed to save at least £325 to buy a car when all he was doing was selling fruit and veg on a stall?

Why didn't anybody in Hessel Street know that Slotkin was also treasurer of PLATA, the Petticoat Lane Traders Association?

And why didn't anybody in Hessel Street know that Rene Slotkin was the treasurer of WHISSA the Whitechapel Shop and Stallholders Association?

And why didn't anybody in Hessel Street know that Slotkin's brother was treasurer of KBAB, the Kosher Butchers Association of Brighton?

And why didn't anybody know that by Monday afternoon, Slotkin, Rene and Slotkin's brother and wife were three-quarters of the way to Monte Carlo in an open-topped Bentley?

Two years later, a sum of £400 was transferred into the HESTA bank account by persons or person unknown. It also transpired that a similar amount had been transferred into the PLATA, WHISSA and KBAB accounts.

A couple of days later, Joe received an envelope from Monaco. The only thing inside was a piece of fancy headed paper, which read as follows:-

Association Boutiquier de Monte Carlo
24 Rue de Dai
Monte Carlo
Monaco
Madam President Rene Zlotkin
Tresorier David Zlotkin

And why was it that Joe Gorminsky and Sol Zimmerman had no need for the French to be translated into English?

No Gossip Today

"Did I ever tell you the Hal Levine story?" asked Doris.

"What Halloween story? You've never told me a Halloween story," replied Hannah.

"Not Halloween, Hannah. I never said Halloween. I said Hal Levine. If I wanted to say Halloween I would have said Halloween not Hal Levine. I always pronounce my 'v' like a 'v' should be pronounced and my 'double-u' like a wer sound. I'm talking about Harold Levine who called himself Hal because it sounded posher than Harold and not so Jewish. That Hal Levine."

"Why didn't you say Harold Levine in the first place?" Not that Hannah had heard much about Hal Levine or Harold Levine. All that she knew was that he had lived in Hessel Street before the war, made a few bob and disappeared off the scene. In those days she didn't get involved with other people's affairs. However, under Doris's tutelage matters changed somewhat.

She'd heard of Alf Levene with an 'e' not an 'i', and she also knew Yetta Levine, who had a fish shop in Hessel Street, and she knew Manny Levine and Sol Levine. Neither, as strange as it may seem, were related to Yetta Levine, nor to each other. And she definitely knew Sid Levene with an 'e' and with whom she was desperately in love. Sadly for Hannah, though, Sid's loves were lodged elsewhere, with Marie Gorminsky and the Communist party, but not necessarily in that order. So Hannah ended up with Norman Woolf. Not that he was a bad catch, but compared to Sid Levene with an 'e'....pha!

"Is he related to Lennie Levene?"

"No, he's not related to Lennie Levene." replied an exasperated Doris. "You spell that Levene with an 'e' not an 'i'."

"They could be related by marriage."

"But they're not."

"That's all I wanted to know. Thank you."

"Can I carry on with the story now?"

"Who's stopping you? Carry on. You know I love your stories."

"Thank you."

Doris's notion of Hell was a world without gossip, and gossip had been less than thin on the ground, and the outlook was bleak. Not a hint, not a whiff, not even a glimmer of a whiff of gossip on the horizon. But things could change, just like that, with a blink of an eyelid. In the meantime, Doris was having withdrawal systems and needed somebody to talk to and take her mind off this tragic state of affairs. And as luck would have it, Hannah was on hand. Hannah's husband, Norman, had gone with his friend Barney Goldstein to see his beloved Spurs play a floodlit match, whatever that was, against some team from France called Racing something of somewhere or other; she wasn't sure and, in truth, couldn't care less. He was out of their flat and she had the evening to herself - with Doris, in Doris's flat.

Now, without gossip, Doris could easily have started a rumour about somebody having a you-know-what with you-know-who and you-know-where, but that was beneath her. She had her pride to consider and her standing in the community. Whatever one could say about Doris, which was plenty, she was not a rumour-monger. Gossip was based in truth but a rumour was just that - a rumour - without foundation. So, in the absence of gossip, a story would have to do. And who better to tell the story to than Hannah, who would believe every word.

"Okay, this is the story, but I'm going to call Hal Levine, Levine to save time. There's only one Levine in this story so I don't have to keep saying Hal Levine or Harold Levine, Levine will do."

"It's fine by me. You're telling the story not me."

"Good. Now, according to somebody I knew very well and never lied unless they had to, this is how Levine became a very rich man and went to live in a posh house in Golders Green with his floozy wife and two kids and never came back, not even for a pound of mince. Nobody knows what happened to him after he moved."

Hannah needed to know a little more information before she could let Doris continue with the story. "Is the fact that his wife was a floozy important to the story?"

"No."

"That's all I wanted to know." That's definitely not all she wanted to know, but it would do for the time being.

"Can I continue?" Hannah's nod of the head gave the answer. "Thank you. Now, before the war he was just a bit of a wheeler dealer, buying bits and pieces from junk men and the like. Shmochners, old bits of brass, copper and silver and other stuff, a bit of old furniture –

anything he could make a profit on. Of course, he never asked where any of it came from. If you don't ask. . . if you know what I mean."

Hannah wasn't quite sure she knew what Doris meant, but was certain she thought she knew.

"And he was also a knocker. He'd knock on people's doors, usually out in the sticks somewhere and ask them if they had anything they wanted to sell or get rid of."

"If he'd knocked on my door, he could have had everything for nothing for what it's all worth."

"If he'd knocked on your door, he would have had to bring things with him to leave behind."

"That's not a very nice thing to say."

"I'm joking, Hannah." Hannah wasn't sure that Doris *was* joking. "And sometimes people would ask him to come to a house or flat and buy old stuff they didn't want any more. Maybe somebody in the family had died and they needed to get rid of things they thought weren't worth a candle. Of course, everybody thought that everything was worth something, except you according to you. Anyway, Levine would go round and buy what he could. He'd clean some of it up and sell it in the market in Cheshire Street, you know, just off Brick Lane."

Hannah had to interrupt again. But this time there was a little annoyance in her voice. "I know where Cheshire Street is, Doris, you don't have to be so pacific."

Doris was beginning to wonder whether she had done the right thing inviting Hannah over for the evening - she could have been listening to 'Take it from Here' or 'Ray's a Laugh'- but she continued. "Anyway, he seemed to be making a living out of it. He even bought old clothes if they were in good condition, which he sold straight away to Al Martin the shmatta man - another man who made a fortune that nobody knew about. So all in all he was doing okay. Then one day a solicitor he knew…"

"Jewish?" interrupted Hannah.

"What's that got to do with it?"

"I just wondered if the solicitor was Jewish, that's all."

"Does it matter if he's Jewish or not?"

"Only because I might know him if he was Jewish."

"How many Jewish solicitors do you know? Better still, how many solicitors do you know?"

"None…yet, but I might do in the future."

"In the future, in the future! It's still to come. Worry about it when it does. I'm talking about the past. You know something, Hannah. By the time I finish this story the whole of the future would have come and gone."

Hannah looked apologetic. "I'm sorry. I won't interrupt again, but before you continue I need to do a pish, if you'll excuse my language."

"Go, you know where the toilet is but don't get busy with the papers. And on the way back, put the kettle on, we'll have a cup of tea."

Hannah made her way through the scullery and forced her way into the toilet. It was crammed from floor to ceiling with back copies of the East London Advertiser and the Jewish Chronicle. She sat opposite the stack praying it wouldn't collapse on her, killing her mid-flow, and she would never find out what happened to Hal Levine with an 'I'. And why did Doris ever need to buy toilet paper? she thought to herself. On the way back to the dining room, Hannah washed her hands, filled the kettle, placed it on the stove and lit the gas with a new-fangled fancy battery operated gas-lighter. Gas, gas-lighter and a million tons of paper? Another thought ran through her mind. Although she had been into Doris's flat a thousand times before, this was the first time she had needed to use the toilet. She would make sure it was the last.

Doris was waiting patiently for her in one of the two brown rexine-covered armchairs. "Feel better?"

"Much, thank you. I've put the kettle on like you asked."

"Did you put the whistle on the kettle?"

"Of course I did. Safety first." The last thing Hannah needed was for the kettle to boil over, the water to boil away and for the kettle to get red hot. Then there would be a fire in the flat and before you could say stick that in your salmon beigal and smoke it, Hessel Street would be up in flames and confined to the history books along with her and Doris. Norman Woolf would be beside himself with grief that he was watching Spurs fiddling around in front of goal whilst Hessel Street was burning and he couldn't save his wife. And every yachna in town would be pretending to mourn the loss of its greatest, Doris Feldman.

Hannah sat back in her armchair and made herself comfortable. As she sat, she made a mental promise that she wouldn't interfere with the story again. A promise she knew she had no chance of keeping but had to try. "I'm ready for you to continue, but we're going to have to have a break when the kettle boils, which will be any minute now because I only filled it halfway."

"Why are you being so mean with the water? It's not as if it's *your* water. Right, I've decided not to continue this story until we've had a cup of tea. Is that okay with you?"

"It's fine by me, you're telling the story."

Doris eased herself out of the armchair and made her way slowly into the scullery. She took a teapot and two Queen Elizabeth 11 commemorative coronation mugs off the shelf above the sink and heated them by using the water from the Ascot heater. She then took out a tin of tea from the cupboard and a Queen's coronation commemorative teaspoon from the drawer- why waste a perfectly good teaspoon? Whilst waiting for the kettle to boil she placed two heaped teaspoons of tea into the teapot and waited for the whistle.

"Do you want a slice of lemon in the tea?" she shouted.

"No thank you, Doris," Hannah yelled back.

"Just as well, I don't have any left. Do you want milk?" shouted Doris again.

"Yes please, but just a little." And the shouting continued.

"Do you want sugar?"

"No thank you."

"Do you want me to drink it for you?"

Hannah laughed. "No thank you. I can do that for myself. But I wouldn't mind a biscuit if you have one."

"All I've got are digestives. Will they do?"

"They'll do fine...if you don't have anything else a little more upmarket," Hannah chuckled.

Doris, insulted at the comment, thought that if she rushed quickly into the dining room with the teapot, she could smash Hannah over the head with it, kill her there and then and not have to worry about telling her the story, or make the tea. How can you beat a digestive for dunking? The fact that she had a packet of Bourbon biscuits in her cupboard was not the point. Why should she waste quality Peak Freans Bourbons on Hannah when she could waste them on herself?

Then the whistle blew.

"The whistle's blowing, Doris." As if Doris was oblivious to the fact.

A minute or so later a smiling Doris walked back into the dining room carrying an old wooden tray with all the necessaries resting on it. The two mugs, each with a drop of milk, the teapot, a strainer, a plateful of digestives and the Queen's commemorative teaspoon to stir the tea. She placed the tray on the dining room table and sat on one of the oak dining chairs. "I don't want to get too comfortable in the armchair because I'm only going to have to get up again to pour the tea."

Very reasonable, thought Hannah, but why bother to say it? Instead she said, "Are they what I think they are?"

"It depends on what you're looking at and what you think they are."

"Two coronation mugs and a spoon. That's what I think they are."

"Well then, that's what they are."

"So why are you using them instead of keeping them safe as an investment?"

"Because they're fakes. They're copies. The mugs cost me threepence each and the spoon, a penny. The real ones, the posh Doulton ones are hidden away in my bedroom. Now can I pour the tea?"

"Of course, now that I know you're using fake mugs and a fake spoon." Hannah looked quite upset that Doris hadn't used the real ones. How important does a person have to be before she uses the real ones? Obviously far more important than Hannah.

"What about the photo of the Queen on the wall in the kitchen?"

"What about it?"

"Is that a fake?"

"What are you talking about? How can it be a fake? It's a photo of the Queen."

"Well, if the mugs and the spoon are fake, the photo could be."

"But it's a photo of the Queen."

"The photo could be of a double. Film stars have doubles, so why can't the Queen?"

"Hannah, the photo of the Queen is genuine." Doris was quite hurt that Hannah had thought the photo could have been of a double.

"So what's the Queen doing in the kitchen?"

"Checking I'm not using the genuine mugs, that's what. Now can I get on with the story?" answered a despairing Doris.

"Of course. Who's stopping you?"

Only a meshugena, thought Doris.

Having stirred the tea with the fake teaspoon, she filled the two mugs and handed one to Hannah, who looked carefully to see if she could tell if it was a fake. Unfortunately, as she wasn't quite sure what a genuine one looked like, there was no hope of her telling if it was a fake.

Doris returned to her own armchair with her fake mug and a couple of genuine digestives. She would let Hannah stretch across to get her own. "So, where was I?"

"You got to the part where Levine was contacted by a solicitor friend of his who may or may not have been Jewish but it doesn't matter."

"I never said he was a friend. I just said that he knew him. Anyway, this solicitor had a client…and before you ask, I don't know if he was Jewish."

"I wasn't going to ask."

Of course you were, thought Doris. "As I was saying, this client had died and had no relatives to leave anything to, but owned a house in Stamford Hill that needed clearing. After all the legal problems were sorted out, Levine was given the job of clearing the place."

"If it was in Stamford Hill he must have been Jewish."

"What is it with you and everybody being Jewish? There are people who aren't Jewish, you know."

"In Stamford Hill?"

Point taken. Doris decided not to continue that part of the conversation, as there was no chance of her winning. "As I was saying, the house needed clearing and Levine got the job. He agreed to pay £100 for everything, which in those days was a lot of money."

"It's a lot of money today."

"Very true, Hannah. But he must have seen things in there that were worth a few bob for him to pay so much. It took him days to clear. He hired a van and a couple of old men to help him. He took everything back to his lock-up garage at the back of Vallance Road until he had time to sort it all out. The garage was full with furniture, pictures, crockery, clothes; all sorts of stuff. Now, what he had forgotten to do was look in the loft, which he remembered to do on the last day. And there, stuck in the corner, was nothing but three old tea chests, which he, and his helpers, managed to get down and put into the back of the van."

"This is a long story," said Hannah after dunking and eating her last digestive.

"It would have been shorter if you hadn't kept interrupting. Anyway, I'm coming to the best bits in a minute."

"Good, because I want to hear the rest before Norman comes back from his football match."

Doris thought about the teapot over the head again.

"After a few weeks he had managed to sell almost everything, and it seems he was into a handsome profit. The only things he had left were the three tea chests and an old chest of drawers. He had tried to sell the chest of drawers to loads of people but no-one was interested. He even brought the price down to £2.00."

"What kind of chest of drawers?"

"What kind? How do I know what kind of chest of drawers it was? All I was told was that it was old, very old. That's it. Anyhow, why does it matter what kind it was?"

"Of course it matters. I could have been interested in buying it if it was only two pounds."

"But . . .forget it." Doris shook her head in disbelief. What was the point? she thought. She took a deep breath and continued. Whatever happened, Doris was determined to get to the end of the story that evening or, by the latest, the end of the world. "So, it was time to look in the tea chests."

"And what did he find?" asked an excited Hannah.

"Rubbish, absolute rubbish. The chests were full of old irons and bits of old weights and scales. The scrap man wouldn't have given five bob for the lot."

"So why take them in the first place?"

"First, because he had to clear the house, and second, because he thought there might have been some good stuff in them, that's why. You never know."

"He should have looked in them before he brought them down."

"He didn't want to draw attention to them just in case there was something worthwhile in them."

"But there wasn't."

"But he didn't know that at the time." Doris heaved a big sigh and looked at the teapot on the table.

"So that's the end of the story?" Hannah looked disappointed.

"Of course that's not the end of the story. If it was the end of the story I wouldn't have bothered to tell you because it wouldn't be worth telling. Remember, he still had the chest of drawers."

"But nobody wanted it."

"True. So he thought he'd smash it up and use it for firewood."
"So he ends up with a pile of rubbish metal and some firewood?"

"Not quite. He takes all the drawers out and puts them to one side. He picks up a large sledgehammer and …"

Another interruption. "Did he find the sledgehammer in one of the chests?"

"Does it matter?" If only Doris had the sledgehammer in her hand it would have been put to good use. "Who cares? Nobody, apart from you. Anyway, he smashes the top of the chest of drawers and as he does," Doris paused for dramatic effect, "a secret compartment springs open just below the top."

"And?"

"And there it was."

"There was what?"

"Everything. Jewellery, gold and platinum rings, diamond rings, gold coins, sovereigns, half sovereigns, gold this and that, and to crown it all, £1000 in crisp five pound notes."

Hannah slumped back into the armchair. "Phew! That is some end to the story."

"Which, again, according to this person, is how he managed to buy the house in Golders Green, and never be seen in the East End again."

Hannah shook her head in disbelief. "Boy oh boy, that is some story. I'm so pleased you told me."

And the story of Hal Levine had come to an end just in time. There was a knock on the door. "It must be Norman," said Hannah. "I told him I was coming here, and you know what he's like? Worried that I might not be safe walking the twenty yards back to the flat. There's a better chance of my protecting him than the other way around."

Doris got up from the armchair and opened the door. "Hello, Norman, hold on a moment, she's on her way. I was just telling her a story about the old days before the war. How was the football?" As if she cared.

"Good. It's really exciting going to a floodlit match. I remember going a couple of years ago to see Spurs against the same team. That was the first ever floodlit match Spurs played."

"That's interesting to know," replied a completely uninterested Doris. What gossip was there to be had in talking about a football match? Now, Jewish footballers doing something wrong on Hackney Marshes. That's a different story altogether, especially if it involved fighting and somebody getting hurt and then not inviting the person who hurt him to his son's bar mitzvah even though they'd been friends for years. That was something she could really get her teeth into - if she took them out of the glass.

Hannah stood up, thanked Doris for a lovely evening and made her way to the door, where Norman was waiting for her.

"Doris was telling me a fantastic story about someone she knew before the war. I'll tell you everything I can remember when we get home although I'm sure you must know about it anyway, but just in case."

As they were about to walk out, Norman stopped, turned to Doris and said, "By the way, Doris, talking about people from before the war, you'll never guess who's gone mechullah and is now's selling football programmes outside the Spurs ground."

The Legend of Nat 'Shush' Shapiro

If something unusual doesn't happen at least once a week in Hessel Street, it's time to do two things. Number one; worry and, two, start looking at what's unusual about the usual things that have happened. And, as Yoseler the Philosopher once said in his early days as a philosopher, "It's what's usual about the unusual that makes it so unusual or usual, usually, so you must always look behind whatever is in front to see what is hidden."

So, the thing that happened that wasn't unusual on that Sunday in June 1954, was that somebody died of natural causes. It was what happened afterwards that was so unusual.

But first, the man who died.

His name was Nat 'Shush' Shapiro. Nat had been given the nickname

Shush because of his habit of nodding off to sleep at any given moment or after the downing of a glass of cherry brandy. Even as a kid he was known for falling asleep when he should have been wide awake. Maybe it was the noise of his mother singing late into the night that stopped him sleeping, so the only time to sleep was during the day. Or maybe he just liked sleeping.

"Shush, Nat's sleeping. Keep your voices down," was often heard, even at work. However, because he was such a hard worker when he was awake, not even his boss complained. But that was a long time ago. Now, at the ripe old age of 81. Nat had dropped dead in front of half a dozen witnesses. Money Mishkin was there, so was Ronnie Flaxman, Joe Gorminsky, Morry Gold, Alf Silverman the egg and cheese seller and, of course, Doris the yachna, who was always everywhere.

All of them, apart from Manny 'Money' Mishkin, the spiv, had been standing around complaining, as usual, how bad business had been, although it might well have been good. Even Doris was complaining about the lack of real gossip. Business was never as good as it used to be, even if it was good or bad back then, whenever back then was. Mishkin, probably the most disliked person in the street, had just turned up, with the usual smirk on his face. His black-marketeering during the war had made him a lot of money, and even more enemies. But he still lived in a flat in Hessel Street. Why? Nobody knew and nobody cared. And what's more, he wasn't married and deserved to stay unmarried. Nobody could think of any woman who would want to marry him, even with all that money, and no woman would think of marrying him. He was such a no-good he made your normal no-goods look good.

Joe Gorminsky, one of the kosher butchers in Hessel Street, was an eminent expert on dead bodies, so when Joe proclaimed that Nat was dead, there was no-one around to argue.

Nat had just purchased his regular ration of vegetables from Morry Gold: a couple of pounds of potatoes, a pound of carrots, a couple of large onions, four tomatoes and a half pound of sprouts. Morry knelt down by the side of his barrow and looked at the crumpled body, then the carrier bag of vegetables, then back at the body, and sighed with relief that Nat had the decency to pay before dying. His next thought was obvious - for Morry. If he's dead he won't need the vegetables, so why not put them back on the barrow? Who's going to know he paid? He looked upwards and knew the answer immediately.

The thought disappeared as quickly as it came. It would never do to have God's wrath down upon him for the sake of a few lousy pennies. Pounds maybe, or even just a pound. Anyway, Nat was a good man, and to Morry's knowledge nobody ever had a bad word to say about him and nobody had ever wished him ill let alone dead.

Then, of course, he *could* have been ill and kept the news to himself, not wishing to cause any upset or inconvenience to his family or friends. Nat was, as everyone in the street knew, a proud man. His wife had died some nine years earlier, knocked down by a runaway barrow in Petticoat Lane. *"I told her she shouldn't go that far on her own, it's another world. But would she listen? - No."*

He had lived on his own ever since; never asking for favours or special treatment. Both his children had grown up, married, had children of their own and moved to the more upmarket area of London, Stamford Hill. In time they hoped to move to where some of the biggest bigshots lived – Golders Green or even Hendon. They rang Nat every day to make sure he was okay and they also visited him regularly, and he them, but they could never persuade him to move out of the street. *"I've lived here all my life and this is where I'll die."* And so he did.

Within seconds other witnesses had gathered round the body and Joe re-affirmed his opinion that Nat was dead.

Money Mishkin was the next to open his mouth. "If I'd known he was ill, I would have done his shopping for him."

Mishkin got the right response from Joe. "Mishkin, you've never helped anybody in your life unless it was for your own benefit. Now, all of a sudden because you don't have to, you would have. Good. Do something useful and help me move the body into my shop. We can't leave him in the street. It's not dignified.

So shlepping him into a butcher's shop is?

Doris was in a state of suspended animation. She had known Nat all her life, and the sight of him lying dead turned her normally cacophonous voice into silence. In the meantime the vegetables had broken loose from the bag and rolled into the gutter behind Morry's barrow. Nobody bothered to pick them up.

Wait until nobody's looking.

By this time, a large crowd of busybodies and nosey parkers had arrived. Most of them crying or pt pt pt ptutting or oigavulting or oivayzmeering. And those that weren't, were comforting those that were.

> "Don't worry, it's only a dead body. It could have been much worse."

> "How could it be much worse?"

> "It could be you or me lying there."

> "Thank you for those words of comfort. I really needed them."

> "You're welcome."

> "And if I was dead you wouldn't be talking to me like this."

> "But I am."

> "Oi! I wish I was dead."

Morry and Mishkin helped Joe carry the body into the shop. For a small man he was quite heavy. Morry held his head, Mishkin and Joe took an arm each and Flaxman took both legs. Alf, too upset to help, went back to his shop, closed the door behind him and cried; another lifelong friend gone. As the others carried the body into the shop, a thick brown envelope fell from Nat's inside jacket pocket. Morry signalled to Joe as to what had happened. Mishkin also noticed. But then, Mishkin noticed everything.

"What was that?" he asked.

"When we put him down, we'll find out," replied a puffing Joe.

Joe's son-in-law, Reuben, who had been serving a couple of customers whilst the commotion had been going on, cleared the counter of chicken quarters, minced meat, a couple of giblets and other off-cuts of meat, some carving knives and a steel. The customers took a quick look at Nat and disappeared as fast as they could.

"Lay him on the counter," said Flaxman.

"How can you lay him on there?" asked Reuben, "It's kosher."

"Well, he's been koshered, so what's the difference?" replied Flaxman. "Anyway, the chickens won't mind, will they Joe?

"Let's not ask," replied Joe. Nat's weight was getting too much for all of them, so with a quick nod from Joe, they heaved the body onto the counter and then sighed with collective relief.

"How can such a little man weigh so much?" asked Morry.

"Dead weight," laughed Mishkin. The others looked at him in disgust.

Joe needed a cigarette, but decided against lighting one, and Morry went back to his stall to sort out the fallen but not forgotten vegetables.

Just then, Joe remembered that the envelope was still on the pavement. He walked outside quickly, picked it up and returned to the shop.

"Gorminsky, what's in it?" asked an eager Mishkin. It had to be Mishkin to ask first.

"How do I know? You can see I haven't opened it."

"So open it," said Mishkin, his impatience getting the better of him.

Joe told him that it was none of their business to open other people's private envelopes.

"It might be full of money," was Mishkin's response.

Joe decided, with some reluctance, to open it. The look on his face said it all. Mishkin was right. The envelope was full of battered five pound notes. Dozens of them. No, maybe hundreds of them. Well, somewhere nearer the dozens than the hundreds.

Mishkin grabbed the envelope. "Oh, my God! There must be at least two to three hundred pounds in here, if not more."

Ronnie looked at the envelope, so did Reuben. Joe looked again, as did Morry, who had decided to come back into the shop to see what all the commotion was about. Ronnie looked again just to confirm what he had seen first time. They were all amazed at the sight of so many fivers in so small a space. In the meantime, the body was being ignored. Gorminsky took the envelope, with the money, from Mishkin, who, naturally, was not particularly happy about handing it over. Joe placed it back into Nat's jacket pocket. "We should never have opened it. It's an invasion of someone else's privacy," he said.

"Are you crazy or something? Who's going to know? Let's divvy it up and keep quiet about it," said an irate Mishkin. "And anyway, Mr Knowall, you've opened it now. How are you going to explain that?"

"I'll tell them nothing, and neither will you. You'll keep your big mouth shut. For all they'll know it was already open. In the meantime we say nothing to anybody else and when his kids get here they can go through his pockets and find it. Now we need to call the rav, and the hospital to come and take the body. Joe was really busy being a bigshot.

Flaxman offered to go to Nat's flat to see if he could find a telephone number for his son or daughter. He must have it somewhere. He had checked his pockets for a notebook or telephone book, but nothing. He did, however, find a bunch of keys.

"I'll be five minutes. If I can't find a phone number, I'll see if I can find it in a telephone book. I'll also ring the rav.

Mishkin's eyes said only one thing: "Let's take the money and spend it. Nobody will know."

"No," Joe's eyes replied. He would hear none of it, although he could have done with a few bob to pay for a nice holiday somewhere. However, to steal from the living is one thing, but from a dead friend? Never, and certainly not somebody as loved as Nat 'Shush' Shapiro. Mishkin, of course, couldn't care less. Dead, alive, half way between, money was money and take it when you can.

Whilst he and Joe were out-eyeing each other, two flies had taken time out from the dustbin to see what the fuss was all about. They had been rummaging around and noshing on decapitated chicken heads and bones of recently departed lambs and cows, and fancied a change. They decided to check on Nat's deteriorating body. Nowhere near bad enough yet, they decided, and went back to the hors d'oeuvres in the dustbin. They would make a note to come back later - with a few friends.

Some of the onlookers had moved on, had wiped the false tears from their faces and got on with their shopping. But Doris was still in the street, standing as stationary as a petrified beigal, when Mishkin came out of the shop and whispered in her ear. The transformation back to her normal verbose self matched the speed of light.

"How much?" she shouted.

Mishkin told her what he reckoned was in the envelope.

"I don't believe you. Where did he get it all from?"

"Who knows? Who wants to know? Who cares? All I know is that he's got it and doesn't need it anymore, but we do."

"Since when do you need money? You've got plenty."

"Listen, plenty of money is never enough, and there's plenty more where that came from and I, sorry, we could do with it more than him. Anyway, how should I know where it came from? Maybe he robbed a bank."

"Maybe it's his life savings and he didn't like keeping it in a bank just in case it got robbed," answered Doris.

"Life savings don't come in old five pound notes."

"Why not? And, anyway, who cares?" she replied, shrugging her shoulders and nodding in agreement. "So you reckon there's more? Where, in his pockets? In the flat?" Now she was changing into top gear.

As Doris asked the questions, Mishkin remembered where Flaxman had gone. To see if he could find a phone number for Nat's son… in the flat…where the rest of the money was hidden. . .where all the jewellery was stashed away…where untold wealth was stored… under beds....in cupboards. . .under the sink… in the toilet cistern – if he had a toilet…in every nook and cranny. . .and to make matters worse, Flaxman had got there first, the bastard.

Mishkin told Doris that he had important matters to attend to in respect of Nat's death, and dashed off to find Flaxman. "So that's why he was so keen to help," muttered Mishkin to himself. "Bastard, bastard."

Meanwhile, Doris, who had been thinking what a lowlife Mishkin was, decided it was time to play Yiddish Whispers.

Hooray! At last, a yachna had come out to play. And the top-of-the-class one at that.

By the time the details had passed through a dozen different mouths and twice as many ears, Nat had become a multi-millionaire. He had at least three Daimlers stashed away somewhere in Hendon, two houses in Westcliff, three in Bournemouth, a guest house in Brighton and a holiday home in Cannes, wherever that was. There was also a suggestion that he owned a hotel in Cliftonville but didn't want anybody to know because he would have to give them discounts when they went there on holiday. Not only was he a multi-millionaire with a young woman on the side in Golders Green, he was also a shnorrer. And before his death, nobody had a bad word to say about him but now… His death might have been natural, but his wealth. . .unnatural.

All this in only fifteen minutes and the body still warm.

Mishkin found the door to Nat's flat open. Flaxman was looking through the drawers of an old oak sideboard. "Ronnie, have you found anything yet?"

"What do you mean? I'm only looking for an address book."

And I'm Alice in Wonderland, thought Mishkin. He was convinced that Flaxman had found money or jewellery or both. "Where is it then? Come on. Let's share."

"Where's what?" Flaxman replied, looking through the next drawer.

"The money, the jewellery. I know you've found it. Come on, we'll share it and won't tell anybody. It'll be our secret."

Flaxman, as honest as a person can be in a dead man's flat, was furious. "Mishkin, you know, you're the lowest of the low. You're a good-for-nothing bastard. I came to find a telephone number and all you're interested in is Nat's money. Worse, a dead friend's money, that's if you have any friends. Get out of here before I give you a smack in the mouth."

Mishkin was shocked by Ronnie's outburst. "Alright, I'm going, I'm going. Don't get so busy." As he walked out of the flat, he turned to Flaxman and said, "but if you do f…" when Flaxman slammed the door in his face.

Well done, Ronnie.

He continued to search for the book and finally found it in an overcoat hanging on a hook on the back of the kitchen door. He also found another brown envelope.

Which he left behind. And never told a soul, ever.

He returned to his own flat, sat down at an oak dining table and looked through the telephone book to find Nat's son Steven's number. It didn't take long as there were only half a dozen or so numbers in it, including Ronnie's. That's nice, he thought to himself, he saw me as a good friend. He rang the number and gave Steven the sad news. Steven said he would contact his sister and that they would be over as quickly as they could. Even in shock, Steven managed to say that he would have to arrange the funeral as soon as possible. Ronnie's wife, Gertie, was out. She had fancied a trip down the Lane to meet her best friend, Bella Katz. It was a pity she wasn't around. She would have broken the news to Steven in a much calmer and more understanding way. And she would definitely have hit Mishkin straight between the eyes or legs, or both.

By now, those that were left of the crowd had moved on. And so had the vegetables, and Gorminsky decided to shut the shop for the rest of the day. Who was going to buy meat from a counter with a dead body on it?

Isn't that what everybody does in a butcher's shop?

The rav came and so did the ambulance. The body was taken to the hospital where it would be examined and then moved to the morgue.

Why bother with a doctor when Joe had already pronounced Nat dead? Just hand over the death certificate and stop wasting time.

As part of Jewish ritual, the rav would arrange for somebody to sit with the body until the time of the funeral. Joe said he would ring the Federation of Synagogues to see if the funeral could take place the following day or the latest, the next. It would be nice to be able to tell Nat's children that they needn't worry about that side of things. And Joe knew people, so he knew it wouldn't be a problem. It might have been a problem if he knew people who knew people, but that wasn't the case. Anyway, the Federation was used to arranging burials at short, sometimes very short, notice.

However, before the body was placed in the ambulance, Joe suggested to everybody that the contents of Nat's suit be removed and placed with the rav for safekeeping. He realised just in time that it might not be such a good idea after all to leave things where they were until Nat's children turned up. Not that he distrusted the ambulance men or the hospital staff. But just in case. This way there could be no argument.

They removed everything from the pockets. A well-pressed fresh handkerchief, a packet of Polo mints - unopened, some loose change amounting to 4/3d and, of course, the infamous brown envelope. Nothing else. A lifetime and you end up with gornisht in your pockets...except... Joe went back into the shop, picked up a paper bag and placed the contents into it. He then handed it over to the rav, telling him that Flaxman had the keys to the flat and he'd arrange for him to bring them round to the rav's house, which was situated next to the synagogue in Cannon Street Road. Joe did not tell the rav what was in the envelope, just in case.

The rav, of course, could be trusted, but just in case, Joe found some sticky tape and wrapped it round the bag - just in case. That's all, just in case. A rabbi, as is well known, can also have urges.

By the time Nat's kids arrived and the paperwork completed, the funeral had to wait just a little longer. The body was buried at Rainham Cemetery on the Wednesday. The cemetery was home to a host of dead souls who had paid throughout their lives and through their noses to the Federation of Synagogues for the privilege of having a permanent resting place in the heart of the Essex countryside.

Instead of "Please God, next year in Jerusalem," it should be "Please God, not next year in Rainham."

In addition to the hearse and four cars, four coaches were hired to take hoardes of relatives, friends, mourners, half friends, half mourners and not a friend but a friend of a friend, to the grounds. Who was to know who was who and who knew who? Nobody knew everybody but everybody knew that there would be a free nosh-up at the end. And there was also a trip into the Essex countryside. Well, it was a warm summer's day.

One demented coach driver even suggested to his passengers that instead of going straight back to the East End, for an extra 1/6d per head he would take them to Southend for the rest of the day.

Doris suggested that for 1/6d each they could send him to Plotsk. That kept him quiet.

As a mark of respect for Nat, the stalls and shops in the street were closed for the day - an unheard of occurrence - save for Max Foxman, who owned one of the fruit and vegetable shops. He had no time for funerals. "They're for the dead," he would always say, "not for the living." He believed that it was more important to remember the person for the good or bad they had done in life, rather than have to cart off to some miserable windswept burial ground just to throw half a ton of earth over a dead body.

Nat's children, Steven and Eva, decided that it was only right and proper to have the shiva in the East End. After all, that's where most of his friends, those who were still alive, of course, lived. They hired the hall underneath the Grand Palais in Commercial Road so that as many people as possible could pay their respects after the funeral.

Later, Steven and Eva would go back to the flat in Hessel Street and spend the rest of the week there. Not very comfortable, but still. And Steven's wife and their two daughters would make their own way back and forth to Stamford Hill each day. Eva was happily married to an accountant - naturally - and their only son was in Israel. He was contacted straight away and was returning as soon as possible. Eva's husband would also make his own way home each night. There would never be a problem in making up the number for a minyan to say prayers. In fact, there might have to be an overflow service as the flat was so small.

The coach-loads and car-loads of mourners unloaded themselves outside the Grand Palais hall and made their way downstairs to the food. Beigals, platzels, bridge rolls, brown bread - naturally - were the order of the day. Smoked salmon, chopped herrings, schmaltz herrings, sweet and sour cucumbers, pickled cucumbers, haimisha cucumbers, fish balls, cream cheese, eggs and onions, honey cake, fairy cakes, plaiva, kichels and strudel all adorned the tables. Glasses of wine, cherry brandy, with or without advocaat, and whisky were also laid out. The shikas went one way and the chazas the other.
"Is this all a millionaire like Nat can come up with?" said somebody who didn't even know Nat.

"Nat who?" asked someone else.

In truth, the mourning was over for most of them. It was time for gossip. News of the envelope had spread beyond the confines of Hessel Street. Tales of fantasy were now the order of the day. Even Steven and Eva had no idea where the money had come from. Yes, he had worked hard all his life - as a pattern cutter - so there was no way that he could have saved that amount. True, he didn't need a great deal to live on and, again, he had taken very few holidays, none, in fact, since his wife had died. So the mystery deepened.

The yachnas, of course, had all the answers.

"I reckon that he had a rich woman who liked older men and paid him for you know what regularly," suggested Minnie Feld, a somewhat minor player in the yachna league.

"Nat couldn't even do it irregularly with his problem," replied Doris.

"What problem?" asked Minnie.

"I don't want to say." So she told them and then continued, "I think he was a gambler on the quiet. Somebody I know said that somebody they knew saw Nat at Clapton dogs every week. He must have got lucky a few times."

That's better, much better. Somebody knows somebody who knows something.

Hannah, a senior member of the team, picked up a smoked salmon bridge roll and said, "The way I see it is this. The money wasn't his and he was looking after it for somebody else when he dropped dead. One day some gunnuf will come looking for the kids and demand his money back. They'll deny all knowledge of it whilst cleaning their new cars outside their new houses and there'll be trouble. Mark my words. And believe you me, before you can say Jack Rubenstein, they'll be joining the old man at Rainham."

Doris, who by now had filled her plate with an assortment of everything said, "Now you're talking silly. Nat would never get mixed up with characters like that. Why would Nat be holding money for a crook? The man was as straight as an arrow."

"For a percentage," replied Minnie, "and no-one would suspect him of doing anything wrong…and…to be honest, what else is there to do at his age?"

"I'm nowhere near his age but nobody has asked me to hold any money for them," said Hannah, who had just been handed a cherry brandy and advocaat by an unknown passer-by on his way to the beigals.

"At your age, nobody would ask you to hold anything for them," smiled Doris. "Anyway, you don't move in the right circles."

"So you know the right circles?"

"How should I know what the right circles are? I don't move in them. All I know is that we keep going around in circles and we're getting dizzy going nowhere fast."

It's not the circles, yachnas, it's the drink.

In the meantime, old man Kopel, the street shika, had fallen off his chair and started to mumble, "I know, I know where it comes from, from the pin cushion, that's where it comes from, from the pin cushion. All of it."

Flaxman helped him back onto the chair.. "Kopel, you've had enough to drink. Stay here and I'll get you a cup of tea."

Kopel replied, "I've not touched a drop since I got here, out of respect for Nat. He was a good friend."

"So what are you going on about?"

Kopel realised that he had said the wrong thing. "Nothing. I said nothing. I promised to keep my big mouth shut. I think I need a drink."

Ronnie went off to get Kopel a strong cup of tea. "Stay there, I'll be back in a minute."

Mishkin, living up to his weight, had already downed four salmon beigals, four bridge rolls with eggs and onions, three pieces of honey cake and three large whiskies, and was just about in earshot to hear what Kopel had said. He went on the attack. "What are you talking about? You know where what comes from, the money? Come on you old shika, out with it. What are you talking about, pin cushions, what pin cushions?"

Kopel, totally confused and scared by the verbal assault, placed a finger to his lips. "I promised not to say a word. I promised Nat I wouldn't say anything to anybody and a promise is a promise till my dying day."

Mishkin, having been thwarted left, right and centre in all his efforts to get the money, lost his temper and grabbed Kopel by his lapels. "Listen here, you drunken old fool, if you don't tell me everything you know, this could be your last day." Poor Kopel was terrified.

Ronnie came to his rescue. He had had enough. He pulled Mishkin away from Kopel and hit him straight on the chin. Mishkin staggered back into the only table left with food on it, broke it in two and found himself surrounded by a mixture of herrings, cucumbers, cakes and beigals. "So help me, Mishkin, if you open your mouth about this once more you're going to wish you were never born."

The crowd broke out into spontaneous applause. Everybody who knew Mishkin hated him, and those who didn't know him hated him because the others did. Steven and Eva, who were being comforted by friends at the other end of the hall, came over to see what the commotion was all about. Ronnie, not wanting to cause any more grief, explained that Mishkin had slipped on a runaway piece of smoked salmon and had fallen over.

Having satisfied themselves that Mishkin was okay, more's the pity, they made their way back to the other end of the hall.

Mishkin wiped the blood from his lip and staggered to his feet. Nobody could be bothered to help him up. As he left the hall wiping the residue herrings from his suit, he shouted to Ronnie, "I'll get you for this, mark my words I will." Mr Big mouth. All words.

Ronnie was too busy examining his grazed right hand to hear the threat.

"It's about time somebody gave him a good hiding, Ronnie, well done," said Morry Gold.

His own explosion of rage shocked Ronnie. "You know something, Morry. I'm 62 and I think that's the first time I've ever hit someone. I've always preferred other ways of resolving problems."

Ronnie's wife, Gertie, rushed over to see if he was alright. "Never felt better, Gertie, never felt better." And he gave her a big hug. "That man's a low life. Look, I feel great but I'm still shaking. I think I need a drink."

A weak voice that emerged from Kopel's face said, "I'll drink to that. After all, you saved my life."

Ronnie decided not to ask Kopel what the hell he had been talking about when he said he knew. The answer wouldn't have made any sense.

Unbeknown to anyone, Steven and Eva had spent the previous evening going through their father's belongings. It helped pass the time. Having been given the bag from the Rav they thought they should check the flat carefully. To their shock and horror they found eighteen envelopes containing at least £200 in each. It was enough to give them and their children a cosy future.

"What do we do now?" asked Eva

"Simple. We split it between us. That's what we do, and keep some by for the kids." Steven answered, "What else. I don't know where any of it comes from but knowing dad it must be straight."

"And the taxman?"

"Since when is the taxman straight? What the taxman doesn't know, the taxman won't miss. If we tell them about this they'll only nosey about and call the police. Dad's name will be dragged through the mud and we could get nothing. Not that they could prove anything against anybody. But we won't tell them, just in case. Anyway, if God didn't want us to have this money, he wouldn't have invented brown envelopes."

They laughed, cried and wrapped their arms around each other for comfort. "Who would have believed it?" Eva whispered.

The rest of the week passed without problem. Friends and acquaintances came and went, remembered, laughed, cried, talked of the old days, of schooldays and of holidays. Of weddings and honeymoons, and of births, bar mitzvahs and deaths. Nat Shapiro was remembered warmly; with love and affection.

But Mishkin was still fuming. The chances of getting his hands on all that money had gone. Not that he knew that there was any more, but he was sure. And all he could do was blame Flaxman, who, he knew for certain, had pocketed all of it. He was now plotting his revenge.

Four weeks later, a tall slim, pale-faced stranger in his early thirties entered Hessel Street in the early hours of Sunday morning. He was wearing a long black coat over a pair of black trousers and black patent shoes. A white silk scarf was wrapped neatly around his neck and tucked into the overcoat. On his head he wore a black fedora hat. Strange, considering it was the middle of summer. Across his left cheek was a four-inch scar that, to the initiated, explained the uniform.

Mishkin was returning from his regular early Sunday morning walk to get a newspaper when the stranger stopped him.

"Excuse me, sir," the man asked, in a heavy New York accent. I wonder if you can help me. I'm looking for a guy called Nat, Nat Shapiro. Supposed to be kinda short, round about 80 years old. Do ya know anyone with that name who lives round here?"

Mishkin was scared. "Nat, yeah, Nat Shapiro. I know him, no, I mean I knew him. He doesn't live here anymore. He doesn't live anywhere, he's dead. He died a few weeks ago.

Why? Did you need to see him?"

"I did."

"Can I be personal and ask why?"

"Why do you want to know?"

Mishkin stepped back a pace. "No reason, just curious, that's all."

"Ya know what curiosity did? Now, can ya tell me where he used to live?"

Mishkin pointed. "At number 24, in the flats, but the whole place has been cleared out by his kids. Somebody else is living there now."

The stranger's tone hardened. "I hope you're telling me the truth. I wouldn't like to…"

Mishkin interrupted. "Why shouldn't I?"

"Why should you?"

"No reason why. Go see for yourself."

"I'll take your word for it. I wouldn't want to cause damage to an innocent party. But if I find out you've been lying…" He gently stroked his scar with his right forefinger.

Finally the penny dropped for Mishkin. This was the truth, his truth, the moment the truth of all his evil deeds and thoughts had finally come to get him in the guise of an American hitman. But which maker was he going to meet? The one up or the one down? He felt a damp patch between his legs and he started to sweat. He looked around to see if anyone could help. The street was still empty.

The stranger asked another question. "Well, if he's gone, do you know where his kids live?"

"Th…th…they live in G. . .o gone. They've gone. They've left the country. They've gone to live in Austria, No Australia, both families. . .to start new lives now the old man is dead. They all went last week." Mishkin was stumbling and stuttering over his words.

"Well, that is nice and convenient for them. Of course, I hope you're telling me the truth again."

"Why would I lie?"

"Why not?" asked the stranger. "Everybody lies."

"But I'm telling the truth."

"Whose truth? I'm sorry, what was your name?" Mishkin didn't like the word 'was' in the question. The stranger placed his right hand into his coat pocket and pulled out what looked to be the nastiest of flick knives. And still the street was empty. Where is everybody? thought Mishkin, the stalls should be out by now.

"Mishkin, Manny Mishkin. My name's Manny Mishkin. Ask anybody here. I wouldn't lie about my name."

Liar.

The stranger flicked the knife open. "So you're Mishkin eh? Well, well, well. I can kill two birds with one stone. Well, one actually, the other's already dead."

That did it. Mishkin threw up on the spot. He was going to die and not be given a chance to atone for his sins. He was on a collision course with God. He took a handkerchief from his now sodden trouser pocket and wiped his mouth. "What do you mean kill two birds with one stone?"

"Just a figure of speech. Just a figure of speech, my friend. That's all." And the stranger began to clean his fingernails with the tip of the knife.

The 'friend' bit. Mishkin really didn't like. He paused for a moment to reflect on his previous statement. "Well, when I said they had gone to Australia, what I meant to say was that they're going to Australia. They've booked but they haven't gone yet. I think they're going in a couple of weeks."

"So you lied, yes?"

"Only to protect them."

"That was noble of you. But now you've decided not to protect them anymore. Right?"

"Right."

"Why?"

Mishkin could only come up with the truth. "To protect myself. I'm scared, that's all. I don't want to die."

"We all have to die sometime, Mr Mishkin. It's just a matter of when."

"But I don't want the when to be now."

"And that's fine by me. All you have to do is to let me know where they live...and you can." With those words he closed the flick knife slowly, very slowly, and put it in back in his coat pocket slowly, very slowly.

Mishkin sighed. "Thank you, thank you very much. I'll find out today or tomorrow the latest. How can I let you know?"

The stranger put his hand into his inside coat pocket and pulled out a small brown paper bag. "Inside this bag is a brown envelope. All you have to do is to put the address on a piece of paper and place it in the envelope and send it. It's already stamped and addressed. You won't even have to send a covering note. I'll know who it came from. And if your information is correct you'll never hear from me again. Of course if…" He placed his hand back into the pocket with the knife, slowly, very slowly.

Mishkin took the bag and put it into his jacket pocket. "I promise that it'll be done by tomorrow."

The stranger turned his back on Mishkin and started to walk away. He then turned again and said, "Don't promise, Manny, I can call you Manny, can't I? I would hate it if you broke that promise."

"I'm sorry," he replied, "I'll try my hardest to have the addresses by tomorrow."

The stranger smiled. "That's all we can do in our short or for some, very short lives, Manny, try our hardest."

With those parting words the stranger walked slowly out of Hessel Street.

In a state of near hysteria, Mishkin slumped to the ground, still alone in the street. Where is everybody? he thought to himself. He was shaking with fear. What had he done to deserve this visitation? The front of his trousers was now sodden and stained. Somebody, no, everybody was right. He was a good-for-nothing. The lowest of the low. Ronnie Flaxman was right. He was a good-for-nothing lowlife who had never done good in his life. It was time to change. Somehow he would have to change. Somehow he would have to put matters right. Become a human being – a mench.

He would start off by tearing up the envelope. Even if it cost him his life, he would protect Nat's children. He took the bag from his pocket and removed the envelope. He would definitely tear it up.

But curiosity got the better of him. He had to know who wanted their information. He read the address on the envelope.

MICHAEL FLAXMAN
The Actors Studio
24 East 56th Street
Manhattan
New York
NY
USA

The second penny dropped. "You bastard, Flaxman, you bastard. You had me scared to death. I'm going to kill you for this, you bastard."

The stranger had turned at the top of Hessel Street and headed towards Cannon Street Road. As he did so he removed his hat and peeled the fake scar from his cheek. At the traffic lights he stopped and shook hands with a 62 year old man.

"He's all yours, uncle Ronnie, all yours."

In the January of the following year, the body of Hershel, otherwise known as Purple Nose Pincus was found face down in a gutter in Cable Street. The body of one of East London's leading crooked bookies was riddled with bullets. The police, looking for clues as to who could have killed the 80-year-old went to his flat in Stamford Hill. He had lived alone since his wife ran off with another bent bookie from Brighton some twenty years earlier. It's a pity, Pincus always thought to himself, that she didn't run off years earlier. It would have saved him a fortune.

Whilst looking through the drawers of the Epstein - only the best for Pincus - sideboard and then the dressing table, they came across nothing more sinister than a notebook and twenty-four unused brown envelopes. The notebook dated back to the 1930s. In it they found a series of numbers and initials. At the time it made no sense to the police.

But 2763450SH, the first number and initials in the book, had made perfect sense to Purple Nose Pincus, or the Pincushion, as Kopel and Nat had always referred to him.

27th June, 1934, £50/-/-, Shapiro.

Simple. But not to the police.

On the morning of June 27th 1954, Nat 'Shush' Shapiro woke up to celebrate a most unusual anniversary. He got up early, as usual, dressed, and had breakfast. He then went back into his bedroom and took out a small leather bag from beneath his bed. He then removed two small brown envelopes, put them in his inside jacket pocket, closed the bag and put it back under the neatly-made bed. He then walked out of the flat, locked the door and took a casual walk to Brick Lane to talk to the stonemasons who had made the stone for his wife.

"I want to pay for a stone."

"Who's it for?"

"Me. I don't want my kids to have to pay for it when I go."

"But that could be years off. Prices could have gone up by then."

"Trust me," said Nat, "it won't be a problem. I'll pay you plenty more than you'll ever need." He took one of the envelopes from his pocket and handed it over. "Is that enough?" he asked.

The man looked in the envelope and said, "This is more than enough. This could pay for two, even in five years' time."

"Don't worry about it. It's nearly all my savings, but I've still got enough to get by. Don't even give me a receipt. Just write the details down in a book. I trust you. You've always been the best stonemasons in the area so I know you'll do the right thing. When my kids come to arrange things, and they will, you'll know what to do. Thank you."

After all the paper work had been done, Nat made his way back to Hessel Street with a brown envelope in his pocket, happy in the knowledge that his future resting place had been settled, next to his wife.

Which is why he had so much money on him when he died, and why, when Steven and Eva went to organise the stone, they didn't have to pay a penny.

Oh, by the way, that Sunday in June 1954 was twenty years to the day that Nat had carried out his first contract killing for Purple Nose Pincus.

The New Hen Berg Trial

Moishe Berg the shochet was terrified, and with good reason. He was about to be grilled by three ferocious looking featherless chickens.

"Sit down," came a booming order from the largest, seated in the middle of the three on a large luxurious armchair made of the finest chicken feathers Berg had ever seen - and he had seen millions in his time. The other two were sitting on what looked like top of the range very comfortable large white satin pillows. What they were filled with he would never find out but he had a pretty good idea.

"I said sit down, Berg," repeated the chicken sternly.

He looked around nervously for somewhere to sit.

"In there," replied all three chickens, as each one raised a wing and pointed.

Berg looked shocked. "You. . .you. . .you expect me to sit in there?

It's a… a… it's a wooden cage. It's not even fit enough for a..a..a.. ch." He decided to hold his tongue.

The three chickens nodded in agreement.

"And it's disgusting and filthy and… and…it's got bits of straw on the floor…and it's . . .so….so . . . small."

The three chickens again nodded in agreement. And Berg could just see a glint of absolute pleasure in their eyes. Not that there was much of their eyes to see.

"And what if I refuse?" Brave words, Berg, now all you need is brave deeds to back them up.

The three chickens stood up.

Berg looked around to see if there was a way out. Not a chance. No doors or windows. The only light coming from a single-centre pearl drop bulb dangling precariously from a threadbare wire. Hell was the only word that came to mind. And wait a minute, how did this chicken know his name? And hold on another. What was he doing talking to three chickens and what were three chickens doing talking to him? And why was he still wearing his pyjamas? Something was very wrong.

"Okay, okay. I'm going, hold your horses, don't get into a flap, I'm going." Berg crawled slowly and nervously into the cage and sat facing them with his knees pressed up against his chest. There was no space to do anything else. So much for brave deeds. "Now what do you want me to do?"

The three chickens sat back down and made themselves comfortable, too comfortable for Berg's liking.

"Nothing for the moment, Berg. Just relax and try to make yourself at home." Fat chance! "Now, before we get on to the official proceedings," said middle chicken, "let me tell you who we are. My name is Jezebel and to my right is Tallulah and to my left, Fanny. Hens, as you will by now have gathered. We are the official three-chicken tribunal acting on behalf of ASLAC, the Association of Slaughtered Chickens, and to put it in simple terms, we are here to decide your fate after hearing evidence from the thousands of victims and witnesses."

"Fate? What fate? And what victims and witnesses? What are you talking about?" asked an even more terrified Berg, with sweat beginning to trickle down the back of his neck. And then something even more bizarre crossed his mind; what sort of chicken would call their daughter Jezebel? He decided not to ask.

Jezebel, Tallulah and Fanny looked at each other and started to laugh. Well, it sounded more like a cackle to Berg. "All in good time," said Jezebel. "You can't rush a three-chicken tribunal, especially one made up of three hens."

"Definitely not," said Tallulah, or was it Fanny? Berg wasn't sure and in truth didn't care; fear had seen to that. He looked around and realised he was in the most disgusting place he had ever seen or been in and yet it seemed strangely familiar, as did the stench.

"Please pay attention," said Fanny, or was it. . .? "And don't think you can escape. There is no way out. Well, not the way you're thinking."

Jezebel, who was obviously top dog in the pecking order, said, "Now, Mr Berg, you don't mind us calling you 'Mr' do you, even though it's way above your standing in the Jewish community?" Berg thought this to be a little unkind and insulting but shook his head and shrugged his shoulders. Why get involved in an argument over a 'Mr'?

"Good, now before this tribunal decides on your future we need to ask a few questions for our official records."

Then suddenly, from out of nowhere, a fourth featherless chicken

- another hen - appeared with a pencil in her mouth and a notepad tucked under a wing. She placed it on the floor, opened it out with both wings and poised herself in a highly professional manner, ready to take notes.

Jezebel continued, "Now, just to keep you up to scratch, as they say in chicken parlance, Henrietta, who has just joined us, is the clerk to the court and she will be taking down a complete record of what is said and you will be able to read it prior to your sentence to confirm that no mistakes have been made in the proceedings, and that there have been no misunderstandings. Do you understand?"

Did he have a choice? No. He was facing four hens and not a male in sight. So he agreed to agree.

"Good. Now, what is your occupation?" asked Jezebel.

Then, having realised that the word 'sentence' had been mentioned, and obviously wanting to save himself from whatever fate was to befall him, Berg plucked up enough courage to fight back. "Wait, wait, wait," he shouted, shaking the bars of the cage. "Before I give you an answer, don't I have the right to consult a solicitor? Surely a man's got a right to a solicitor, no?"

The four chickens started to laugh even louder than before. In fact, Tallulah was laughing so much she fell off the back of her cushion.

"What's so funny about asking for a solicitor?"

"A solicitor?" asked Fanny. "That's the funniest thing I've ever heard. It's so funny my kishkas are hurting. We should have hired you for one of our hen nights. A solicitor? We didn't know you were a comedian as well as a mass murderer. A solicitor? Whatever next, an accountant and personal tailor?"

Tallulah jumped back on her cushion and apologised for her unprofessional behaviour.

"What are you talking about, a mass murderer?" asked Berg. "I wouldn't even kill a fly."

"You rotten piece of kreplach, Berg, we're not talking about killing flies," screamed Henrietta.

"Potz," cried Fanny.

"Mumza," cackled Tallulah.

Henrietta said nothing. She was too busy looking important, writing and misspelling. But she was slowly coming to the boil.

Jezebel resumed, "If we were talking about killing flies, we would be a three-fly tribunal. But we're chickens so we're talking about killing chickens. You are here on a charge of mass murder, Mr Berg, the mass murder of innocent chickens. So genug with the flies, enough already. The flies can talk for themselves when the time comes, please God."

Poor Berg. Things were going from bad to worse and to cap it all, the chickens were now talking Yiddish. Where did they learn that? But what was the point of even thinking about it? He had bigger problems to worry about rather than concern himself as to how three chickens learned to speak Yiddish. But, as ever with Berg, curiosity got the better of him, so he had to ask. However, this time he decided to ask in the most deferential way he could.

Why make matters even worse?

"Excuse me, your honour, but can I ask you a simple question just out of curiosity?"

Unfortunately, he did make matters worse. Jezebel was not at all happy. "You do NOT refer to me as 'your honour' but as 'your Henour' with a capital 'H'. Do I make myself perfectly clear?"

"Yes, your errm, Henour. I'm sorry for the mistake. But how was I to know?"

"How were you to know? By knowing, that's how. Now, as for your simple question, it all depends on how complicated it is. Please ask away.

"Thank you your….Henour. All I want to know is where you learned how to speak Yiddish."

Jezebel replied, "Well, as you've asked a simple question, Mr Berg, I can give you a simple answer. You see, when you spend as much time as we have listening to it, you pick up a few words here and there. Although to be honest, the words 'as much time' should be 'as little time' considering how short our lives are. And that's another thing we might well take into consideration when deciding your fate."

Why did Berg open his big mouth? Because he has a big mouth, that's why.

Now, Mr Berg, we come to the official part of the proceedings. Tallulah, Fanny, are you both ready?"

"We are," they answered in unison.

"Henrietta, are you ready to take down every word spoken in this session?"

"I am, Jezebel. I have been learning shortbeak for the past two weeks, and I can now take down 200 words a minute."

"Wonderful. Then we can begin." Jezebel sat up straight, wriggled her bottom and began. "Mr Berg, for the record, and before we call the first witness for the prosecution - by the way, there are none for the defence, can you please confirm that your full name is Isaac Berg, your address is 14 Morgan Houses, Hessel Street, London E.1 and your occupation is that of a shochet, an official ritual slaughterer?"

Berg had a problem, a serious problem. He couldn't remember. "Errm, I'm sorry your Henour, but… but… I can't remember what my name is or address or even my job." And it was genuine. He really couldn't remember. Maybe it was the precarious position he had found himself in that caused his partial and, hopefully temporary amnesia. Only time would tell, if he lasted that long.

A look of shock and disgust came over Jezebel's face and the others started shaking their heads and tutting and clucking in mock disbelief. "What do you mean, you can't remember? I've just told you."

"I know, but I've forgotten, just this split second, honest, your hon… hen…Henour, honest. If I could confirm it I would but I can't."

Tallulah said, "I think he's lying. He's just stalling for time."

"I agree," said Fanny. "I think we should kill him here and now. Why bother calling any of the witnesses, they're all going to tell the same story?"

Henrietta's boiling point had been reached. "Quite right. He didn't waste any time with my mishpocheh, so why waste time on him?" The knives were well and truly out. The chickens were restless and were baying for blood.

Suddenly, Berg's partial and very temporary memory loss evaporated and he realised he was fighting for his very existence. He knew he had to come up with a plan to save himself. But there he was, locked in a cage being closely watched by four crazed chickens. No - hens! Even worse. There was no escape. And then, as if by some miracle, it came to him, in a flash. "Wait, wait, wait a minute. I can prove I can't remember."

Jezebel was not convinced at all but she had to be seen to be beyond reproach as chairhen of the tribunal. "Very well, Mr Berg. We will give you one last opportunity to prove that you are telling the truth about not being able to remember."

"One chance," added Tallulah, even though she didn't sound too happy about the prospect. Never trust a caged shochet, she thought to herself.

"I wouldn't give him a half a chance," muttered Henrietta under her breath.

"Thank you, your Henour. Now, all you have to do is ask me my name, address and occupation."

But we've already done that," said an angry Fanny.

"You said you'd give me one chance. And that's all I'm asking for."

"As you wish," said Jezebel, "but be warned, it's your future at stake, so no trickery. Now, for the second and final time what is your name, address and occupation?"

"I can't remember."

"But that's the exact same answer you gave the tribunal before," shouted a furious Henrietta.

"Correct. And now I'm confirming it, it must be true. Why would I lie twice? Once you could understand, but twice?"

Poor Jezebel looked confused. Why did they give him another chance to prove that he had lost his memory? Tallulah had a dizzy spell and fell off the cushion again, Henrietta picked up the pencil with her beak and started to break it into little pieces in anger, and Fanny, now in a hot sweat, started flapping her wings in front of her face to cool herself down. It was turning into a chicken-tribunal disaster. Berg had managed, in one fell, no, fowl swoop, to create a havoc of hens. Jezebel quickly beckoned the other three into a huddle. "He has a point, you know," she said, "and the rules clearly state we cannot sentence a man who has lost his memory."

"So what? I'm sure he's lying. I think we should kill him anyway," said Henrietta.

Tallulah and Fanny looked at each other and then at Jezebel. Tallulah was the first to speak. "I think Henrietta is right. Let's do him in here and now."

Fanny was up next. "I'm not so sure. What would the Council say?"

Henrietta, although not a member of the tribunal, certainly had a lot to say for herself. "You were appointed to the tribunal as decent, upstanding chickens. The members will go along with whatever you decide to do. They trust you to do the right thing. And the right thing to do is to KILL HIM."

Well, the other three certainly knew what Henrietta's views were, but in fairness to her, she was emotionally involved, having had most of her relatives slaughtered by Berg. Jezebel was about to take a more detached and reasoned approach to the problem when she, for no particular reason, turned round to look at Berg. There he was, grinning to himself. A look of self-satisfaction on his face. As far as he was concerned, he had won the battle and probably the war. A mistrial would be declared on the grounds of his loss of memory and he would be released immediately. He had managed to complicate the matter and send the tribunal into complete disarray. He couldn't see a way back for these cocky, chicken upstarts. Who did they think they were messing with?

But, and it was a big and important 'but', he couldn't see what they could see.

The face of a shochet. The face of a cold-blooded chicken killer from Hessel Street.

Jezebel was now in no doubt, and nor were the others. "Henrietta, you were quite right. We are the decision makers. We shall vote with a show of wings. All those in favour of killing Berg in the time-honoured tradition raise your right wing?" It only took a couple of seconds for the result to come through. "There you have it, a unanimous and resounding 'yes'. Mazeltov. Thank you one and all for your careful consideration in this matter."

There was an instantaneous flapping of wings from all four chickens. Henrietta even tried to fly she was so excited. Berg's look of smugness turned immediately to doom and gloom. What was to become of him? A few seconds later he was to find out.

Jezebel, again perched on her armchair, and now looking even more regal than ever was ready to give Berg the tribunal's verdict, but instead of having a crown on her head she had a small piece of black cloth - an ominous sign for Berg. "Now, Berg - we can dispose of the 'Mr' - this tribunal has unanimously found you guilty of mass-murder and has decided to sentence you to death in the time-honoured manner. You will, therefore, be suffocated to death by exactly one million white chicken feathers. Not a feather more or a feather less."

Henrietta butted in. "Hopefully it will be as painful and uncomfortable as possible."

Poor Berg was in a state of utter despair. His plan had backfired terribly and now he was to meet his fate at the wings of four chickens. "Do I have the right to appeal?" he asked, with tears welling up in his eyes. He was a broken man. The cage he was cooped up in felt as if it were shrinking by the second and the room looked even more terrifying and threatening than before. And that stench!

Henrietta was at it again. "Did my parents have the right to appeal? Did my booba or zayda? No. So shoin, why should you?"

Both Tallulah and Lily nodded in agreement, but Jezebel, as ever, the most compassionate of the four, was beginning to feel a little sorry for Berg. After all, he was only doing his job, it was nothing personal. "Tallulah, Fanny, Henrietta, I know we've made a decision and normally it would be final. But look at him, he's pathetic. He's a whimpering mess, a nebbish. I'm sure deep down there's a good kind man trying to get out. Okay, so he's a mass murderer, but sometimes you have to forgive. So I think we should give him a chance to save himself and his soul just one more time."

"You're too soft," said Tallulah.

"I agree with Tallulah," added Fanny. "We've already given him too many chances."

"And you know what I feel about the piece of dreck." More vitriol from a bitter Henrietta. First he was a piece of kreplach and now he's a dreck. What next?

"Well, you're the chairhen, Jezebel, you have the final word," said Tallulah.

"And so I have. Therefore, by the powers invested in me, I have decided that I am going to invoke Rule 7b subsection 40 of the 1842 amendment to the ASLAC rule book concerning the death penalty."

"But no tribunal has used it since it came into force all those years ago. You will be creating a precedence," shouted Henrietta, as she slammed a wing on her notebook.

"I am well aware of that, Henrietta, but there's always a first time for everything, and sometimes we need to show some compassion, even to those we have very little time for, such as human beings." Henrietta shrugged her wings in utter disgust at Jezebel's sudden change of heart. Jezebel turned to Berg and said, "Berg, as you might have overheard, I am going to give you another chance to live, much to the disapproval of my colleagues, but what happens to you from now on is down to you. You can save yourself. In a moment or two, pure white chicken feathers of the finest quality are going to descend from the ceiling, first in a trickle, then in a cascade and finally in a torrent. For you to survive you are going to have to escape from this room before they consume you, and suffocate you to death. Do you understand?"

Berg, too upset and shivering with fear to say anything, and still in the cage, nodded in agreement. But at least there might be a way out. His way.

"Good, and remember, we have given you one final chance to redeem yourself."

Henrietta had to get the last word in. "Which is more than you gave my family. And what about all those chickens we had to say Kaddish for? You didn't give a flying fliegl about them." Then she gave Berg the highest insult a chicken could give to a human being. She turned away from him, leaned forward and exposed her backside. Jezebel gave Tallulah and Fanny the nod of approval, and the three of them quickly followed suit.

A few seconds later, Fanny turned back and pressed a previously unseen very large red button with her beak. Berg looked up and saw a single white feather floating down towards him. Then another and another. After a minute or so, the floor had a snow white covering. He began to panic and closed his eyes, fearing the worst. When he opened them a few seconds later, to his surprise the cage was gone. He looked around. So were the chickens. However, the feathers were still coming down, but now faster than ever. He had to do something. Then he noticed a door - which had definitely not been there before - and decided to run towards it. Unfortunately he was now up to his waist in a sea of feathers so running was out of the question. He pushed as hard as he could using all the strength his arms and legs could muster and just as the feathers were about to cover his neck, he managed to stretch out and reach the door. He realised very quickly that this was the last chance to save himself from suffocating to death. There was only one thing to do. He took a deep breath, closed his eyes, put his head under the feathers and charged at the door.

A split second later he found himself face down in his single bed ripping his pillowcase and inner case to shreds. He was now covered in duck down - more bloody feathers - as was the bed and half the floor. He was sweating and screaming. "Help, help, oi! Somebody save me. They're going to kill me. The meshugena chickens are going to kill me. Help me. Is anybody there to save me? Oi! I can't breathe. I'm choking to death. Help."

His wife, Ruth, shot up in bed, looked at poor Berg and rushed over to him. "There, there, Moishe, take it easy. You were only having a bad dream." She helped him to turn over on his back and started to stroke his forehead to calm him down. "Okay, take some deep breaths, good, that's better. It's okay, you'll be fine. Just relax."

"Ruthy, it was a nightmare. They were going to kill me. Four lunatic chickens, all of them hens, wanted to do me in. They wanted to suffocate me to death with a million chicken feathers. That's it, I'm giving up my job straight away. I'm finished being a shochet. I swear I'm never going to kill another chicken in my life. In fact, I'm never going to eat another chicken in my life. No more meat either, just in case a dozen cows or sheep want to trample me to death. I'm going to stick to fish in future. At least I wouldn't be responsible for their deaths, and even if I were, they wouldn't remember."

"Listen, take it easy. We'll talk about it in the morning when you feel much better. As you said, it was only a nightmare, and you'll soon forget all about it. Now, go get into my bed and try and get back to sleep. I'll clear up this mess."

Berg wiped the sweat from his brow on the sleeve of his pyjama top, gave his wife a gentle, grateful smile and kissed her on the cheek. "Thank you, Ruthy. I'm already feeling much better." He made his way gingerly to the other bed, tucked himself in slowly and rested the back of his head on the soft, welcoming pillow. Unfortunately, it was another feather-filled one. As he closed his eyes and drifted off to what he hoped would be a peaceful night's sleep, he heard some familiar voices.

"I'm pleased he made it through the door, Jezebel," said Fanny.

"So am I," she replied. "And you know we did the right thing, giving him another chance, even though he is a member of the lowest form of life on earth."

"And let's hope that now he's decided not to kill any more of us, he'll become a mench, get himself a decent job and lead a good life," said Tallulah.

Berg gave a sigh of relief and smiled. Then he heard the fourth familiar voice. "Not if I have anything to do with it. Get ready, everybody. It's soon going to be time to say kaddish."

Oi!

Doris Feldman's trip to Sainsbury's in Watney Street market to buy a block of salt yielded far more than expected. After mishearing - badly - a private conversation, she scurried off back to Hessel Street as fast as she could, desperate to tell Hannah the bad and sad news.

Oi!

And, of course, the joyous combination of bad and sad news is the first thing that any yachna worth her salt wants to hear, and as quickly as possible. Good news can always take a leisurely stroll along the seafront at Westcliff, and even find time to stop for a toffee apple or some candy floss.

By the time Doris got back she was exhausted and in a thoroughly bad mood. Hannah was still at work and so she would have to wait. Ten minutes to get back from Watney Street plus another fifteen minutes. Not good for her blood pressure and far longer than Doris would normally have to wait to pass on news of major importance. She would pace up and down Hessel Street looking the picture of innocence and pounce the moment Hannah got back. Fifteen or so minutes later, Hannah returned to find a worn-out Doris sitting on the steps outside her flat tapping her watch.

"Doris, what are you doing here at this time of the evening? It's a bit early for you."

Doris ached herself up with a couple of 'ois' for good measure and replied, "Quick, don't ask complicated questions. Just open the door, I've got news and it's not good."

Oi!

"What is it?" asked a flustered Hannah as she struggled with her mortice and Yale keys.

"Keep your voice down. Let's get inside first. I don't want to talk in public. Stairs have wells and wells have ears. Everybody knows that."

Hannah finally managed to open the door and walk in. "Come in, Doris. Oh, you're already in. Let me hang up my coat and take my shoes off. Sit down and make yourself comf…you're already sitting. Of course you are. Now, what's the not good news you're dying to tell me?"

"Sit down, I don't want you to fall over from the shock…Good. You know Millie Franklyn?"

"Of course I know Millie Franklyn."

"Well, it's about her youngest grandson, Jack, who's coming up to his bar mitzvah in a couple of weeks' time."

"I know him; he's a lovely boy. I sometimes see him on his way to school in the mornings. What about him?"

"He's been diagnosed."

Hannah slumped back in her armchair. "Oi! If I wasn't already sitting I'd have to sit down. Oivay! Oh, my God. This is terrible. When did you overhear the news?" History had taught Hannah that Doris would never have heard it straight from the horse's mouth; not even from the horse's trainer or jockey.

Doris looked at her watch. "Ages ago in Sainsbury's in Watney Street and I've been waiting to tell you ever since." Obviously, she had to exaggerate the time factor, but as every top class yachna knows, exaggeration is the cornerstone to any good story. Not too much exaggeration, though, just enough to make it still believable.

Hannah took a handkerchief from her handbag and started to dab her face. "Oi, this is terrible, terrible. And he's just a kid. Oi! I don't feel good. Couldn't you at least have given me a few minutes before telling me?"

"News like this can't sit around waiting for you all day and night. It does have other customers, you know. Anyway, if I'd waited you'd only have a go at me for not telling you straight away."

"Do they know what's wrong with him?"

"Of course they know what's wrong with him. I told you, he's been diagnosed."

"Was he diagnosed by a Jewish doctor?"

"How should I know? And, anyway, what difference would it make?"

"Well, at least if it was a Jewish doctor you'd know it was kosher, a proper diagnosis. That's all I'm saying." Then there was a brief pause. "So?" Hannah wiped the crocodile tears from her eyes and cheeks and gave Doris one of her 'well, come on then,' looks and gestures, to which Doris duly replied.

"He's got ambi - errm -ambidextrous. That's it, ambidextrous."

Poor old Hannah was beside herself with grief, and waved the flimsy handkerchief across her face. "Oi, I can't believe it. Oivay! And he's so young." She paused for a moment to catch her breath. This was the most shocking news she had heard in years, but naturally, it didn't stop her from wanting to hear all the sordid details. "So, where's he got it?"

"In his hands."

"Oi! Oi g'valt. Of all the places to get it, in the hands. The family must be beside themselves with worry. Are they going to have to cancel the bar mitzvah?"

"Who knows? If it's catching they may have to. It's just as well we haven't been invited. At least we won't catch it, thank God."

"True. But the poor boy. I'll have to pray for him when I go to shul on Shobbus."

"But you don't go to shul."

"This week I'll make an exception…if I've got time. Anyway, more importantly, can the doctors cure him?"

Doris, of course, hadn't a clue, but that didn't stop her from giving a professional opinion. "I don't think so. I think he's got it for life, and they also say it might spread to his legs." More exaggeration and fabrication was obviously needed to add a little spice to an already shocking piece of news.

That did it for Hannah. The bad news just didn't stop coming. First it was the hands, then the legs and now for life. And far worse still, he'd been diagnosed by a Jewish doctor - no, consultant, possibly. "Oi, I need smelling salts, Doris, please, there's some in the sideboard drawer. I need to use them to clear my head before Norman gets back from work. We're going to Johnny Isaacs for some fish and chips."

Doris didn't move an inch to help poor Hannah in her moment of need. Instead she went on the attack. "How can you afford to have an appetite to go out and eat after what I've just told you?"

"What's one thing got to do with the other?"

"Everything."

"It's got nothing to do with it. Are *you* going to eat tonight?"

"Of course I'm going to eat. But I'm not going to eat OUT."

By now, Hannah had forgotten all about the smelling salts. There was a row going on, and the last thing you need when you're in the middle of a row is smelling salts. It could knock you back for a couple of seconds and you would lose all momentum. And, anyway, a row is far better for you than smelling salts. "But you're still going to eat. So what's the difference?" Hannah had raised her voice.

Doris raised hers even more. "In and out. O U T. That's the difference. Anyway, don't say a word to Norman. You know what men are like - big mouths, every one of them. They can't help themselves."

Hannah wasn't having any of it. "Not my Norman. If I tell him not to say a word to anybody, he won't."

"Especially if you don't tell him in the first place," replied Doris.

"But if I don't tell him, I wouldn't have to tell him not to say anything because I wouldn't have told him in the first place."

"Exactly. Now you get my point."

"What point?"

"The point of you not telling him because it could be the point of no return."

"Ah! Now you're talking sense I get your point. You should have said that in the first place."

Another circular, dangerous and disturbing tour around two of the most complex minds known to man, beast and kosher chickens. If only there had been someone around to write it all down, turn it into a book and then a film they could have made a fortune.

Hannah continued. "Are you sure it's catching?"

"I never said it was catching."

"But you said it's just as well we weren't invited."

"Only just in case it is. You can't be too careful. We might have to keep washing our hands."

Hannah was beginning to believe that Doris hadn't overheard the whole conversation. Could she be losing her finely tuned listening powers? "Are you sure they used the word 'diagnosed'?"

"I'm sure they did."

Aha! A chink in Doris's armour. 'I'm sure they did' wasn't good enough for Hannah. 'Of course' would have done, so would 'I'm not deaf, you know.' But 'I'm sure they did' wasn't the definitive answer she was hoping for.

"And anyway," continued Doris, "if he wasn't diagnosed how did they know he's got ambiwatsit?"

Now Hannah wasn't convinced at all, especially as Doris couldn't remember the word. "I think you said something like ambi - ambidextrous."

"Exactly. That's what I just said."

Hannah suddenly clicked her fingers, "I've got an idea. We'll look the word up in a dictionary. Then we can find out all about it."

Doris gave a cursory glance around the room. "Have you got one?"

"Got what?"

Doris shook her head in disbelief. "A dictionary, Hannah, a dictionary. That's what we were talking about. Have you got one?"

"I used to, but I don't remember where I put it."

"Wait a minute. I've just realised, it doesn't matter."

"Why?"

"Because we don't know how to spell it, and if we don't know how to spell it, how can we look it up?"

"How do you know we don't know how to spell it?"

"Do you know how to spell it?"

"No."

"That makes two of us."

"But we know it begins with an 'a'."

"That's if I heard it properly. Don't forget I was overhearing from a little bit of a distance. For all I know it could begin with an 'e'".

So the conversation had moved on from discussing what was wrong with poor young Jack and Hannah's desperate need for smelling salts, to how you spelt the word that Jack had been diagnosed with that neither of them had heard of before, but couldn't look up in a dictionary because they weren't sure if it began with an 'a' or an 'e' or any other letter of the alphabet. And anyway, Hannah couldn't remember where she had put the dictionary, that's if she had one.

"I'll ask Norman where it is when he gets in, and if I find it we can look up all the 'a's and 'e's."

"Then he'll want to know why we need it."

"So we tell him."

"But we agreed not to tell him."

"No, you agreed with yourself for me not to tell him."

So for the next few minutes they continued to disagree about the agreement they may or may not have agreed about when it came to telling Norman - or not. In the end Doris called a halt to the proceedings. "That's it, that's enough already. If you want to tell him, tell him, but don't blame me if he tells the whole world the wrong story."

"But what happens if we tell him the wrong story but he thinks it's right? You can't blame him then."

"Why should we tell him the wrong story?"

"Because you might not have got the story right in the first place. Don't forget, you overheard it."

"The only reason I would have got the wrong story is if the people I overheard got the story wrong. Otherwise it's right, but as I said, to make sure, we shouldn't tell him anything."

As ever, Hannah gave in and agreed with her. "Okay, so we don't tell him. But what happens if he asks what you're doing here?"

"Why would he ask? I'm always popping in for a chat about this or that."

Of course, Doris should have thought about leaving the flat before Norman got back. That would have been the simplest thing to do but that would be too simple. No, much better to stick around and dig a hole for themselves and then find they can't get out because it's too deep and filled with chicken livers. Anyway, it was too late to do anything about it. Just as Doris finished talking, Norman came home.

Hannah gave him an uncomfortable smile and a gentle kiss on the cheek. "Norman, looks who's come to say hello. It's Doris."

"Really? I never noticed. Hello. Doris, it's nice to see you," he lied. "I haven't seen you in ages. Sorry you have to leave so soon but Hannah and I are going out to Johnny Isaacs. I'm just going to have a good wash and change."

Doris thought, who changes to go to Johnny Isaacs? A wash, maybe, but a change? The world was obviously going mad.

It wasn't as if Norman didn't like Doris. On the contrary, he had a lot of time for her, especially as she had been a very good friend to Hannah and deep down, hidden amongst the thick layers of gossip, there was a good and kindly soul fighting to get out into the fresh air. But he wanted to go out and soon. He certainly didn't want Doris sitting around for hours, yachnaring to Hannah. He was hungry.

As he left the room he asked Hannah if she was ready to go out.

"I'll get ready soon. I've only been in five minutes. And anyway, Doris's just leaving."

"I am?" asked a surprised Doris.

"You are."

"I didn't know."

"I didn't tell you."

"Nobody tells me anything." Doris was quite put out. Not only was she told that she was leaving, she wasn't even invited to go to Johnny Isaacs for fish and chips.

"Nobody needs to tell you anything, you already know everything." Hannah gently pushed Doris towards the door.

"So when can we talk about it?"

"In the morning. I'm not working till lunchtime. I'll knock on your door about ten. In the meantime just give me a chance not to say anything to Norman."

It was going to be a difficult night for Hannah. For some unknown reason, a good helping of fish and chips always loosened her tongue.

Twenty minutes later, she and Norman were on their way to Johnny Isaacs whilst Doris was having to make do with a cold piece of chicken she had left over from the previous night. She might add a couple of sweet and sour cucumbers or some chrayne or both, and then she remembered that she still had a piece of chola sitting in her bread bin - a veritable feast was in the making. Doris couldn't make up her mind what to eat; she was still upset about not being invited out for the evening. And if she had been invited out, she wouldn't have had to make a decision as to what to put on her plate. Decisions, decisions, so many decisions to be made and so much time. Never mind, she thought, who needs to go to Johnny Isaacs when I can sit at home with my cold chicken and listen to Donald Peers on the radio?

But if Doris was having a problem deciding what to eat, Hannah was having an even bigger problem to cope with. And it had nothing to do with telling Norman about young Jack, although it was to do with poor little Jack, the poor little mite with an affliction - a terrible affliction that had been diagnosed, according to Doris.

As they were finishing their meal, who should walk in to Johnny Isaacs? None other than Millie Franklyn and her husband Bernie. And what were they doing? Laughing their heads off, that's what.

Something was very wrong. How could they be laughing away when their poor grandson had just been diagnosed with ambidextrous? They should be ashamed of themselves. And. . .and…and, they were going OUT to eat. How could they? Hannah was about to have more than a few words to say when she remembered she had managed not to have said anything to Norman. Mmmm, that could cause a serious problem.

"Look, there's Millie and Bernie Franklyn queuing up. We'll have to say hallo to them and congratulate them on the bar mitzvah. We haven't seen them in ages," said Norman.

"I'm not going to," replied an angry Hannah.

"Why not?"

"I don't want to say."

"What's wrong with you? You always say hallo to people you know."

"Not this time."

Then the penny dropped. "Has this anything to do with Doris turning up this evening… early?"

Hannah dropped her head slightly. "I told you, I'm not saying."

"Then it must be. Come on, out with it. What did she say to you?"

"I promised not to tell you."

"Not to tell me what?"

Hannah paused for a while before giving in to the fish and chips. "About Millie Franklyn's grandson, Jack."

"What about him?"

"He's been diagnosed."

"With what?"

Hannah paused for a few moments before giving in to the fish and chips. "With ambidextrous, that's what," she blurted out.

"So what? What's the problem?" Norman gave Hannah a dismissive shrug of his shoulders.

Hannah was furious. "You as well? What's wrong with everybody? The poor boy's got ambidextrous and all you can ask is, 'So what's the problem?' and the Franklyns are laughing away. The bar mitzvah's probably going to be cancelled because of it, even though we haven't been invited. Everybody's gone meshuga. You wouldn't be laughing if someone in your family had it."

"They have."

Well, that stopped Hannah in her tracks. "You never told me."

"What's the big deal? My cousin Lennie's son, Simon, is ambidextrous. And it's been really good for him, especially with his sport."

"How can having ambidextrous be good for you?"

It was only then that Norman realised that Hannah hadn't a clue what the word meant. "Do you know what being ambidextrous means, Hannah?" Hannah looked a little embarrassed and shook her head. "I thought as much. It means you can use both hands equally. You can write, catch a ball, anything like that, with either hand. They're just as good and as strong as each other. So if you hurt one hand, you can use the other one without any problems."

"What about legs?"

"I'm sure it hasn't got anything to do with legs."

Hannah sat in silence for about ten seconds. Then, "I'm going to kill Doris with my bare ambidextrous hands, both of them, the moment I see her. Just you wait and see, putting me through all that worry and stress." Then she paused for a few seconds before smiling, waving and shouting out, "Millie, Bernie, it's good to see you. How have you been? And mazeltov."

Millie called back, "Thank you, Hannah, thank you. We're fine. Sorry we have to rush but we have to go over and see Jack. He's just done a couple of paintings for us. One with each hand. He's a genius. His art teacher reckons he could be the next Ron Brent. Bye-bye." With a wave of her hand she and Bernie left Johnnie Isaacs. Bernie, of course, couldn't wave goodbye as he had his hands full with bags of fish and chips.

Poor Hannah's face was as red as a beetroot. She had never been so embarrassed and angry in her life. And all Norman could do was to laugh.

"This is no laughing matter, Norman."

"True, but it is funny," he replied as he continued his way through the remainder of his meal.

And all Hannah could do was to blame the fish and chips for forcing her to reveal the secret.

Meanwhile, back in her flat in Hessel Street, Doris had been rummaging around her spare room and, as luck would have it, came across a battered old dictionary tucked under a pile of back copies of the Hackney Gazette. She began to look through the 'a's hoping to find 'ambiwhatsit', that's if it started with an 'a', to confirm what she already knew to be terrible news about young Jack. If she couldn't find it in the 'a's, she would jump to the 'e's, and if necessary, to the 'i's. Well, what else was there to do when you weren't invited out to eat? Within a couple of minutes of her finger wandering down the columns, Doris came across a word that she was convinced was the one she was looking for although she had, obviously, not seen it written down before. This word needed serious consideration so, full of confidence and excitement, she rushed to the toilet, sat down, made herself comfortable and read the meaning. Ten seconds later, shocked and stunned, she dropped her head and shoulders and cried out, "Oi!"

Then, without a second thought, cursed and blamed those good-for-nothing yachnas in Sainsbury's.

Ice Cream Crackers

Everybody was shvitzing, which is why everything that happened, happened the way it happened, possibly…

A gentle, but very hot mid-summer breeze was trundling its way up the Commercial Road from Aldgate, heading for the tranquillity of the Essex countryside when, for some unknown reason, it changed its mind and course, and turned right into Hessel Street. What a mistake!

By the time it had passed five kosher butchers, four fishmongers, a pickled herring seller, two fruit and vegetable stalls and a couple of bakers it was on the verge of throwing up. As it reached the end of the street, it recovered its senses, picked up speed and made its way to the Thames via Cannon Street Road - why it was a street and a road was anybody's guess. It skirted Rogg's delicatessen on the corner of Burslam Street and by passed another potential poisonous place, Langdale Mansions, blocks of bathroom-free flats built a million years ago, but given the grandiose title of 'Mansions'. For a rat it might have been a mansion, but for a human being?

The breeze took a sharp intake of breath and continued its journey along the river as fast as it could and headed for the estuary. Not much better, it thought to itself, but *anything* was an improvement on the amalgam of smells coming from Hessel Street.

Whilst nature was taking its new course towards Westcliff - a welcome relief - Sid and Abe were discussing the weather. They were taking an almost stationary stroll along New Road on their way to the London Hospital to visit a good friend, Lou Levitt.

Now poor old Lou was always ill, even when he was fit and well, but nothing could withstand the full force of his hypochondria. The first sneeze would always lead to a fatal bout of pneumonia, and the first cough of winter was always a sign of imminent death. A small cut would naturally lead to gangrene and the cutting off of a leg or legs. And whatever ailment somebody else had, he had it far worse, which is one of the reasons why he had never married. Every woman he went out with steered cleared of his marital approaches, worried that any potential wife would have to look after him every day for the rest of her life. A night out with Lou could easily end up at the London Hospital, or him ending up in bed for the wrong reason. And as for work, well, that was another plate of chopped and boiled fish. He worked part-time as a bookkeeper for a local kosher meat wholesaler. Three days a week was enough. Any more and exhaustion would have set in and, at his age, whatever it was, it would be very bad news and possibly fatal. One close friend, and he had a few, even went to the lengths of pinning a notice on the door to Lou's flat that read, "Lou Levitt, Never Knowingly Well, Lives Here - Just".

This time he had been admitted to hospital with a serious bout of dehydration caused, unsurprisingly, by not drinking enough during the very short heat wave. He was concerned that if he drank too much his stomach would expand to such a level that it would cause a massive explosion, sending his internal organs in a thousand different directions, thus rendering him dead. This time, however, to the shock of everyone he knew, he was genuinely ill. The heat had really laid him low, and Sid and Abe were most concerned. Not just with Lou's condition, but with the weather.

"This has got to be the hottest few days since the war, I'm sweating like a pig." said Sid, wiping his brow with the back of his hand.

"Never! 1947 was much hotter. It was so hot even the sun was shvitzing." replied Abe, who was really feeling the heat, but had no intention of admitting it. He didn't have to.

"I'm not convinced you're right, but if you're so certain, when in 1947?"

"How can I remember exactly when in 1947? I'm not Leslie Welch the Memory Man."

"So if you can't remember when in 1947, how do you know it was hotter?"

"Because I remember, that's all and just because I can't give you the exact dates doesn't mean to say it wasn't. All I can remember is that it was very hot for a long time, and it was in the summer.... definitely, I'm sure."

Sid decided to ignore his friend's heat-induced last comment and said, "Just because it was very hot for a long time, doesn't mean to say that it was hotter, it was just longer." The argument was now building up a nice head of steam, and, of course, had to continue.

"So you think it was colder?" asked Abe.

"I don't think, I don't know," replied an exhausted and exasperated Sid.

"So if you don't know, I could be right."

"Ah! Now you've used the word 'could' you could be."

"Thank you."

"I only said 'could'. That's not a definite."

"But it could be."

"Possibly."

One of them was winning the argument, but which one? It didn't really matter because it wasn't the winning of the argument that was important, it was the taking part.

They then discussed the possibility of contacting the Meteorological Office to get confirmation as to which was the hotter year but decided, after much deliberation, that they couldn't be bothered. It was too hot to care, and who cared anyway? Well, neither of them anymore.

They continued their crawl to the hospital. If they had walked any slower, visiting time would have been over. Lou might have expired, his vital organs having stopped suddenly and without permission, and the outing would have been a waste of time. Not only that, they would have to cart all the way to Rainham Cemetery for the funeral on yet another baking hot day.

Meanwhile, Hessel Street was, on the surface, in a benign and benevolent mood. It was a hot summer's Monday afternoon, normally the quietest day of the week bar Saturday when all the shops and stalls were closed, but this one was quieter than usual. It was the heat. Nobody could be bothered to do much business or to argue, row or cause any sort of commotion that could disturb a sleeping fly or cause an argument. An argument could lead to a row, which could lead to a commotion, which could lead to a confrontation, which could lead to a fight. And it was too hot to fight. It was too hot to do anything other than sit, drink, drink some more and sit and sleep.

Even the shvitzing cats, dogs and the odd rat were too hot to run around.

Every now and then, however, the odd meshugena, oblivious to the heat, would come by Morry Gold's stall and ask for a couple of apples or oranges or pears or a half a pound of potatoes, or this or that, which was worth nothing to him. Or even ask for a single piece of fruit. Resting and sleeping on a semi-deformed Bentwood armchair was what Morry enjoyed and did best, so the effort of moving, let alone getting up to serve a customer, was one exercise too many.

So why did he stall out? Ask him, but he won't know the answer.

"I'd like to buy a lemon."

No reply.

"So you don't want my business?"

Morry pushed back his flat cap and opened an eye.

"You call buying a lemon business?"

He opened the other eye.

"Of course it's business. It could lead to bigger things. Who knows? Tomorrow I might want two lemons and three apples, and maybe the next day I might want to buy two pounds of apples and three pounds of pears *and* four lemons."

"And maybe by this time next year you might want to buy everything on my stall and set up your own business. Anyway, you've woken me up and all you want to do is to buy a lousy lemon, which is worth umpence to me."

"So you don't want my business and my potential business?"

Potential was the last thing that Morry wanted. The first thing that Morry wanted was this lunatic's money, however little it was, and go back to sleep. But he had to stand up.

"Here, take a lemon, give me the money and stop driving me round the bend. I'm a very busy man."

"You know something, if there was another stall open I would have taken my custom there."

"And if there was another stall open, I'd have sent you there."

But there wasn't, so another pathetic piece of business was done and Morry became a richer man. He went back to the armchair and busied himself thinking how many lemons he would have to sell to become a really rich man. It was like counting sheep and within seconds he was asleep. His bigshot client went away to make himself a glass of lemon tea. Ideal, so somebody told him, for cooling himself down in such hot weather.

There was always somebody in Hessel Street who had a cure or an answer for every ailment known to man.

"So what's wrong with you?"

"I don't know. I don't feel good. I've got pains."

"Where?"

"All over."

"All over where?"

"All over means all over. It means everywhere."

"Have you tried Epsom Salts?"

"I've tried everything."

"But have you tried Epsom Salts?"

"No."

"So you haven't tried everything."

"Okay, I've tried everything apart from Epsom Salts. But I know they won't help."

"How do you know?"

"I just know. That's how I know."

And the discussion had to continue until there was a vague chance of a solution.

"Have you been to the doctor?"

"Are you mad or something? Every time I go there he gives me cherry linctus. Even for a back-ache he gives me cherry linctus. If I take any more, I'll look like a cherry. The man should be locked up for our own safety."

"Then change doctors."

They're all the same, cherry linctus pushers, every one of them. If I've told you once I've told you a thousand times, going to a doctor is a danger to your health. Anyway, I'm off."

"Where are you going?"

"To get some Epsom Salts."

Who needed a doctor with so many experts about?

Hessel Street was almost deserted. Those who weren't in their shops waiting for the lone demented customer to come in, were either sitting and sweating at home or had opened their ice boxes and stuck their heads in to keep themselves cool. At least four women and six children were suffering from sunstroke or sunburn, having gone to Southend the day before on a charabanc outing organised by the

Cannon Street Road Synagogue Ladies Guild.

> "The sun's good for you and plenty of it. It can't do you any harm. Alright, so you might get a bit of a headache. Just take a couple of aspirins and you'll be as right as rain, and if your kid's burning up put him in a cool bath with some olive oil and in no time he'll be fine, but maybe a bit red."

Every hot summer the same advice, and every hot summer, sunstroke, and every hot summer, sunburn.

As Morry dozed off, there were rumblings of discontent coming from the sweetshop. Peace and tranquility were about to be broken. And the cause of these rumblings? The ice cream. The ice cream was going soft, very soft.

The sweetshop was about fifteen-foot long, and nowhere near as wide. At the rear was a small room that housed boxes full of reserve but not reserved stock and the odd piece of black-marketed gear. Even in peace time there had to be some perks for the hard-working shop owner. The shop itself was divided down the middle lengthways by a 9ft long glass counter, behind which old man Mendel would sit most of the day. The counter had two glass shelves packed with packets, cartons and jars of sweets. Bars of chocolate nestled next to gobstoppers, whilst flying saucers snuggled up to sherbet dabs and four a penny chews. Packets of sweet cigarettes were surrounded on all sides by blackjacks, bubble-gum, liquorice sticks, dolly mixtures and Smarties. A glorious tooth-rotting gathering. Sugar rationing was well and truly over. The shelves were also at the perfect height for kids to come in and place their grubby little fingers and hands on the glass and point to whatever they wanted.

"I'll have three of those and two of them and four of them, Mr Mendel."

"Where's the please?"

"Please."

"That's better." And Mendel would place the purchases in a small white paper bag and hand them over.

"Can my mum pay at the end of the week when she gets paid?"

"No she can't, you little gunnuf. I know you've got the money on you, otherwise your mum wouldn't let you come in. Now give me the twopence."

"Alright then. Here's your money."

And two grubby pennies would be handed over by a scruffy looking kid.

But Mendel loved children, so he would always put an extra chew in the bag. Maybe he thought that if he did this one kind and simple thing, God would recognise his good deeds and persuade his children to have children. His greatest joy, he thought to himself every time a child came into the shop, would be to have grandchildren of his own.

When he closed up for the day, Mendel would spend a little time counting his takings. It wasn't a question of greed, it was a question of division. How much he should tell his wife he'd taken and, far more important, how much should he put in his pocket for himself, just in case.

Mendel, as ever at the end of the day, would talk to himself. "Four pounds for me, three for the wife. No, five for me and two for the wife. That's much better. No, I'd better make it one more for me and one less for the wife, just in case."

Just in case what?

There was always a just in case. And today was a perfect case of just in case. Just in case he took too much money. It had been one of the busiest days he had ever known, and his was the only shop in the street taking any money. And all because it had been hot, very hot.

Ice-creams and ice-lollies were flying out of the shop at the speed of sound. In fact, there were no more ice-lollies, and there were only a couple of cartons of vanilla ice-cream left, sitting in the freezer waiting to be scooped up. Bottles of soft drinks couldn't get into the fridge quick enough. As one went in, another came out. Hessel Street had gone cold drink mad. Somebody should have told them that they would have been better off drinking lemon tea. The so-called meshugena who bought the lemon from Morry knew. They should have asked him how to keep cool.

The high shelves on the wall behind the counter were full of cigarettes and tobacco, cigars for the Somebodies and packets of Woodbines for the Nobodies. Boxes of chocolates and packets of ageing sweets for those with poor eyesight, even poorer pockets, and dead taste buds. The lower shelves had bottles of Tizer, lemonade, cream soda and other soft drinks resting on them. In addition there was a hotchpotch of regular necessities such as writing paper, envelopes, pencils, boxes of crayons and ancient boxes of Windsor and Newton charcoal strips.

In all the years he had been there, he had sold just one box of charcoal, but he kept a supply - just in case.

Daily newspapers, comics such as the Beano and Dandy, The Radio Times and some periodicals rested on one end of the counter, with one of each tucked into a rack that hung on the wall near to the entrance. Every Friday the Jewish Chronicle and the East London Advertiser would take pride of place, relegating the likes of the Daily Worker to the back of the shop.

A single one hundred-watt bulb hung from a broken bakelite holder in the centre of the ceiling. By its side dangled a mangled piece of sticky flypaper, the final resting place of a thousand or more flies. It was changed every six months or so, give or take six months.

A small fan had been plugged into a highly dangerous looking socket on the wall behind the counter and sat precariously on a three-legged high stool. The fan's air reached just far enough into the back of the counter to keep the contents cool. Another fan rested on the top shelf, ready to topple over at any moment. To his credit, Mendel was more concerned for his stock's welfare than his own. Of course, it might have had something to do with not wanting to throw melted chocolate bars and sticky sweets away thus losing potential profit.

Mendel had owned the shop since the late twenties. He had run it with his wife, Rose, until she decided that enough was enough. Living with Mendel was one thing but working with him for the rest of her life was another. After their two children had left the family flat she retired to concentrate on doing nothing that required effort, which she did with a great deal of style. Even at the end of a hard day, Mendel would go home and cook for both of them. Why? Why? Who knows why? He did it because he did, that's why.

Her argument was always the same. "I spent the best years of my life working and looking after the kids, now it's your turn." Tonight, he decided, he would not take an ice-cream back for her. He would tell her that he had run out. When he thought about it, it was nearly true.

Mendel was glad to be out of the flat anyway. He had often thought about moving out and living in the back room of the shop. All he needed to do was to move a couple of boxes, put in a bed and a sink and he would be fine. But…

But he never did. People would only talk. They talked anyway, so he might as well have moved out.

The chest freezer stood by the small drinks fridge beside the door that led to the back room. And it was this dilapidated piece of equipment that would cause the commotion.

Jackie Rifkin came into the shop and asked for a vanilla ice-cream cornet. Mendel obliged. He scooped out a large single spoonful, placed it gently into the cornet and handed it over. As he did so the ice-cream began to melt and drip onto Jackie's hand. Jackie gave Mendel a look that could kill.

"Look what's happened," said an irate Jackie.

"It's not my fault," said Mendel.

So whose fault is it?" asked Jackie.

"It's the freezer's fault. I had to turn it full on. The weather's too hot for it to cope all day what with having to keep the ice-cream cold enough not to melt."

"So how cold does it have to be for the ice-cream to stay cold enough not to melt?"

"Colder than it is now. If you had come in earlier, the freezer would have been working properly and the ice-cream wouldn't have melted."

"So it's my fault? What's the point in having a freezer that doesn't keep things freezing cold when it's hot?"

And the ice-cream continued to drip.

"This is the first time it's been so hot since I got the freezer. How was I supposed to know it wouldn't keep the ice-cream cold all day? It's only just happened. I'm sorry but I can't read the freezer's mind."

"You should have read the instructions; that's what you should have done."

"What instructions. It's second-hand."

Third or fourth more likely, thought Rifkin.

He had taken a day off work, feigning sickness from his job in the sales department at Buck and Hickman in the Whitechapel Road, in order to do some holiday shopping. The following week, he and his wife, Maureen, would luxuriate in the comfort of the Normandy hotel in Bournemouth. Nobody was ever sure how they could afford it, but then again, nobody asked, especially when they wanted to buy a brand-new hammer or screwdriver. Anyway, with a bit of luck Rifkin would be able to find something to complain about at the hotel and get a discount.

But the commotion in the shop had now turned into an argument and was building up into a right royal row. Even more of the ice-cream had trickled down Rifkin's hand and on to the floor.

"Now look what's happening?" shouted Mendel, "You're making a mess on my floor with your ice-cream."

"What are you talking about, you meshugena? It's your ice-cream that's making the mess, not mine. If it wasn't melting so much it wouldn't be making a mess."

"And if you'd have eaten it instead of going on and on about my freezer, the ice-cream wouldn't be melting at all because you would have eaten it by now. As it is, it's still making a mess on my floor."

As their voices grew louder and louder, Cyril Berner walked in. "Mendel, give me an ice-cream in a cornet, please."

"Don't have one," said Rifkin.

"Why not?"

"Look what's happening to mine. It's dripping all over the place. The freezer he's got is as useless as him. All the ice-cream is melting."

Mendel interrupted. "Thanks very much. First of all you complain, then second of all, you don't know that all my ice-cream is melting because it's still in the freezer, and now you're trying to drive my customers away. What sort of person are you?"

"You don't deserve customers with a freezer like that." At least half of the ice-cream was now on the floor. The remainder was dripping through the bottom of the cornet and on to Rifkin's hand.

"Again look at the mess on my floor?"

"I don't care about the mess on your floor."

"And I don't care about the mess on your hand. Just pay for the ice-cream and get out of my shop. And what's more, don't bother to come back."

That did it.

"If you think I'm paying for an ice-cream I can't eat you can think again," yelled Rifkin.

Mendel, usually the most passive of people had had enough. He charged into Rifkin with his fists flying. Rifkin, in turn, clattered into Cyril, who, not being able to keep his balance, fell into the street and onto the pavement, quickly followed by a shocked and stunned Rifkin. The only one left standing was the smallest, Mendel, who ran into the street after them.

"Get out of my shop you good-for-nothing good-for-nothing. Even when you were a snotty-nosed kid you were no good and you haven't changed one bit. A cheapskate, depriving an old man of a lousy couple of pence for an ice-cream. That's what you are, a cheapskate."

Rifkin, full of rage and ready to kill, managed to get to his feet and was about to hit Mendel with the full force of his fifteen stone when a dizzy Cyril stood up and staggered between them. Unfortunately for Cyril, Rifkin's right fist, with the cornet still attached, caught him square on the chin, returning him to the ground speechless and senseless. The meagre remains of the ice-cream squirted out of the cornet and landed on Mendel's nose. An incensed Mendel took an almighty swing at Rifkin, missed completely, fell over and found himself lying next to the comatose Cyril. Rifkin, now in full command of his stupidity, stormed through the shop, lifted the lid to the freezer and removed what was left of the ice-cream and threw it all on the floor.

Mendel, seeing what was happening, rushed back into the shop, shouting and cursing, trying to stop Rifkin.

"Meshugena, bastard, lunatic, what do you think you're doing?"

"What I should have done straight away," answered a demented Rifkin.

Unfortunately, Mendel had forgotten about the melting ice-cream on the floor, slipped and knocked himself unconscious on the glass counter. The shock waves sent the cartons of sweets tumbling into each other. Rifkin, satisfied with his efforts, turned around to leave the shop, tripped over Mendel, and slid across the pool of melted ice-cream into the street, where he collided, headfirst, into the recovering Cyril.

All three were now unconscious, and nobody in the street could be bothered to do anything about it. There was no blood to be seen so it couldn't have been that bad. A stray dog, however, sensing that there was no danger of a kick in the rear, managed to get up the strength to wander into the shop and help itself to the melted ice-cream.

What was a balmy day for most of the residents of the street had turned into a barmy one for two meshugenas and an innocent by-stander.

Mendel was the first to come to. He looked at Cyril and Rifkin, gave a loud 'pha!' and then staggered back into the shop and started to clear up the mess. There was definitely no chance of his wife getting an ice-cream. In fact, there was no chance of anybody getting an ice-cream that evening.

The other two finally woke up, both with terrible headaches.

"What happened?" asked an aching Rifkin.

"I can't remember too well, Jackie, but I think you and Mendel might have over-reacted to a very difficult situation. You need to talk to him but don't do it until tomorrow," replied Cyril, rubbing his jaw.

"I think you might be right. I'm going home to have a cold wash and clean myself up."

"That's exactly what I'm going to do, even though I would have much preferred an ice-cream."

They nodded to each other, stood up a little shakily, brushed themselves down and went their separate ways along a now almost deserted Hessel Street.

But things were happening elsewhere.

By the time his two friends arrived at the hospital, Lou was well on the way to making a remarkable recovery.

"We're pleased you're looking so well, Lou. We thought that, God forbid, these were going to be your last hours on earth," said Abe.

"Dying on the hottest day since 1947," Sid continued.

"That's true, but only if. . ." added Abe.

"Don't start that again, Abe. It's too hot."

"Anyway, we've come all the way here from Hessel Street to see that you're okay, even though it's hot enough to fry an egg on the pavement."

"And we're shvitzing," said Abe, wiping his forehead with his shirt sleeve.

"But that's what friends like us are for," smiled Sid trying to loosen his shirt from his body.

"Thank you, thank you both for coming," replied Lou, who,

according to both Sid and Abe, had never looked healthier.

"I'd like to say it's a pleasure, but in this weather I'm not so sure. It's a pity you couldn't have become ill on a colder day. Then we could have got here quicker, brought something with us, like some fruit, and we wouldn't be sweating so much. But carrying something, anything, even ourselves, in this weather is too much," said Abe.

And poor old Sid was worn out. "Is there any chance you can move over a bit on the bed so we can lie down? We're exhausted from all the travelling."

Lou didn't move; it was too hot. But he could talk.

"Listen, it's a miracle what a few supervised glasses of water and tea can do for you. You should try it one day. It'll do you the world of good, especially if it's supervised by one of these nurses. First, they bring you out in a sweat when they tuck you in, even in just a thin sheet, then they cool you down with some water and a nice cup of tea, sometimes with a slice of lemon. I didn't realise that tea can cool you down. You learn something new every time you go into hospital."

If you'd have spoken to the lemon buying so-called meshugena in Hessel Street you would have found out much earlier.

"And now I feel so much better, you know what? I really fancy one of Mendel's ice-creams. Is there any chance you can go back and get me one?"

The Wedding List from Hell

Sometime during the middle of the night at the flat in Hessel Street of Barney and Lily Goldstein, parents of their articled-but-soon-to-be-qualified-as-an-accountant son Daniel who, at this particular moment in time was staying, for his own sanity and other matters of a private nature, with a friend in Bournemouth, Lily woke up shouting.

"Oi, Barney, wake up right now, we've got a problem. We've got a problem with the Greens." Lily shot upright in bed and switched the bedside lamp on. Her long-suffering husband was still fast asleep, facing away from her for his own safety. It was hair roller night and he didn't want to be blinded by an escapee from the hairnet. "Barney, wake up, it's the Greens." She shook him as hard as she could to wake him up.

"Mmmm ...what...? What are you talking about? I don't have any problems with the greens," Barney mumbled, drifting in and out of consciousness. "I'm dreaming of winning at the dogs and you're going on about the greens. I told you not to eat so much pickled cabbage. It's your own fault. Try and go back to sleep. It'll pass." He then prayed quickly to himself that he wouldn't be around when the greens did pass.

"Listen to me. I'm not talking about those greens. I'm talking about the Greens from Streatham. We forgot to invite them to the wedding." This was bad news, very bad news; especially for Barney.

He gave a large sigh. "What are you talking about? What are you worrying about in the middle of the night?"

"The wedding!" she shouted, "We forgot to invite Manny and Becky Green from Streatham to the wedding." Lily was beside herself with grief. How could Barney forget to invite the Greens? How could she forget to invite the Greens? Why didn't one of them remember? But, regardless as to who was to blame, without question it was Barney's fault for not checking the list. Of course she should have checked that he had checked, so it was both their faults, but she would never admit to that. She was, as ever, blameless and, as far as she was concerned, Barney was useless, clueless and brainless, and she would make sure that the rest of his night would be sleepless.

Barney, now just about awake, stretched his arms, rubbed his eyes and forced himself to sit up. "So you woke me up in the middle of the night to tell me that we forgot to invite the Greens to the wedding. Why couldn't you wait 'til the morning to tell me? It's not as if we can do anything about it at," he squinted at the bedside clock, "at half past two in the bloody morning. And anyway, the invitations haven't gone out yet."

Lily was in a bad mood and there was only one person who was to get the full force of her anger. "You don't understand. You men are all the same – dreamers. That's what you are, all of you, dreamers. You dream of this and that and dream of winning the pools and winning at the dogs and having an affair with some floozy film star, but when it comes to real things, important things like wedding invitations, you don't want to know. This is serious stuff. This is our only son's wedding we're talking about and all you can say is 'can't it wait 'til the morning?' Always putting things off! That's why women always have to take control. Men are useless. The quicker a woman runs this country the better, and it'll happen, trust me, it'll happen, one day."

"Sure, and Spurs will win the league and cup in the same year."

What the hell is he talking about? What league and cup? thought Lily, as she got out of bed, put on her dressing gown and made her way to the lounge-cum-dining room. Whilst she was rummaging through her handbag looking for the wedding list, Barney had taken an executive and potentially disastrous decision to try to go back to sleep. "Dear God, was it the 4 and 6 reverse in the 7.10 or the 2 and 5 at Clapton?" he muttered to himself, throwing the sheet and blankets over his head. With a bit of luck, he wouldn't be able to hear Lily going on and on about the bloody list and the bloody Greens from bloody Streatham.

"Where is it? I know I left it in the bag." In fact, she kept everything in her bag. Birth certificate, wedding certificate – may it burn in hell - old ration books, stamps, shopping list, lipstick, hairbrush, a couple of spare hair rollers. Hair rollers? Why? Just in case, that's why. You never know when you're going to need something, especially spare hair rollers. "Ah! Here it is," she muttered to herself. "Okay, let's have a look." She ran a finger down the page, knowing full well what she wasn't going to find. "I was right, they're not on the list. Barney," she shouted, "they're not on the list. The Greens aren't on the list. I knew it. I knew I shouldn't have bloody-well trusted you."

Barney, of course, wasn't listening. He was too busy confirming with God what the bet was in his previous dream.

Lily stormed back into the bedroom, sat on the bed and gave Barney another shove. "Come on, wake up, we've got work to do."

"It's the middle of the night and I don't work nights. Besides, I need my rest. It's shobbus and I have to go to shul later."

"What are you going on about? It's Saturday. You never go to shul unless it's yomtov or you have to for some bar mitzvah or wedding."

"You know I go to shul every other Saturday, and today's the every other Saturday. So I have to go."

Of course Lily knew, but that wasn't going to stop her going on and on and on. "Why?"

"You know why. To meet Norman Woolf to arrange going to Spurs this afternoon."

"You're supposed to go to shul to pray, not to arrange to meet to go to a bloody football match."

"We will pray. We'll pray that Spurs win this afternoon and that my dogs come in tonight at Clapton."

"Why can't you just ring him up?"

"What, on shobbus? I don't use the phone on shobbus."

"So it's okay to go to football on shobbus but you can't use the phone?" And on and on and a half-dozen more 'ons' for good luck. When will it ever stop?

"There are some things you have to keep, like kosher at home. Anyway, I think their phone is out of order. I tried ringing yesterday and there was a funny noise on the line and I never got through."

"That was yesterday. It could have been fixed by now. And by the way, stop changing the subject. I know how your mind works." It's a pity she didn't know how her own mind worked. "Right, out of bed, now. Go and put the kettle on and make a cup of tea while I start looking at the list and pray I can sort the mess you've got us into, out."

"Why is it my fault?" Because it was always Barney's fault.

"Because you didn't put their names on the list." So it was his fault.

"But you were calling out the names." Why couldn't Barney have called the names out?

"And you were writing them down." In Lily's mind, the person writing the names down was always to blame. And Barney was writing the names down.

"So why didn't you remember to call out their names?"

"Why did you forget to write them down?"

"How could I forget when you didn't tell me in the first place?" Always excuses, always. As far as Lily was concerned, Barney was a walking excuse for a human being.

"Can't you think for yourself? Why do I have to think for both of us?"

"Because if I had thought for myself, you would have told me that I wasn't thinking straight and whatever I was thinking was wrong." At last, he was right.

What had started off as a dream had turned into a nightmare. It was bad enough being woken up in the middle of the night, but to be physically confronted by a hair-rollered wife ranting and raving over a lousy wedding list was too much for any sane man.

"Anyway," continued the much–maligned husband, "why do you want to invite the Greens? We haven't seen them for years or spoken to them. Not since they moved overseas to Streatham and he got that posh job working for whatever-their-names-are."

"Just because we haven't seen them, doesn't mean to say we shouldn't invite them."

"Hold on a minute. Wait. Did they invite us to their daughter's wedding a couple of years ago?"

"No."

"Aha! They didn't invite us to their wedding do, so why should we invite them to ours?"

"Exactly. That's the whole point." But obviously Barney had missed the point completely. "That's why we have to invite them. To make them feel bad about not inviting us." To Lily, this seemed perfectly reasonable and logical.

Another one for the looney bin, thought Barney. "So what you're saying is that you want to invite them but you don't want them to come because they didn't invite us."

Now you understand, Barney. What took you so long?

"Correct, now you're beginning to think like a woman."

"I'd rather die than think like a woman," said Barney under his breath. "I'd go mad."

"What did you just say?"

Barney needed to think quickly. "I said, 'Who says they're going to feel bad?' Maybe they'll think that the only reason we're inviting them is so that they'll feel bad, so they won't feel bad. They'll think that we're only inviting them out of spite, and then they'll come."

"Mark my words," replied Lily, pointing the finger of fact at Barney, "they won't come, but they might send a good wedding present with a letter saying they can't make it because they've already been invited to another do, but hope we can get together soon."

"So all of a sudden the wedding list is based on presents and who can cough up the most."

"That's how it works. We go to a do and give a five-pound present, so when they come to our do they feel obliged to give six pounds, and so on and so on, and it's even better when they don't or can't come. Then they feel they have to give more than if they did come. Not only that, they save money by not having to hire dinner suits and dresses. So everybody wins." This made perfect sense to Lily and it was something a man would never have thought of.

"What happens if you're very poor and can't afford a present?"
"You don't get invited, that's what."

Barney put on his dressing gown and slippers, shook his head in disbelief and made the short walk into what was laughably called the kitchen. He popped his head round the kitchen door into the lounge-cum-dining room, where Lily had her head buried in the wedding list. "So what you're saying is," he said, rubbing his hair, "that it's better that nobody comes and they just send a present."

"Now you're being stupid. Of course you need people at a wedding. You can't have a wedding without guests."

Barney put the kettle on the stove and lit the gas. He then opened the kitchen cabinet, found a couple of aspirin and swallowed them whole without using water. That's how bad he was feeling. I might need the rest of the bottle, very soon, he thought to himself. "Can't you invite them not to come?" he shouted.

Lily decided to ignore the stupid question. "Make sure there's enough water in the kettle," she shouted. She had work to do, and it was all to do with the list for the do.

She was seated at the dining table with the old list to her left and a blank piece of paper to her right - pencil in hand ready to attack. A few minutes later, Barney came in carrying two cups of tea. "Did you use the pot or the strainer?" Lily asked.

"Does it matter?"

"It tastes better from the pot."

"So I used the pot," he lied.

Lily was in no mood to be lied to. "If I go into the kitchen and find tea in the strainer that hasn't come from the teapot, there's going to be big trouble." Barney, however, was no fool, and he had already washed out the strainer with cold water, leaving just a few tea leaves behind and had also put hot water in the teapot, swilled it around and emptied it, again leaving just a few leaves, so if Lily went into the kitchen to check, she would have found a warm pot and an almost empty tea strainer, proving, without doubt, that Barney had used the teapot. For all his messing about, he might as well have used the teapot. But no, this was done out of spite, and to prove a point. Not that he knew what the point was, so what was the point?

Lily sipped her tea. "I told you it tastes better from the pot. Right, sit down and concentrate, we still have a couple of weeks before the invitations go out."

"That's what I said before but not in the same way. So why do we have to do it in the middle of the night?"

"Because it's still fresh in the mind, that's why. If we leave it we might forget somebody else."

"But we don't know anybody else to forget."

"We know lots of people we could have forgotten to invite. Just because we don't want to invite them, doesn't mean to say we don't know them not to invite them to the wedding we don't want them to come to."

If only Barney could find someone to translate what his wife had just said into English.

Lily handed the piece of paper and pencil to Barney. "Now, just write down the names I give you. Ready? Your mother and father and my mother and father."

"Do I write their names down or just mothers and fathers?"

"Names. I told you to write down their names." Barney, why don't you just listen instead of asking questions all the time?

"Surnames or just first names or both?" Another question, but Barney wanted to make sure he was doing the right thing.

"Does it matter?" replied Lily, ready to rip her hair rollers out.

"Not to me."

"Then both."

"What's your father's middle name?"

Lily gave him a look.

"Okay, I'll forget middle names."

So Barney wrote their names down in full, excluding middle names. He made sure, of course, that Lily's parents' names went first. The last thing he needed in the middle of the night was an argument as to whose names should go top of the list.

"How many does that come to?"

"What are you talking about? It comes to four."

"Good. Write the number four after their names. Your sister Maureen and her husband Monty plus their two kids."

"Done."

"My brother Tony and his wife and their kid."

"Done."

"Your cousin, Mavis and her shmendrick of a husband, Lew."

"Why is he a shmendrick?"

"Does it matter? We're making a new list for the wedding not a list of reasons why he's a shmendrick. Put the number two after their names. And remember, at the moment we're not inviting their kids so don't put their names down."

Barney had already decided not to put any names down that hadn't been called out. Thinking for himself could easily cause permanent self-inflicted mental damage and a fitting for a strait-jacket.

"My cousin Doreen and her husband Geoffrey, and their two children, Lennie and Michael. That makes four."

"Wait a minute. If you're inviting their kids, why can't I invite Mavis's kids?"

"Do you remember what happened the last time we saw them at a do?"

"Good point. Carry on." For Barney to agree with Lily meant that something was wrong, but he had no idea what.

"Your uncle Dave and aunt Gertie. My aunt Helen and her husband Phil. How many does that come to so far?"

"Slow down, slow down. Wait. I need to put their names down and then I'll count." Barney wrote down their names and started to count and then, just to make sure, he re-counted. He definitely did not want to make any miscalculations. "It comes to twenty-one."

"Write down the number twenty-one so we don't have to keep counting from the beginning. Joe and Leah Gorminsky, Flaxman and his missus, Norman and Hannah Woolf, and then put down

Solly and Marie Barron. Now what does it come to?"

Poor old Barney was writing and counting as fast as he could. "Twenty-nine exactly to the penny. It comes to twenty-nine."

"Doris Feldman." Doris, of course, had to be on the list. The last thing Lily needed was for Doris to tell everyone some booba meise as to why she hadn't been invited. It was better to invite her and keep her quiet - fat chance.

"Next the Levis and the Levys. Another four."

"Do the Levis with an 'i' come before the Levys with a 'y'?"

Another look! If one look could kill, what would two or three or even four do?

"Ok! Done."

"Good. Your uncle Cyril and my aunt Joyce. They could sit together like a couple."

"Wait. We're only doing the list, not the table plan."

"I'm just saying they could, that's all. That's not making a table plan."

Why did he have to mention the table plan? Why? Anything but the table plan, Barney, anything. It was bad enough sorting out the list of guests, but where they were going to sit was a whole new plate of chopped liver that nobody wanted to eat. This one doesn't like that one and that one wants to sit next to this one, so why can't the couple they don't like sit on a table with people who do like them instead of our table? Barney, you can't satisfy everybody.

"You'll never guess who I had on my table.

"Who?"

"Guess."

"You told me I'd never guess, so what was the point of guessing?"

"The Glicksteins."

"I'd never have guessed."

"That's what I said."

"How could they do that?"

"Because that's what they're like."

By the time he had to get ready for shul, the aspirin bottle would be empty and Barney might be on the way to the London Hospital instead.

In truth, he couldn't have cared less as to where people sat, as long as he didn't have to sit next to people he didn't want to sit next to. Not that the parents of the bride and groom had much of a choice. They would be sitting on the top table. He dismissed it from his mind seconds after it came into it; he knew it was something he didn't have to worry about.

"Is that it? Is that the lot?"

"We need to cross check."

So the next few minutes were spent cross-checking and, surprise, surprise, the names on both lists were exactly the same. And the same total, thirty-six not including the two of them.

"So we've spent ages confirming the list. Why didn't we just tick off the names on your piece of paper?" asked Barney, finishing off his tea that had been made through the strainer.

"Just in case it was different."

"How could it be different if you called the same names out?"

As ever, Lily had an answer. "But we didn't know until I finished calling out all the names. Now we have to add the Greens."

"Have we agreed to invite the Greens? I can't remember agreeing."

"Did you disagree?"

"No."

"Then you must have agreed." Another dose of Lily's logic.

"But we need to discuss it before we agree or disagree."

"Why?"

"Because that's what people do, discuss."

"But we haven't got time to discuss. We've only got time to decide. And I've decided we invite them. You can, of course, disagree."

"I disagree." Just for the sake of disagreeing, no other reason, no logical reason. It wasn't as if he didn't like the Greens.

"Good, disagree, but it's not going to get you anywhere." Neither was this conversation. Lily was going to have her way, whatever.

"So how many does that make?"

"It makes thirty-six plus two which makes thirty-eight." And he wrote the Green's name down at the bottom of the list. "What about their daughter and son-in-law?"

"What about them?"

"Are we inviting them?"

"Did I call out their names?"

"No. But that might have been because you've forgotten their names."

"I don't forget names."

"But you forgot the Greens."

"I never forgot the Greens; you forgot to put them on the list. And anyway, I didn't have to remember their kids' names because we weren't going to invite them." Aha! So Lily had forgotten their names. Barney knew full well that she had forgotten and chalked up a victory for himself. Not that he was going to push the matter any further. A victory is a victory even if the other side knows nothing about it. Then he decided to follow her lamentable answer with his next question; one that he knew would really rile her.

"Lily, my dearest, would you like me to write the list out again in alphabetical order, including the Greens, so they're not at the bottom?"

"Don't get sarcastic with me. Remember, this is all your fault. And I've told you before, don't be so clever, it doesn't suit you."

Barney was slowly getting the upper hand although it didn't show, but he needed to push home his advantage. It then came to him in a flash. "I think there might be a problem."

"You're the only problem here. What other one could there be?"

"Numbers. How many people can we invite seeing as we're not paying?"

"How should I know? I never asked, and, by the way, neither did you." This was very true. But they should have asked before writing the list. "Anyway, I'm sure thirty-eight is not going to be a problem; the Gilberts are loaded with gelt, ever since he...never mind, I don't want to talk about it. They could even afford Ambrose and his Orchestra."

"But the hall might not be big enough."

"What are you talking about? It's the Majestic, it can take plenty more. Anyway, if the Queen and Prince Philip wanted to come, would the caterers be able to make space in the hall?"

"Of course they would."

"There you are then, they're not coming so there'll be enough space for a couple more." The mind of a woman is a wonder to behold. "Is there anything else you want to say before you make some more tea?" Barney, of course, didn't know he was going to make some more tea.

"Yes, if we've invited thirty-eight people, what happens if they've only invited thirty-six?"

"That's up to them. I didn't ask them to only invite thirty-six."

"I didn't say they had, I said, 'what if?'"

"What if? What if? What if they invited the Pope?"

"That would make thirty-seven, so it's not so bad. They'll only be one short because the Pope's not married. Then again, they could invite the Greens instead of us inviting them and then they would have thirty-nine and we'd only have thirty-six because we're not inviting the Pope."

"I don't even know if they know the Greens. Anyway, why should we have fewer guests than them? We need to find three more people to invite, but three's an odd number so it won't be easy without upsetting somebody."

This question and answer session was obviously put together in a lunatic asylum situated somewhere between The Isle of Dogs and The Isle of Wight.

"All I was doing was just putting forward a hypothetical problem about numbers, that's all."

"Don't worry. Leave the problems to me as always. And don't use clever words like the one you just used. Tomorrow morning I'll ring the Gilberts up and tell them how many people we're going to invite and that'll be that, no more problems, and in the afternoon, you'll go over on the tube with the list of names to make sure we haven't invited the same people. It's not safe to do it over the phone. You never know who's listening."

"And if we have invited some of the same people?"

"Go and make another pot of tea. Stop driving me mad."

Barney got up and was just about to walk into the kitchen to do Lily's bidding, stopped and said, "Wait a minute. What about the kids?"

"What kids?"

"The kids. Daniel, our son, the one that's getting married to Deborah. What about all their friends?"

Lily dismissed Barney's question with a wave of the hand. "Don't worry about it. There won't be many of them, anyway. They can make their own list. Daniel will invite a few of his best friends from school and club, and a couple from work, and no doubt she'll invite some stuck-ups from Yetta Barnet School or whatever it's called in Hampstead Garden Snoburb. And you can bet a pound to a penny their zaydas used to pluck chickens for a living."

Barney knew he was a beaten man and went off to make more tea, this time in the teapot. Why bother with subterfuge?

Well, the rest of Saturday went as bad as could be expected. Barney and Norman's prayers in shul landed on deaf ears, or God was an Arsenal supporter, God forbid. Spurs lost - again, and on Sunday morning Barney's dogs were still running around Clapton dog track like headless chickens. More money down the drain. But Barney had the sense not to tell Lily how much he had lost. He also had the sense not to tell her when he had won. Some things have to be kept secret. Winning and losing at the dogs were just two of them.

Late Sunday morning; it was time for Lily to ring the Gilberts and time to put on the posh voice. "Hello, Myrna, it's Lilian here... Lilian...Lilian..." So much for the posh voice. "Lily.....Lily Goldstein, your soon to be machatunim . . . Yes, that Lily. . . How are you?" As if she cared.

"I'm fine, Lily, it's nice to hear from you, and how are you and Barney?" Myrna put her hand over the receiver and mouthed to her husband that Lily was on the phone. He picked up the News of the World, tucked it under his arm and signalled that he was going to the toilet and might be some time.

"We're all well and looking forward to the simcha even though it's a long way off. And how's Mickey?"

"Michael's fine, thank you." Michael? What happened to the bugger of a kid from Langdale Mansions called Mickey? Now he's a big-shot freemason, all of a sudden it's Michael, and, what's more, when did Myrna get such an up-her-own-tuchas posh voice?

"And the lovely soon-to-be-my-daughter-in-law Deborah?" Lily smirked down the phone.

"She's away for a couple of days, but she rang this morning and she's fine."

"Good. So everybody's fine, good. Now, before I come on to what I want to tell you, I have to say the Majestic is not a bad choice, not as nice as the King David, true, but never mind, and the caterers,

Goides, are fine, maybe not as good as Schaverien but beggars as they say. Barney and I went to the Barrons' son's bar mitzvah there a few weeks ago and the food was very nice. And the band you've picked, Sammy Solomon and his Swinging Seven aren't bad. They're not as good as Issy Geiger or Nat Temple and his Orchestra, of course, but you get what you pay for, I suppose. It's funny, we thought you might have been at the bar mitzvah."

"Of course we were invited, but we had to go to Michael's Ladies Night do at the Café Royal. And it's odd you should mention Nat Temple, he was playing. Wonderful, he was just wonderful."

 The perfect couple of put downs for a Sunday morning. Lily was not happy, not happy at all. It was bad enough when Myrna hadn't recognised her voice on the phone, but then to be told that Myrna had been to a do at the Café Royal with Nat Temple playing, was something else. If only she could have stabbed her through the phone with the knife she had just picked up from the table. There was no doubt in her mind that she would blame Barney for making her call the Gilberts, and for him not being a freemason.

After being far too polite to each other, Lily got down to the real reason for the call. "We've made our list, Myrna, and it comes to thirty-eight people, not including Barney and myself."

Hold on a minute. There's trouble afoot.

"But I'm afraid we've got you down for thirty-six which is what you told me last week. That's it; we're up to the maximum."

Lily could not remember telling Myrna how many people were on their list, though she did remember saying something like it might be around thirty-six. It must have been Barney.

"What do you mean? We're only talking two more people. It's not going to break the bank."
"If it was just the money, we'd say you pay for the two extra places and they could come with pleasure."

"Wait a minute, why should we pay? You're the bride's parents, you're the ones that pay, not the groom's parents." Lily's bloody blood pressure was on the rise.

"Lily, you're not listening. I said if it was only to do with money but it's not. We're full. We told the kids they could invite as many friends as they wanted, and they have. They invited a hundred of them."

"A hundred? A HUNDRED? They don't know a hundred people," shouted Lily. "Impossible. That means the kids are inviting more people than we are. That can't be right. It doesn't make any sense. We're their parents, after all."

"Calm down Lily, you'll do yourself an injury. Remember, it's their wedding."

 The grip around the knife was getting tighter and tighter and Lily's face was getting redder and redder. "But it's ours as well. We should be able to invite who we like."

"And you have, but not as many as you want. It's the same for us. We would like to have invited more but we had to stick to forty."

That did it. "What do you mean, you've got forty? Now we've only got thirty-six? That can't be right, you having more than us."

"Well, we did have thirty-eight until we remembered that we'd forgotten the Greens from Streatham, so we put them on the list before we finalised the figures."

"But we've got them on our list. We can't both have them." Lily looked at the hand gripping the knife. She was convinced she could see blood. And if someone had taken her blood pressure there and then, she would have been carted off to hospital at once.
Myrna, as calm as ever, said, "It's simple, you take them off your list and there'll be no problems. The people we all wanted to invite will be there."

"Of course there's a problem. We wanted to invite the Greens." What's with the 'we', Lily? Barney never agreed.

"But they've already been invited. Michael invited them when he met Manny at a lodge meeting the other day." The bloody freemasons again! "And they're really looking forward to coming and, of course, seeing you after such a long time." Myrna was in her element winding Lily up.

"I didn't even know you knew them."

"What's that got to do with anything?"

"Everything; they're our friends."

"So, if they're your friends why didn't you put them on your list in the first place?"

"Why didn't you?" It was definitely blood on her hand. And if she could get her hands on Myrna, she would have her blood as well.

"They were top of our reserve list."

"You had a reserve list?"

"Of course. Everybody has a reserve list, just in case somebody drops out. And in this case a couple of the kids' friends couldn't come so we put them in."

Reserve list? Why didn't Lily and Barney think of having a reserve list?

"So why didn't you have the decency to ask us if we could invite somebody else?"
"Because your son, Daniel, said you wouldn't mind if we invited the Greens."

"What's it to do with him?"

"What are you talking about? It's got everything to do with him. It's Daniel and Deborah's wedding, not ours."

Barney was hiding in the kitchen waiting for the kettle to boil, listening to one end of the conversation. He knew that Lily was well on her way to boiling over way before the kettle.

And then seconds later it happened. Boiling point had been reached. "There's not going to be a bloody wedding if I can bloody-well help it," yelped Lily, "I'm going to make sure that my Daniel doesn't get married to someone with parents like you and that schnorrer of a husband of yours... Micky, oh, I'm terribly sorry, Michael. Your daughter doesn't deserve a son like my soon-to-be qualified Daniel. And mark my words, Myrna, hoity-toity, 'I'm now living in Golders Green, so look at me' Gilbert, she'll end up just like you, with a fake tan, a fake face and a fake voice. So why don't you just go and f......" And she slammed the phone down. Then it took all her strength to release the knife from her own grip. "Barney," she shouted at the top of her voice, "where are you? I need a word."

Fortunately for Barney, Lily had had the sense to put the knife back on the table.

The smile on Myrna's face was a joy to behold. "Mickey, you can come out of the toilet now, the deed's done." Two minutes later, Mickey, also known as Michael, Master of his Lodge, came out of the toilet, washed and wiped his hands, and went back into the dining room. "It worked like a charm, Mickey. And we were right to do it our way and the kids way and not book anything."

"Did you end up telling her the truth?"

"I didn't have the heart. Anyway, she slammed the phone down on me, shouting and cursing. Besides, I think it's best if it comes from Barney, although he might be hiding under the sheets or living in another country when he does."

"And she'll kill him when she finds out. Then she'll kill us and then she'll kill herself."

"Don't worry about it, she's all mouth. Maybe Daniel will tell her first, when he comes back from the flat in Bournemouth with his new wife."

"Mr and Mrs Daniel and Deborah Goldstein sounds very good to me, and not even a wedding party to worry about. Perfect. We can go to another Lodge do instead."

Sometime late on Sunday afternoon at the flat of Barney and Lily Goldstein.

"L L L Lily," mumbled a terrified, but courageous Barney, hiding under the bed. "There's something I need to tell you."

Doris's Dream

Mr Johnny Walker was sitting and waiting patiently on the table, as was a glass and four pieces of Miriam's finest honey cake. Yoseler the Philosopher was ready for a night of tranquility only to be broken by the occasional sound of the bottle tinkling against the glass. Peace and quiet were to be the order of the evening. Not even the sound of the radio. Silence. He might, only might, browse through last week's copy of the Jewish Chronicle. But only might. It might be too much of an effort.

His wife, Miriam, was off playing cards with friends, so the evening was his - alone, apart from Johnny, that is, but he was one of his closest friends, a friend who demanded nothing but loyalty and the right to be drunk, so he didn't count. It was bliss, pure bliss; whisky and honey cake. Who could ask for anything more? He could close his mind to the problems of the two previous evenings and concentrate on himself for once.

No chance. The knock on the door put paid to that. It was getting on for eight-thirty and he really didn't want to open the door, especially as he wasn't expecting anybody. But it could be someone in trouble. How could he not open the door? Then again, it could be someone wanting to rob him, so opening the door would not be a good idea. If, of course, they knew what sort of person Yoseler was, they would know there was nothing worthwhile stealing. However, if they didn't know what sort of person he was, they might have thought there was something worth stealing. But wait, this was Hessel Street, so what was worth stealing? A dead chicken? A plate of chopped liver? Some lokshen pudding? He decided to open the door.

It was Doris. Of all the people he could think of who would be knocking on his door at this time of night without an invitation, the last person that would come to mind was Doris. But there she was in all her ample flesh.

"Doris, what a surprise." And it was. "Have you come to see Miriam? If so, I'm afraid she's out playing cards somewhere."

"No, Yoseler, I've come to talk to you. I need some help with a problem I have."

Doris with a problem? This was something new; this was a first. He had to invite her in. "Come in, come in, Doris, please sit in the armchair and make yourself comfortable. Can I take your coat?"

"No, I'm fine thank you, Yoseler."

"A piece of Miriam's honey cake maybe, or a glass of lemon tea?"

"No thank you, not for the moment." She had noticed the bottle and the glass on the table, and Yoseler noticed that she'd noticed the bottle and glass.

"How would you like to share a drop of Mr Walker with me? You look a little flustered if I might say."

"You know I don't drink, Yoseler. But if you're pushing me to have a little affair with Johnny, then maybe I will. Thank you."

Who was pushing?

Yoseler was about to take another glass from the sideboard when he noticed that there were already two glasses on the table. He couldn't remember taking two out. Maybe Miriam had put one on the table before she left which he hadn't seen. At least it would save him having to bend down. He poured the whisky and handed one glass to Doris. He then sat opposite her and, holding his glass in one hand, placed the bottle on a small side table to his right with the other, just in case an emergency top up was needed - for both of them.

"Now what's this problem I might be able to help you with?"

"Well, it's not so much a problem I need help with, but advice. Advice about a very strange dream I had last night. I've been worrying about it all day and haven't had a minute's peace, and I came to the conclusion that you're the only one who can possibly help me. So here I am."

Yoseler should have known. If the two previous evenings were anything to go by, he should have known. But for the time being he would say nothing. He would just listen. "I'm not a great expert on dreams, Doris, but if I can help I will. So tell me, what was it all about?" He just hoped it wasn't going to be too personal and involve bodily functions.

Doris made herself comfortable in the armchair whilst Yoseler placed another small table to her side so she could rest her glass. Now she was ready to begin. "As you know you don't often remember your dreams very well, but this one was so vivid that I remember every single detail. But you have to promise not to laugh when you hear what it was all about."

Yoseler said he wouldn't dream of laughing. Dreams were no laughing matter unless they were funny, and even then…

"Well," said Doris, after taking just a little more than a sip of the whisky, "this is what happened. I woke up at about eleven o'clock in the morning, in the dream, that is. Don't ask me how I knew it was about eleven, I don't know. Anyway, I walked down into the street from my flat and I saw that the market was empty. Not a person, not a stall, nothing. None of the shops were open. The whole street was deserted. Not even a dog or a cat. I'd never seen anything like it before in my life, not even on a shobbus. I thought to myself, where is everybody? Has something happened that I don't know about? Had everybody been evacuated? I didn't know. I knew nothing which, for me, as you know, is unheard of. So I decided to walk to the top of the street and see if there was anybody about in Commercial Road, but before I could get there I saw it, there in the middle of the street, all on its own. And it stopped me in my tracks."

"Saw what?"

"Well, at first I wasn't sure that what I was seeing was what I thought I was seeing, if you get my meaning. But it was. It was a matzo. I saw a matzo in the middle of the street, all on its own - wobbling, and there was no wind or breeze. It was a very still day."

"What do you mean by wobbling?"

"It was moving from side to side and up and down - just a little. I thought it was my eyes playing tricks on me, but it wasn't, it was wobbling."

Yoseler cleared his throat. "Was it a Bonn's matzo or Rakusen's?" he asked, trying to hold back even the tiniest hint of a chuckle in his voice.

"How should I know? It wasn't in a box. It was a single matzo, on the ground - wobbling. Why does it matter if it's a Bonn's matzo or a Rakusen's one? Is it relevant?"

"Of course it's relevant. Everything in a dream is relevant. Even the tiniest thing has relevance. A Bonn's matzo could mean one thing but, depending on the situation in the dream, a Rakusen's matzo could mean something completely different. Then, of course, they could have the same meaning. It could also depend on whether the dream was in black and white or in colour or a mixture of the two. These are all very important matters that have to be taken into consideration when considering the meaning of the dream to the dreamer and also to the person who is trying to translate the dream."

Yoseler hadn't a clue as to what he was talking about but sounded very convincing, so that was good enough for Doris. After all, this was Yoseler the Philosopher we're talking about not your run-of-the-mill know-all philosopher who knows nothing but sounds as if he knows everything.

"Please continue, Doris."

"Well, now we come to the strange bit." As if it wasn't already strange. "As I got closer to the matzo, it got bigger and bigger until it was at least, I should say, about seven feet by five, even bigger, but I can't tell you how big exactly because I didn't have a tape measure with me. And by now it had stopped moving or wobbling. Anyway, as I got very close to it I had this funny urge to sit on it, which I did, and I wasn't even scared. In fact, it felt quite comfortable even without a cushion."

Yoseler decided to down his whisky in one gulp and pour another. Needs must in times of need. "And what happened next?"

"It gets even stranger, Yoseler." Doris lowered her voice, raised her right arm slowly and gazed at the ceiling. She continued talking in a very slow and deliberate voice. "It then took off into the clear blue sky like a magic or flying carpet, except this was a flying matzo, a flying matzo, Yoseler, with me sitting on it. Can you believe it?"

Yoseler was transfixed by Doris's description and Oscar-winning hand movement, and had to wait a few seconds before replying. "Of course I believe it, Doris, this is a dream you had. This was very real for you." He paused for a second time to compose his thoughts.

"Now, I believe this to be good news because while you have been talking, I have been thinking. We can, for certain, rule out Bonn's and Rakusen's matzos."

"How come?"

"Because to the best of my knowledge neither company makes flying matzos."

"Now you're joking with me."

"Doris, I'm not joking with you. As I said, dreams need to be analysed very carefully. So it's possible that this matzo might have been hand-made by somebody in Baghdad or somewhere and a thief stole it and brought it back to Hessel Street. As yet we do not know. Please continue." For someone who knew nothing about dreams ten minutes ago, Yoseler was quickly becoming an expert and by the time the evening was out he would be Hessel Street's leading, and only, dream analyst.

"Well, The matzo took off with me on it and the next thing I know is that we're flying all over the East End, along Commercial Road, round the back of the London Hospital, down the Whitechapel Road and up New Road, then up to Poplar and back till it gets to Cannon Street Road. Then it goes all the way down to Cable Street where it turns right before it turns again into Christian Street and makes its way round the back-doubles and ends up back in Hessel Street. By the time it gets there, the streets all around are packed with people waving to me and cheering. Some even had different sorts of flags in their hands and others were even waving boxes of matzos, Bonn's and Rakusen's. When I took off the street was empty, now it was full. I don't know where all these people came from in such a short time."

Yoseler wondered how somebody could remember so much of a dream and in such perfect detail. "Did you recognise anybody?" As he asked the question his thoughts turned to the conversations he had had over the two previous nights. He still said nothing about them.

"It was too high and I wasn't wearing glasses. Anyway, within seconds, the flying matzo sped off towards Commercial Road and turned off into Alie Street. Then it went over Leman Street Police Station, where dozens of policemen were throwing their helmets in the air, and headed off to the river. Wherever I went there were people waving and cheering. It was like the coronation. When it got to the Thames, the flying matzo turned right and followed it until it reached the Houses of Parliament." Doris paused to get her breath back. "I'm sorry I'm talking so fast, but I don't want to forget anything and this is the only way for me to do it."

Yoseler's calming voice allayed any fears. "Don't worry. You're doing very well. In fact, remarkably well." In truth, Yoseler thought that if Doris could get through the dream quickly he would still have time to himself after she had gone. But at the same time, he thought the evening was becoming quite interesting.

"Where did you and the flying matzo go from there?" Yoseler was convinced he knew the answer but needed confirmation.

"Buckingham Palace."

He was right. "Buckingham Palace?" he questioned in mock surprise.

"That's what I said, Buckingham Palace. It flew, well, we flew, over the gates, over the top of the palace and then, suddenly, it stopped and we hovered over the garden, looking down on a great big swimming pool. Now, to be honest, by this time I was feeling quite hungry and I know it sounds even crazier than the crazy things I've already said, but I started nibbling at the ends of the matzo, and then ate more and more until it got much smaller. In the end it got so small I couldn't balance on it any longer and I fell off - into the swimming pool full of beautiful clear water. But unfortunately I landed on somebody. I don't know who it was. It could have been a man or a woman. It could even have been a dog or dogs for all I know. And from that height I could have killed whoever it was. Who knows? Anyway, the next thing I do know is that I'm sinking to the bottom quickly, but when I come up gasping for air, the person or whatever I landed on had disappeared and the clear water had changed. It was no longer water."

This time Yoseler did not know the answer. "So what was it?"

"Borsht," exclaimed Doris, sending a startled Yoseler back into his armchair. "Borsht! The water had turned into borsht. And if I had to choose one thing to really hate apart from the Nazis, it would be borsht. I hate it with a passion. It makes me feel sick. I sometimes throw up just thinking about it. Unfortunately, I swallowed a mouthful trying to save myself from drowning and I started to choke. I thought I was going to die, and that's when I woke up, catching my breath, feeling very sick and sweating like a pig, if you'll excuse the language." She paused for a moment, hoping she wasn't going to throw up all over Yoseler's spotless flat.

She took a deep breath and then continued, "And that's it. That was my dream, or as it turned out a nightmare, because the last thing I would ever want to do is die drowning in a pool of borsht. Chicken soup or barley soup I could live with if I had to die drowning, but borsht? I would rather wash my mouth out with carbolic soap."

It was time for Doris to take a deep breath and finish the remnants of the glass. "Now maybe you can understand why I needed to talk to somebody about this meshugena dream. This is not a normal dream. This is something very particular, or do I mean peculiar?"

"In this case," said Yoseler, "I think both."

"So?"

"So, have you always hated borsht?"

"Always. My mother, may she rest in peace, always forced me to have it at least twice a week. And I've hated it ever since."

"Ah!" exclaimed Yoseler.

"Ah! What?"

"Nothing. Just 'ah!' We'll come back to it later." Yoseler wished he had never said 'ah' and hoped Doris would forget all about it. The last thing he needed was for an 'ah!' to turn into an 'aha!' Not quite on a par with an 'oi' turning into an 'oivay', but not far off. However, Yoseler had a bigger problem than worrying about 'ahs' 'ahas' 'ois' and 'oivays'. He was considering whether or not to tell Doris about the two previous nights' discussions? It didn't take him long to decide. The answer was definitely yes. Although he had promised not to mention the dreamers' names to anybody, even Miriam, there was no mention of holding back the details of the dreams. So he was free to talk about them. There was, indeed, something strange going on and he was the ideal person to find out what it was. But he would hold back names, as promised.

"Doris, before I give you my thoughts, I need to tell you something which will make the whole thing much more complicated. But it's nothing to worry about."

So there was definitely something to worry about, thought Doris, looking most concerned.

"Let me give you a top up before I continue."

"Thank you, Yoseler." She put her hand up when the glass was about a third full. "Stop, that's enough. We don't want people talking if they see me coming out of your flat, drunk, especially if Miriam isn't here. As you know, Yoseler, there are people round here with big mouths. I'm not saying who, but they know who they are. Now, what did you want to tell me?"

"Well, I'm considering the possibility that we might have an epidemic of strange dreams breaking out in the street. And they might all be connected. I'm not sure yet, so I'll have to do some research."

"I think you'll have to do some explaining first." Definitely, especially as she wasn't a hundred percent certain as to what 'epidemic' meant.

"That I am happy to do. Two people, whose names I can't tell you for the moment because I made a promise not to, have come to see me - separately - over the last two nights. Each of them told me that they had had a strange and very vivid dream the night before and wanted to know if I could help them understand what the dream meant. Neither of them knew about the other one's dream and I didn't mention anything, so they still don't know. Of course, until you told me about yours I didn't make any connections, but now things have changed. They might be connected or might not. Only time and my research will give us the answer. So, would you like me to tell you about the other dreams?" As he asked the question, he realized that he might have made a terrible mistake.

Doris, whose mouth and mind would normally be working at the speed of a rocket, sat in silence. Then her eyes lit up, and her hands answered the question.

"So, this is what the first person told me about their dream. It was coming up to Pesach and this person needed to buy some matzos. Unfortunately, wherever he went, they'd run out. All the shops he went to had run out of matzos. In fact, some of the Jewish shop-owners even said that they were going to stop selling matzos for Pesach because there was too little profit in it so they were thinking of selling beigals and cholas instead."

"What? Selling beigals and cholas for Pesach? They should be ashamed of themselves." Doris was shocked.

"Doris, this was a dream. It was only a dream." Yoseler was concerned that the whisky was having an effect on Doris's state of mind and that she was having problems separating dreams from reality. "In the end, he went for a walk down the Whitechapel Road to see if he could get some."

"And?"

"It seems he saw a long queue for somebody selling something on a stall, so he decided to join it. He asked the woman in front of him what they were queuing for. She said she didn't know but if people were queuing it must be for something worthwhile; nobody queues for nothing. This is, as we all know, not necessarily so, but for once it was true. The man was selling boxes of Bonn's Kosher for Pesach matzos half price. Unfortunately, by the time he got to the front of the queue the man had run out. But he knew this man from years ago and so after a few minutes of persuasive argument, the man sold him a box that he was keeping for somebody else, but charged him a little more for the privilege."

Doris gave Yoseler a somewhat dismissive look. "That's not much of a dream," she said, slumping back into the armchair in disappointment. "The whole dream's about being charged a bit more than half price for a box of matzos? What sort of strange dream is that?"

"Wait. Don't be so impatient. If that's all there was, I wouldn't have bothered telling you about it. I haven't come to the important bit." Doris raised her hands in apology and asked Yoseler to continue.

"Thank you. Now, this man takes the box back to his flat here in Hessel Street pleased that at last he had managed to buy matzos for Pesach."

"And was his wife pleased?"

"He never mentioned if there was a wife in his dream. But it's not relevant."

"But you said that everything in a dream was relevant." Doris was back to her best.

"Only if it's relevant and as a wife is not mentioned it's not relevant."

Doris wasn't convinced by his answer but decided not to force the issue. After all, this was Yoseler the Philosopher she was talking to.

And he was being kind enough to help. "So?"

"So he takes the box of matzos back and after a while he feels a little peckish, but instead of making himself something to eat he decides to have one of the Kosher for Pesach matzos even before Pesach came in. He opens the box and starts to eat one, and it's disgusting, the most disgusting matzo he had ever tasted. He had been duped by the stallholder. Either they were fake Bonn's matzos or they were at least ten years old."

Doris was outraged. "The stallholder is a disgrace. He should be shot and reported to the authorities at the same time, taking advantage of people like that."

"Doris, I keep telling you, this is a dream."

"You can still shoot people in a dream. Anyway, what happens next?"

"Well, he's so upset that he decides to chuck them away. But instead of putting them in the dustbin he decides to throw them out of the window so the birds can eat them. And that's what he does. He throws them out one by one until the box is empty. Next morning - in his dream - he opens the window to see if the birds or maybe the dogs or cats have eaten them, and they have. They're all gone, all except one, which is sitting in the middle of the street all alone, unlikely as it may seem, unbroken. Then he sees someone come along the street, he doesn't know who, and as this person gets nearer to the matzo, the matzo gets bigger and bigger and then. . ." Yoseler decided to stop talking. He could see by the expression on Doris's face that she knew what was going to happen next.

"So you're telling me that the flying matzo in my dream came from a man who bought a box of lousy matzos from a good-for-nothing in the Whitechapel Road, in his dream."

Yoseler was ready with his answer. He wasn't going to be caught out again. "Not necessarily. Remember, these are two separate dreams dreamt by two different people. He didn't know who was on the flying matzo and you didn't know where your matzo came from. The matzo in your dream could have come from somebody or somewhere else. And what's more, his matzo was disgusting and you could eat yours."

"I understand. But it's a bit of a coincidence. Maybe if you tell me who the man is, I might be able to find a connection." Doris was desperate to know who this person was. If only Yoseler would drop his guard - just a little.

"Doris, I said I wouldn't tell, and you know me, if I say a name will be kept secret that's how it will stay, unless I'm given permission. All I can say is that it's someone we both know very well."

"Very well, I won't ask again unless you get permission. So what happened next?"

"Only one last thing. The flying matzo flew past his window at such a speed and far too close that it knocked him out, and that's when he woke up, dreaming of being unconscious. Did you knock out anybody out in your dream?"

"No. Definitely not."

"Aha!" he exclaimed. But at least it was his 'aha!' and not Doris's. "Now you can see what I mean." Doris hadn't the foggiest what he meant but nodded in agreement. Yoseler quickly came to the conclusion that his idea of a quiet night in was gone. But he could only blame himself. He didn't have to tell Doris about the two dreams - he still had the other one to tell - he could have told her that he would think about all three dreams and let her know his conclusions the next day, but this is Yoseler the Philosopher we're talking about not any old hack of a philosopher out of the pages of history. He was keen to understand what was happening and if, how and why these dreams were connected. After all, philosophers need to know more than just on a need to know basis.

Now it was time to tell Doris about the other dream. "Before I tell you about the other dream, would you like a piece of Miriam's honey cake?"

"No thank you, Yoseler, I had something to eat just before I came out."

"Fine. But if you change your mind just help yourself." Yoseler then looked at the bottle of Johnny Walker on the side table and wondered how he had, with a little help from Doris, managed to finish off most of the bottle. Maybe it wasn't as full as he thought it was when he took it out of the cupboard. Never mind, there was plenty more where that came from. He continued, "Now, this person, a woman, again someone we both know very well, came to see me last night and told me about her dream. When I tell you about it, you will realise that there might, I don't say must, be some very strange connection between the three dreams. As I said, I have no idea as yet what the connection is, if there is one, but I will find out after I have looked into the possibility and meaning of intermingling and intercommunicating triple dreams." More convincing words of utter nonsense.

Doris said, "If I can help in any way I will, but I might need to know who these people are." Doris was on another fishing expedition but Yoseler knew better than to be hooked into giving up the names.

He ignored Doris's comment and continued. "We now come to the second dream and you will see for yourself how mixed together they might be. This woman's dream starts off with her buying a raffle ticket from the Cannon Street Road Shul Ladies Guild. They were going to raise money to buy new chairs for the hall."

Doris had to interrupt. "But they don't need new chairs; they bought some a couple of years ago. Something's not right. I think somebody's putting money in their own pockets."

"Doris, for the last time, this is a dream. Please let me continue. She bought a ticket for sixpence. . ."

"Just one?"

"Just one."

"What a cheapskate. She could have at least bought two. They're only sixpence each."

"But she only bought one. And the next thing she knows is. . ."

"Don't tell me. Let me guess. She won first prize and the first prize was a box of matzos."

"Correct and incorrect, in that order. She did win first prize but it wasn't a box of matzos."

"So what was it?" Doris was desperate to know, and it showed by the excitement on her face and the agitated body movement. She was sitting on the edge of the armchair waiting for the answer.

Yoseler decided to wait a few seconds for dramatic effect, and then shot out the answer. "Buckingham Palace."

"What did you say?" asked a disbelieving Doris.

"I said 'Buckingham Palace'. She won Buckingham Palace and everything in it."

Doris slumped back into the armchair again. "Even in a dream I can't believe somebody I know won Buckingham Palace with a lousy sixpenny raffle ticket. Why couldn't it have happened to me?"

"There's more," said a reluctant Yoseler.

"Of course there is," replied a disconsolate looking Doris. "Tell me. I might as well know everything."

Yoseler was beginning to feel quite sorry for Doris, but whatever happened next, he was not going to give her any more whisky. She had obviously had too much and the effects were showing. As he thought about it, he looked at the bottle; it was empty. How did that happen? He couldn't remember pouring himself or Doris another glass. Maybe the whisky was taking its toll on him as well and his memory was slipping. No more for him either, then. The reserves would have to stay in the sideboard. "So, would you like me to tell you the rest?"

"Go on. In for a pound, as they say."

"I will, but if at any time you want me to stop, say so. So the Queen and the family plus all her members of staff had to move out of the palace, and where did they go to live?"

"Tell me." Not that Doris really cared or wanted to know.

"Well, according to this person, she read it in the Jewish Chronicle, in her dream that is, that the Royal Family moved to a couple of flats here in Hessel Street. Obviously, the Queen had to get rid of quite a lot of staff because there wasn't enough room for all of them. But that's where she moved to."

This Doris did want to know. "So you're telling me that this woman swapped homes with the Queen."

Yoseler was being quite specific in his use of language. "That's not what I said. I did not use the word 'swap'. Remember this woman won Buckingham Palace, so the Queen had to move out and find somewhere else to live. There was no suggestion of a swap. But there was a problem."

"For the Queen?"

"No, for the woman. When she moved into Buckingham Palace she realised there were certain things missing."

"But you said she also won everything in it. So how could there be anything missing?"

"There was. There were some very important things that were missing."

"What could possibly be missing from Buckingham Palace?"

"Mezuzahs, Doris, mezuzahs. There were no mezuzahs on any of the door frames anywhere in the whole palace."

Well, well, well. That was something Doris really hadn't thought of. "So, all she had to do was to go out and buy some," replied Doris sounding quite dismissive.

"Do you know how many rooms there are in Buckingham Palace?" Before Doris could come up with an answer, Yoseler told her. "Over seven hundred. Over seven hundred rooms. Where was she going to buy seven hundred mezuzahs?"

Doris was in no mood for sympathy. "Woolworths for all I care. Anyway, with all that money she could buy every mezuzah in the country, even some from Harrods if they sold them."

"I never said she had money. I said she had Buckingham Palace. She still had no money." By this time, Yoseler wasn't sure that everything he was telling Doris was what was told to him but it didn't matter, the story, or the dream, was getting better and better and more absurd by the minute.

"She could get a loan from the bank."

"True. But it didn't matter. It didn't get that far. She was feeling very tired after all the moving and the like, so decided to go and have a few minutes nap in the main bedroom, the Queen's very own bedroom, and when she woke up she noticed that the door frame had a mezuzah on it. So she started looking around the rest of the palace and, surprise, surprise, all the door frames now had mezuzahs on them, all of them made from pure silver, except the front door mezuzah. This one was the biggest she had ever seen and it was made from solid gold."

By now Doris was fed up listening to Yoseler telling her about this remarkable dream. To her it was much better than the one she had had. "I think I've heard enough, Yoseler."

"But you have to hear the rest. It's very important for you to know what happened next because it brings everything together in a neat parcel. After looking around the palace, she decides to go into the garden, and there, according to her, is the biggest swimming pool in the world. Now, I think you know what happens next. All of a sudden, she finds herself in a swimming costume and she jumps into the pool. She has never been able to swim but for the first time in her life she can. She starts swimming up and down the pool on her back without any problems, enjoying herself, and then all of a sudden, she notices something very strange hovering above the pool. She sees somebody sitting on a flying matzo."

"Me," answered Doris, pleased to be part of the proceedings again.

"We don't know that, do we? It could have been someone else. It could have been you. It is relevant but not important for the moment. Then, without a word of warning, this person comes crashing down on her and they both sink to the bottom of the pool. She manages to make her way to the top and when she gets there, she gasps for air. And at that very moment she wakes up sweating, just like you. But she'd been swimming, which is why she was wet."

"Aha!" said Doris, "Aha!" Doris had put two and two together and come up with an answer that certainly did not make four. "That's it. Now I know why this person was gone when I came up for air; she'd woken up. How could she still be in my dream if she was awake?"

Yoseler knew that an 'Aha!' would come back to haunt him, but not in this way. Doris had lost the plot completely, mixing reality with the world of dreams and, probably, whisky. He knew that it was time to bring the conversation to a close. "Doris, as I said right at the beginning, we still don't know what any of this means. It could have been you in her dream or maybe not. There could be thousands of people flying around on matzos in hundreds of different dreams.

I am going to have to go to the library first thing in the morning and do a lot of looking into this, to me, unknown world. Then and only then will we have a better understanding of what has happened. It might be pure coincidence. Then again, it might not. We will have to wait and see. I just hope that nobody else comes to me in the next few days to tell me about their dream."

Doris was still annoyed that she hadn't found out the names of the two others who had had dreams but realised that she too had had enough for one night. She was tired and it was time to go home and, hopefully, have a dream-free night. In the morning, she would find a way of finding out the names.

"Yoseler, thank you very much," she said, standing up, "I'm sorry if things got a bit out of hand with my crazy talking but it was a remarkable evening and I'm very grateful for your help. You must be very tired so I hope you get a really good night's sleep. Let me know what you find out at the library - in your own time, and give my love to Miriam. Oh, and thank you for the whisky, I think it really helped." And you really did help yourself, thought Yoseler, every time I blinked.

"It was a special pleasure, Doris. Be safe when you walk home and get a good night's sleep, and don't worry. Let me do the worrying."

Yoseler showed Doris to the door, waiting until she had gone down a couple of flights of stairs before closing the door behind him; the last thing he need was for her to fall over and crack a dozen bones. He sighed the sigh of an exhausted man. Normally he would wait up for Miriam to come home but his strength had gone. He had lost the will to keep his eyes open. He needed to go to bed. But before that a piece of Miriam's honey cake would not go amiss. But it was gone. All four pieces had gone. He couldn't remember having one piece let alone all four pieces, and he remembered Doris declining, or did she? It had to be the whisky taking it out of him. Johnny Walker should have been ashamed of himself for playing tricks on such a good friend. Yoseler would have to have a word but not until the morning. He made his weary way to the bedroom, changed into his pyjamas, tucked himself into bed and within seconds was fast asleep.

In the morning, still in bed, he apologised to Miriam for not waiting up for her. "I'm sorry, but out of the blue Doris came over to talk to me about something and I couldn't turn her away. She needed my advice. Can you believe it, Doris wanting advice? Anyway, we talked and, I must admit, drank a little, the whole evening. Then I think we finished off the honey cake, I'm not sure. But I do know that by the time she left I was exhausted. I couldn't keep my eyes open. I had to come to bed. I'm sorry. And now I have to get up and go to the library to do some research."

"I don't understand. What's all this about Doris? What research? What are you talking about?" Miriam turned over to face him.

"I'm talking about Doris coming over last night, like I said."

"Impossible, Yoseler, it's an impossibility. First of all, I haven't made honey cake in ages and secondly, Doris was with me all evening playing cards at the Flaxman's."

That night Yoseler had had the most vivid and detailed dream ever.